A FAIR AFFAIR

SARA MADDERSON

For my readers.

Thank you for reading, for supporting, and for returning!

PROLOGUE

HONOR

'Oh my God. Stop flapping, or I swear, I'm going to get out of this chair and do the show with one bare eye. You are killing me.'

I swat away my makeup artist, Elsie, and she giggles. She's one of the best makeup artists I've worked with, and definitely one of the best within ITV's budget, which is why I've kept a tight hold on her for so long despite her biggest flaw. She is a major flapper. Which is irritating at the best of times, beyond irritating when you're preparing to go on live TV, and totally bloody intolerable at five-thirty in the morning.

'You need me. You want him to fancy you, don't you? Even you can't snag Jackson James with one bare eye. Bollocks. Where did I put the mascara?'

'I do not want to 'snag' him. I want to interview him in a professional manner and share his insights from behind the scenes of *Adrenalin IV* with our viewers.'

'You need to share his smile, that's what. That's all they care about. You'd better be really funny or really flirty, so everyone can see his smile. No one cares what Jackson

James says. We all just want to look at him. We want to look at his muscles and see those cold blue eyes heat up as if he's starving and you're a nice bit of steak. I suspect he's a bit thick, but he's so fucking fit I don't care. Ask him about his sex scenes.'

'I wasn't aware you were my producer.' I make a face at Elsie. 'And I can't ask him about his sex scenes on daytime TV. And, for your information, Jackson James is not thick. He's severely dyslexic and highly intelligent, I'll have you know.' I know my stuff on all my interviewees.

'Still, though. Please tell me you're excited. Who wouldn't be excited about meeting *Jackson James*?'

I'd rather die than give Elsie the satisfaction of having me admit it, but I am seriously excited. I eat world leaders for breakfast. I've interviewed Blair and Brown and Merkel and Sarkozy (he was quite sexy, in a wolfish sort of way) and Bush and even Gaddafi. I've also sat on this sofa with Eastwood and Costner and Pitt.

But Jackson James is on another level. I'm not into action movies, but his on-screen presence is seriously potent and so fucking sexy. The camera loves that man, and I can't wait to see what it'll be like to sit a metre or two away from him. Ken and I will hardly have any time to warm him up before we go live—he'll join us on the sofa during the ad break and we'll go straight into the interview after a short intro from us and a look at the *Adrenalin IV* trailer. The conversation will be lightly scripted, with pre-agreed questions, but I suspect my adrenalin will be pumping through me even harder than usual.

I started at Sunrise UK straight out of uni and I've been in front of the camera for three years, first as their Business presenter, and then as one of the two regular anchors. My Economics degree and my ability to assimilate vast quantities of information, relay said information articulately and think on my feet all played less of a part in my rise from runner to presenter than my looks.

I know that, because enough people have told me, with varying degrees of spite and snark, and I'm fine with it. I can't take credit for having won a genetic lottery, but I've certainly cultivated my looks with the attention someone might lavish on their prize racehorse. They're bankable. And I've banked them, over and over again.

I'm far more nervous than I'd care to admit even to myself, but one of the weird and endlessly helpful skills I've honed in the world of live TV is an ability to maintain a remarkably unflappable facade, however much I'm spinning out internally (a skill I wish I could give to Elsie). I suspect I'll put it to good use on the sofa in a couple of hours, because my heart is already racing at the thought of sharing a sofa with Jackson James.

~

Believe me, my heart is still racing when I walk off set, de-mic, and head to my dressing room hours later. Even though we wrapped Jackson James' section forty-five minutes ago. Even though we ended the show talking about eggs, for Pete's sake. Eggs. And still, my heart is hammering in my chest.

Because he didn't take his eyes off me the whole time.

And he didn't stop smiling at me.

And I'm pretty sure he was mentally undressing me for most of our conversation.

And I. Was. There for it.

Don't get me wrong, I didn't show it. The more he flirted and grinned, the more I assumed my impenetrable ice-queen persona. It's my defense mechanism when I feel vulnerable, and the vulnerability I felt when Jackson's eyes were on me was worse than when I interviewed Gaddafi via satellite. And in a far better way.

Besides, I could tell it was driving him mad when I didn't react, and I had a hunch my producer would be loving it. I smiled my aloof, Persian cat smile and kept my legs elegantly crossed and my back ramrod straight (it's amazing how many viewers feel compelled to write in and criticise female presenters' posture). When he addressed a comment to me, I deflected to Ken.

And it felt great.

When we thanked Jackson for his time and cut to the weather, he leaned in towards me. Ignored Ken. Kept his blue eyes trained on me until I felt like Elsie's piece of steak. And he was just about to strike up a conversation when one of the producers materialised to whisk him respectfully off set.

I gave him a final enigmatic smile and a little wave. 'Thanks for your time, Mr James. And best of luck with the premiere on Friday.'

'The pleasure is all mine.' He winked and left.

It wasn't the best interview I've done, not by a long shot. The questions were vanilla and we didn't give him much to run with, which is a good thing, because I'm pretty sure most of the blood in my body migrated south of my waistband when he sat on that sofa and shook my hand. His hand was large and warm and *virile*.

That sounds so pathetic, but everything about the man is so incredibly masculine. It's clear he's pure muscle under that outrageously well-cut suit, he has cheekbones you could cut diamonds with, and his shaved head and carefully cultivated stubble show his bone structure off to perfection.

But it's those blue eyes, that shift from cold to heated in an instant when he fixes them on something he likes the look of, that get me.

He's so different from the nerdy toffs I usually go for. I've always found intelligence incredibly attractive, and I have no doubt that Jackson is a highly intelligent guy, but that's not what turns me on. He wears his sexuality close to the surface, and it's mesmerising. Mesmerising to allow myself an idle fantasy of what he does when he catches his prey. He looks as though he knows exactly what he wants and fully intends to get it.

Which is why it should not surprise me to open the door to my dressing room and see Jackson James sitting on my sofa.

But it does, and the sight of him, and the implication of the fact that he's here, waiting for me, hits me right in the stomach.

He's looking at a magazine, but when he sees me, he jumps up. He's taken off his suit jacket and rolled up the sleeves of the beautiful blue shirt that matches his eyes. And he smiles. It's not the megawatt smile he flashed on-screen, rather a diffident one that my heart responds to with a rush of warmth, and in response I shelve the tight, careful smiles I fed him during the interview and find myself smiling a real smile of delight and wonder. At the sight of it, he shakes his head and his entire face lights up.

Neither of us says a word as I close the door carefully, but he takes a few steps towards me.

'I hope you don't mind.' He shoves his hands in his pockets, and I try to avoid ogling his forearms. 'I wasn't ready to walk away from you after six minutes.'

He's watching my face for my reaction. A million things run through my head at this moment, mainly that I am unlikely to hear a better line ever again. I'm reeling as my brain processes what's happening here: Jackson James has waited forty-five minutes to get me to himself because he wasn't ready to leave me. My ice-queen demeanour has deserted me and there's a large risk of my behaving like a total fangirl. But he deserves the truth.

'I'm glad you hung around.'

'Really? Because I can leave. I can—you must be shattered. I don't know how you do that every day.'

'If someone stood over me at three-forty-five each morning and gave me the chance to sign on the dotted line and terminate my contract, I'd do it. Every day. But I'm fine now. Adrenalin, I suppose. You get used to it. Coffee?'

'I'll take a tea, thanks.'

I bustle around with the kettle, glad for something to do while I pull myself together. I can do this. He's just a man. A very hot man who's a household name. But still. I can do this.

'I'm a big fan of yours, you know.'

'Seriously?' I turn around from making tea and glance at him.

'Yeah. I've watched Sunrise for years. I've always admired how you deal with those politicians. You wipe the floor with them.'

'Thank you. That means a lot.'

It's the oddest feeling that he already knew who I was before today. I imagine Jackson James sitting at home in a pair of pyjama bottoms and watching me on TV. It's too weird. And don't think of him in pyjama bottoms; you'll start blushing. Oops. Too late.

'I was hoping it would be you who interviewed me. But I was also a bit scared you'd break my balls.'

I grin. 'I only do that to sleazy politicians. You had nothing to worry about on that front.'

'I know nothing about politics, but I suspect some of the looks I was giving you on that sofa were pretty sleazy.'

'I'm used to it.' I straighten up. 'I'm not easily intimidated.'

'I like that. A lot.'

He comes to stand right beside me as I chase the tea bags around the mugs with a spoon, and his presence does seriously amazing things to my body. It's his size, and the scent of his skin mixed with some gorgeous cologne, and the heat emanating from his body. I'm not usually affected by guys in this way, but he's pulling me in with something that's more than just star quality.

I add the milk, and he looks at the impressive chunk of Swiss craftsmanship on his wrist.

'If you need to go…' I glance up at him. His eyes are back on me.

'No, nothing like that. I was just thinking, I usually make it past 10am before I hit on a woman. But it's not every day I get Honor Chapman alone.'

There's a predatory tone to his voice that gives me the best type of shivers, and I drink in the deliciousness of the moment. I do indeed have Jackson James all to myself, and he seems to be enjoying it as much as I am.

'I have a proposition for you.' He takes his mug. 'Let me take you out for dinner. Tonight, ideally. And if we hit it off, which I firmly believe we will, you'll come to the premiere with me on Friday. As my date.'

I spin and walk to the sofa to buy myself time. Holy shit. Holy *shit!* Dinner alone would be amazing. The idea that tonight I could be sitting across from this man, enjoying even more of this light of admiration in his eyes, has my stomach churning in the best way. But the premiere! That's another level of exposure he's proposing. Stepping out of a limo with him to a million blinding camera flashes. Walking up the red carpet on Jackson James' arm. It's… it's enough to take my breath away.

He's right behind me. He's right beside me when I sit. He puts down his tea and slides his arm along the back of the sofa and grins at me. That grin. It's so incorrigible and sexy and utterly impossible to resist.

'What do you reckon?'

I arch my eyebrows at him. 'A premiere is a very public statement.'

'Yep. I'm not afraid of that, but I'm not trying to make a statement.' He lowers his voice. 'I just know I'll have a better night if you're there by my side. It's a big deal for me and I'd like to share it with you.'

What he just said… I have no words. So instead, I let my eyes feast on his beautiful face. On the sky-blue eyes that look grave and vulnerable and utterly sincere. On the blessed ridge of his cheekbones and on those full lips that part slightly under my gaze. They're so hypnotic that mine mirror them. A sensation of overwhelm is flooding my nervous system. The alchemy this guy is capable of is astounding; the heat between us is palpable. I'm suddenly shy.

'In that case,' I tell him, 'I'd be honoured.'

As I stare shamelessly at him, his hand comes off the sofa and his fingers brush my hair back off my shoulder.

'Honor. I have to say, you captivate me. I got a real kick out of knowing I was going to meet you today, but being here with you, right now—you are entrancing. I mean, you're so fucking *beautiful*. I could gaze at you all day. But also…' He pauses, and slides his hand around the back of my neck, and it erupts in goosebumps. 'I really want to kiss you. Like, it's all I can think about. It's all I've been able to think about since I walked onto that set this morning. May I?'

The blood rushes to my head and my heart pounds so loudly in my ears that I can hardly hear him. I can barely process any of this. Presumably, Jackson James is not the kind of guy who needs to wait an appropriate amount of time between meeting and kissing a woman he takes a liking to, but just as I was allowing myself to imagine that he might kiss me later tonight, I'm scrambling desperately to understand that it's going to happen now. In my dressing room. On this sofa.

I nod idiotically and marvel as his face clears, he breaks out that sexy grin again, and he uses the hand behind my neck to pull me into him.

And—*fuck*. His lips. *God*. He's so damn kissable. His lips are pillowy and luscious against mine and they press with such delicious pressure that a little noise escapes me—not a moan, exactly, but a little noise at the back of my throat, and I part my lips for him, and he takes full advantage. Full.

He does this thing where his tongue slides into my mouth and then sweeps, then rolls, and his hand moves down my back, crushing me against him as closely as he can, and then I do moan. Properly. Because he's consuming me, Jackson James is consuming me, and the head rush is unbelievable, and the sensation overload is too much.

I grab at his shoulders, running my hands greedily down his arms. This guy is so stacked it's ridiculous. Unfortunately, my 'research' bingeing of his *Adrenalin* movies leaves me in no uncertainty as to the artistry that lies beneath the luxurious cotton of his shirt.

As I reciprocate with my tongue, he catches it lightly

between his teeth, and his other hand moves to cup my arse, pulling me up onto his lap.

'Fuck,' he groans into my mouth, and he tightens his grip. His arm is around my waist in a vice, the other is familiarising itself pretty well with the curves of my arse. 'This dress is—God, it's—you're so sexy.'

I know my dress is sexy—it's an utterly fabulous pale pink sheath that I wore especially for him—but as his hand slides up under it and hits the lace top of my hold-up, I pull away from him with difficulty.

'Jackson.' I look him in the eye to make sure he understands. 'I'm sure there are plenty of women who would happily fuck you on a sofa minutes after meeting you. But that's not me.'

He leans his forehead to mine, and I'm gratified by how unravelled he is, how hard he's breathing.

'I'm so sorry. Of course that's not you. I have the utmost respect for you; I just got a bit carried away. You know, finally getting my hands on you.' He cups my face and gazes at me. 'I'm going to behave.' A kiss, chaste at first before I feel the tip of his tongue and my fingers tighten on his arms.

He pulls away to look me in the eye. 'I'm going to be so well behaved, and so charming, you won't know what's hit you.'

1

HONOR

FORTEEN YEARS LATER

Jackson's cheating on me. Again.

And Mum is dying.

Though, to be fair to Mum, it's the first time she's pulled this stunt.

Unlike Jackson.

They're just both such unbearable situations, and I don't have the energy to deal with either of them properly, let alone both of them simultaneously.

I'm already a mother of two (three, if you count my husband), CEO of a cosmetics brand that's not far off unicorn status, if the next investment raise goes well, and half of one of the highest profile couples in the country.

Make that on both sides of the Atlantic.

And now I have to deal with fresh allegations—not allegations so much as compelling *proof*—of Jackson's latest shenanigans, and at the same time I have to somehow shift all the above around to make room for the most important piece of the puzzle: that Mum has months, if not weeks, to live, and I have God knows how little time left to spend with her, and that she's deteriorating at a rate that's alarming if not horrifying, and is going to need some kind of specialist care.

I don't know what kind of care she needs, but I've a horrible feeling I'm going to get pretty well versed in the terrifying world of cancer and hospices and Macmillan nurses and palliative care quickly.

The only answer is to pull in serious reinforcements on both fronts. My sister Ally is already doing most of the heavy lifting where Mum is concerned, a fact that makes me feel sick with guilt, although Ally has more slack in her schedule than I do during the summer holidays.

With Jackson, I at least have professional help: our publicist, Mara, and our 'fixer', Alex. Alex is an odious human being who is revoltingly good at his job. Unfortunately, moral bankruptcy and performance do seem directly correlated in his chosen career.

While Alex is technically *our* fixer, he's never had to fix anything for me. *Nada*. Happily for Alex's wine cellar, Jackson's antics keep him busy. You'd think I'd be used to it by now. I've had years to get used to it, after all.

We were married within a year of meeting, and Serena came along a year later, and Rollo two years after that. And the first year was an amazing adventure: heady and crazy and a media whirlwind. It felt like we were a travelling circus: The Jackson James and Honor Chapman Show. But with my first pregnancy came crushing fatigue and seemingly endless nausea, and despite being married to someone whom most red-blooded women would shag in a heartbeat, I did not want to have sex with my husband. Not often enough for his liking, in any case.

As soon as I had Serena, I felt enormous pressure to get my figure back. I'd quashed my nausea with far too many Mars Bars during my pregnancy. I'd quit morning TV when we got married—the wake-up times were too antisocial when married to someone as high-octane and sociable as Jackson. But in its stead I launched my own makeup line, Honor Chapman Cosmetics, and found myself juggling a workforce and factories and can't-make-them-up production headaches. The combination of new motherhood and exhaustion and dieting and work was all-consuming, and there was nothing about that schedule that facilitated having sex as much as Jackson would like: ideally, daily.

The rumours started, small but insidious. I sometimes wondered if the tabloids had given Jackson the green light. His fidelity was constantly being questioned already; what was the point of him keeping it in his pants? Every model he air-kissed at a fashion show, every co-star he worked with: they were all fair game for the press (and, presumably, for Jackson). It caused fights and tears (at my end) and humiliation and millions of occurrences of the paparazzi ruining the few social events we attended together. But under the tears, I was horrified to feel a sort of quiet, guilty relief.

If Jackson really was finding a way to have his considerable needs met, it took the pressure off me. I could sit and rock Serena for longer in the nursing chair that I loved, in the cosy nursery that smelt of talcum powder and lavender and my exquisite baby daughter. I could get up early and do my bootcamp or work without having had to put out the previous night. It became an unspoken, shameful agreement between us.

Things came to a head when I had two kids under three and the business was really taking off and I was in demand as an entrepreneur, and I was so fucking exhausted all the time that my whole life was one enormous contraceptive. I loved him, and he was undeniably gorgeous. And if I had to have sex, I'd obviously want it to be with my husband, but I just didn't need it more than once a week. Max.

So the rumours continued, and we danced this uneasy (and beyond weird) dance around each other, where we both pretended the tabloids weren't full of speculation about who Jackson was fucking this week, until the wife of a premiership footballer pulled me aside at an event.

'You need to decide,' she told me, 'whether you're okay with him sleeping around or not. If you're not, do something about it. If you are, you and Jackson need to take control of this narrative. Find a *good* publicist and get yourself someone who can do your dirty work for you—pay off the right people, make sure NDAs are signed. You know.'

I did not know, but the conversation, and the business card the woman pressed upon me, marked a turning point. Jackson and I had a frank conversation about what the negotiables and non-negotiables for each of us were in our marriage. It was teeth-grittingly tough, but less humiliating than a trip to a marriage counsellor.

The upshot was this: I didn't want Jackson to be unhappy or unfulfilled. Neither did I want to have to put out practically every night. And above all, I didn't want to be humiliated in the press for any reason pertaining to my marriage.

Jackson was clear that he loved me: he adored me. But he loved sex. He needed sex. And he was going to get it from somewhere. I was still the woman he adored, but I couldn't give him the excitement and frisson that going on the prowl still gave him. And, if I was completely honest with myself, I couldn't get as upset as I thought I might about the fact that my husband had transactional relations with other women. The relief that it wasn't all on me was far too great.

The other truth we couldn't quite bring ourselves to

admit was this: as a brand, our family was in the ascendant. We were more valuable together than apart. The press loved us. And so began a new phase in our marriage, one delineated by careful boundaries at home, even stricter boundaries for Jackson's 'pastimes', and a tightly defined, diplomatic relationship with the press, where access was offered and accepted in return for privacy in certain other matters. Super injunctions were rarely needed. The press learnt that to turn a blind eye on one front was to be richly rewarded by the Jackson family on the other.

It all went pretty swimmingly until a couple of years ago, when Jackson pursued—and won over—Rollo's teacher and got stupidly infatuated. Alex paid the girl off and we twisted the headmaster's arm to fire her. I shuddered to think about how close I'd come to losing Jackson, tearing my family apart and devastating our brand.

Since then, things have calmed down, partly because lockdown has cramped even Jackson's style. It's been a weird period of enforced—and surprisingly wonderful—family time when Jackson's been home, and long periods where he's been away. He's been stateside for much of it, filming a US TV series about a veteran, and the kids and I haven't been able to enter the country to visit him.

Now filming has wrapped and he's back in London, but the rumours that have surfaced about him and his gorgeous Iranian-American co-star were seeded in the US press, where we—and Alex—have less sway. They're persistent, and they're worrying, and the paps are hounding us at home and even on the school run. And the worst thing about them is that I would put money on them being true. I have a hunch about this. Filming is so intense, and the necessarily tight bubble of cast and crew this time around made things even more intense for Jackson. He's distant now he's back, I can feel it.

And I have no idea what to do about it.

This shouldn't even be on my mind. Mum is dying. Mum is *dying*. The diagnosis of terminal pancreatic cancer is less than a week old, and Mum and Ally and I are all reeling. It would be nice to think that Jackson's a big boy and can look after himself, but history has taught me otherwise. Even so, I have to leave this to Mara to deal with. It's far more urgent to find the right solution for Mum. Whatever the hell that is. Thank God I have a meeting with my girlfriends tonight. I've never needed a drink more badly.

2

HONOR

When my driver and security detail, Di, pulls up outside Elaine William's immaculate townhouse, I physically sag with relief. It's been a bloody nightmare of a day. I've tasked my executive assistant, Lydia, with researching at-home and hospice care options for Mum. The secret to my efficiency, and kind-of sanity, is having very firm boundaries around the best use of my time. Giving Mum all the emotional support she needs, and taking time to process my own feelings, are things I need to make time for. Researching logistics is not.

Still, it's hard to compartmentalise my worries over Mum and tend to everything else. The paps trailed us when I dropped Rollo off at school this morning in South Ken. Then they trailed us to my offices in Soho. Jackson's been in Manchester today with Leila, his co-star, doing some BBC interview, and the cosiness of their body language on the breakfast TV sofa has sent the tabloids into a frenzy. What *is* it about that man and breakfast TV sofas?

Leila's doe-eyed face and Jackson's best Blue Steel

impression stare out at me side-by-side from this afternoon's Evening Standard, which Di has unhelpfully left on the back seat of the Mercedes for me. I turn the paper over. I can't deny Leila is gorgeous. Jackson's a sucker for a fragile look and a vulnerable vibe. I suspect I had it when I met him. Though he's made me far more vulnerable and fragile after years of infidelity. And that teacher—Jenna—had it in spades. He seems to confuse his on-screen and off-screen identities. He's always the action hero: never able to ignore a damsel in distress.

'There are still some paps around, babe,' Di announces cheerfully. She walks around the car to open the door for me, and as I step out onto the leafy, tree-lined street off High Street Kensington, there's the collective click of several cameras and the sound of my name.

'Honor! Over 'ere, love!'

'How's your day goin', Honor?'

'What do you think of your bloke doing the dirty on you again?'

I ignore the shouts. Keep my head down. Carefully pick my way up Elaine's perfectly even sandstone steps. I'm not sure what's happened to our little arrangement with the press, but everyone seems to regard Jackson and Leila as fair game. Jackson's unlikely to want to cooperate in shutting it down; it's brilliant publicity for the show ahead of its launch this autumn. At least I look perfectly groomed for the paps. One of the perks of owning a cosmetics brand is that I have makeup artists on hand at all times. Before I left the office, I dictated my answers to a US Vogue interview while submitting to a quick face mask and a dewy, iridescent makeup look suitable for this balmy summer evening.

A uniformed server answers the door almost immediately and takes me through to Elaine's beautiful double living room on the upper ground floor. We take it in turns to host these soirees. Experience has taught too many of us that our secrets are safest behind the closed doors of private residences.

The sound of raucous laughter that strikes me immediately is at odds with the decorous surroundings. It appears a few of the others have already arrived. Stacey's guffaw stands out and has the instant effect of helping me mentally change gears. The paps are outside, and that's where they'll stay. I'm here now; I'm with my girls and an evening of laughter and fellowship awaits me, as well as heavenly champagne, thanks to the drinks business Elaine runs with her husband.

The raucousness reminds me of that fabulous scene in *Bridgerton* where the newly wed Daphne arrives at Lady Danbury's soiree for married women and discovers that, behind closed doors, they can leave their carefully curated public personas behind and do whatever the hell they like.

My friends and I are all in different fields, but the parallels between us are striking. We've known each other for years and we meet up monthly, although our schedules are booked up months in advance and closed to mere mortals, because we find each other's company highly gratifying and endlessly entertaining. These women are like a tonic. God knows I need that tonight.

I take a full champagne flute from the server and make my way over to the others, who are gathered towards the back of the room, near Elaine's double doors, which are open onto the terrace overlooking the communal garden behind them. The blossom is long gone, but the French doors frame a perfectly verdant square of a view.

Elaine, always the consummate hostess, notices me first and breaks away to kiss me. Elaine Williams is the oldest in the group by at least a couple of decades, but her perfectly silvered coiffeur is as elegant as those of anyone else in the room. She looks as though she's come straight from the salon.

She puts a hand on my arm. 'How are you doing, my dear? I'm so sorry about the papers. And I'm even sorrier about your mother. You poor little darling.'

The kind words make my eyes sting a little. Elaine does have a maternal vibe.

'Typical of Jackson to add to your plate when it's so piled high already.' She tuts. 'I hope you don't mind, but I've asked my son, Noah, to stop by this evening. Just briefly—he's a palliative care doctor. I thought he might be a useful person for you to meet. Runs his own hospice. No pressure, but he may be able to steer you in the right direction.'

'Goodness. Thank you. That would be—great.' Right now, I'll take all the handholding and free advice I can from people like Elaine and her family. I vaguely knew Elaine's son was a doctor, but the information failed to settle in my brain in the way that most information that isn't directly relevant to me does.

'Excellent. Now, get stuck into your bubbles, and come join in the fun. Stacey's very excited to be here, as you can hear.' Elaine's tone is dry.

Stacey is indeed on flying form. I've known her for years, through Evelyn and Astrid, both of whom are here tonight. Stacey is American, an extremely impressive former Rhodes scholar who runs a FinTech company. She left her husband, Jack, a couple of years back, and fell madly in love with the guy who should have been her plastic surgeon, Ariel Bloch.

She and Ariel seem to do a great job of juggling two big

jobs, as well as Stacey and Jack's four kids—four! I can't even imagine it—and Ariel's two. She's a gorgeous, glossy blonde with an effervescent personality. She's clearly living up to her role as life and soul of the party tonight.

'Hey girl!' She throws her arms around me and gives me a smacker on the cheek. Stacey has never quite adopted the European double-kiss.

'Honor was the last to arrive,' Elaine interjects. 'Shall we do our thing, and then we can have some fun?' She taps a knife against her flute, and the other women drift towards them. 'It's time, ladies.'

We have a little tradition—it sets the tone every time we get together. Everyone takes a second to say one thing that's bothering them, something they're not likely to discuss with their broader circles. It reminds us we all hold each other's confidence in our hands, but on a more practical level, it means we know what's got inside everyone's head. Sometimes we can help each other out—or help each other drink through it.

'I'll go first,' Stacey says. 'A guy at work is being a jackass —my COO. I think he has to go, but he's been at Lokk since the start. It'll be tough.'

She holds up her glass, and we raise ours, murmuring encouragement.

'You want to go next, Honor?' Astrid Carmichael asks. She's the perfect embodiment of her designer fashion brand; her platinum blonde hair is swept back in a chignon and she's in ankle-length, dove-grey silk pleats. She's been a great friend to me over the years and is well versed in Jackson's indiscretions. Astrid is now blissfully happy with her husband Gray Landau, who ran the US private equity firm that bought Astrid's brand right before lockdown and now runs sustainability ventures for Kering out of London.

I take a deep breath. Here goes. 'Right. My current headaches are that my mum's been diagnosed with terminal pancreatic cancer, just this week, and as the entire world is aware, Jackson appears to be shagging his gorgeous co-star from *Vet*, and the paps won't give me or the kids a moment of peace.'

I pinch the bridge of my nose as the others respond in horror. Stacey lunges forward and envelops me in a huge, heavenly-scented hug.

'That guy is such a douche. I know he's divine, and he's Jackson *James* for chrissakes, but he needs to grow the fuck up and remember he has a wife and kids. Get your nasty little pit-bull-fixer-guy to take care of it for you, and I am *so* sorry to hear about your mom, sweetie. That's just awful. What do you need—what we can we do to help?'

'Thanks.' It's lovely to be held and heard, and to be in this safe place with my girls. I feel my shoulders drop a little as Stacey releases me. 'Ally and I are still reeling, to be honest. As is Mum. But Elaine said her son's going to drop in later—he runs a hospice, apparently.'

'Oh, yes.' Stacey winks at Elaine. 'The delicious Dr Noah. He's just what you guys need. Seriously, wait till you see him.'

'Keep your paws off my darling son, Stacey Fisher.' Elaine's tone is steely, but she returns the wink.

We work our way around the circle of women. Siobhan Quinn, event planner extraordinaire, has split up from her husband during lockdown and is struggling to cope with the huge onslaught of events requests that have popped up from so many top brands as restrictions have eased and face-to-face socialising has become possible again. Astrid's dealing with a similar ramp-up in demand for her clothes, which is a high-quality problem.

And wonderful Evelyn Macleod, who I secretly hero-worship, just beams and hugs her glass and tells us she has everything under control. Evelyn is one of the most impressive humans I know. She was one half of a celebrity power couple—a bit like me and Jackson—when her very attractive husband, Seb Macleod, got outed as gay by the paps a couple of years ago (the official story was that he came out, but we have the full scoop: the *Post* got photos of him and his now-husband kissing and forced his hand).

Evelyn and her little boy fled down to her friends' gorgeous resort, Sorrel Farm, in Kent, and promptly fell madly in love with the farm's even more gorgeous farm manager, Angus. She and Angus are now married, and last year they added a baby daughter to their family. Evelyn ditched Seb Macleod Limited, which she had run with Seb, and invested in Sorrel Farm instead. She's the farm's Commercial Director and is in the process of turning it into a mega-brand. It's one of my favourite retreats.

I'm in awe of how endlessly smiley and upbeat Evelyn always seems to be, in the face of everything life has thrown at her in the past few years. Her personality seems to be in stark contrast to mine. I feel like a bag of nerves, even at the best of times. *Neurotic* is how I've been described in the press. *Fragile*. More than once. And I know I do a worse job than others of holding it together, of juggling all the balls, of wearing my privilege lightly and shrugging off the first-world problems and worries and scandals that instead seem to bear down on me all too heavily.

But life seems particularly exhausting at the moment, and as I stand there and drink in the heady company of these incredible women, it's easy to feel fragile and neurotic and inadequate and bloody exhausted. Despite how much I need this evening and this camaraderie (and this champagne), I also need a teeny little break to catch my breath. Gather my thoughts. Be totally alone. And so, after a few minutes of fielding lovely and well-meaning commiserations about Mum and Jackson, I slip off for a moment, to the little powder room downstairs, to pull myself together.

3

NOAH

I stick my head around Mrs Barrowman's door. She's propped up on her pillows, fast asleep, catching flies. The sash window is fully open, and the fine voile curtains flutter in the breeze. The hum of traffic and voices and birdsong carries through from outside, but I suspect they provide white noise rather than a disturbance. I smile and nod, even though she's blissfully unaware of me, and carry on my farewell rounds.

Today has been a good day at the Good Vibes hospice. The weather is so beautiful that all our guests (never patients, always guests) have been able to have their windows wide open, and this has meant that those too weak to leave their rooms can still enjoy the dreamy chords from the string quartet that my team arranged to come and play in the building's garden this afternoon.

We do as much of that kind of thing as possible. Everyone's here because there are very few other realistic options open to them. Some guests have tried everything and nothing has worked, some got remissions and extended life spans that are now in the past, and some have declined treatment on the basis that they don't want their last months on this earth to be spent in a hospital bed, with tubes everywhere.

But my team and I are determined that this is not a place to wait around to die. No matter how compromised their circumstances, no matter how much the quality of life they're used to has been relentlessly chipped away, our guests are still living, and these last few days or weeks or months of life should be *more* precious, and more magical, than before their illness, not *less*. Even if what a person defines as magical or precious now, in these final moments, varies greatly from how they would have defined those qualities when they were in full health.

The staff members at Good Vibes aren't just doctors and nurses. I hope we are friends and family and magicians and counsellors and holders of hands and whisperers of comfort and bearers of tea. Lots and lots of tea. And the building itself isn't a facility so much as a guesthouse, where medical equipment is state-of-the-art but as unobtrusive as possible, and great care and expense has gone into the furnishings and lighting and artwork, and we've designed every detail to soothe and delight and uplift and inspire. For a place people go to die, Good Vibes is a surprisingly happy place.

And indeed, guests and family members and friends always profess their amazement that it isn't depressing or scary or even apologetic for its mere existence, but rather a joyful and peaceful sanctuary where gratitude and the power of human connection reign.

Sure, there are really tough days when guests leave us and their loved ones are unprepared and devastated and wrung-out. But I always find that facing up to death, and grief, and the undeniable fact of our own mortality, is the biggest step we can take to fully appreciating this human experience with which we've all been blessed. There's a reason *memento mori* is the motto of so many people.

I'm thankful it's been an easy, lighthearted day, because I'm due at Mum and Dad's for a quick drink. If I'd had a tough, draining day of assuming the pain and bewilderment of others, I'd probably make my excuses. But as it is, my steps are light as I run down the shallow main staircases and pop my head around the open doorframe of the nurses' station to say good evening.

It's a beautiful evening, and the short walk down from Avondale Park, where Good Vibes is based, through Holland Park to High Street Ken, where Mum and Dad live, is a real pleasure. Apart from a quick bask in the afternoon sun when the string quartet was playing, I haven't really been outside today.

I cut down through enchanting Clarendon Cross, home to my parents' favourite London restaurant, Julie's. The outdoor dining space is full, and the fairy lights strung across the trees will undoubtedly have their moment later, when dusk falls, rendering this little corner of London as pretty as a Working Title movie set.

I stroll down Portland Road, past endless narrow but immaculate townhouses, and once I'm over the main Holland Park Avenue, I'm into the realm of serious money, where enormous stucco-fronted villas border the park.

Oh, to have a hospice here! We could take the patients into Holland Park and sit with them for hours in the Kyoto Garden. But these villas are tens of millions of pounds, and unless your surname is Beckham, they're not an option. Avondale Park works great as a location for us. It's far less posh than the surrounding areas, which means it's actually a (just about) viable base for Good Vibes, but it's nestled right up close to some of the most impeccable and privileged streets in London.

Mum mentioned that one of her friends' mothers has just received a terminal pancreatic cancer diagnosis and she asked if I could pop along to talk to her. I'm not clear which friend. Mum runs in some pretty glamorous, impressive circles. Dad does too, but he's far more introverted than Mum and tends to leave the socialising to her. Mum's zest for life has never waned, and she has more energy in her sixties than he'll ever have. Her girlfriends tend to be as accomplished and driven as her.

I socialise with my parents as little as possible, not because I don't love them, but because being around people who are dying all day means that all you want at the end of a shift is a quiet pint in a beer garden or a home-cooked meal at a friend's house while their kids run around the kitchen table. You want humanity, not high-octane glamour. Not that Mum's friends are remotely vacuous—no one could call them that. These women—the ones I've met, anyway, like Stacey and Evelyn—are powerhouses. They run circles around me.

The park is so gorgeous that I can't face leaving it just yet. I find a bench overlooking the formal flower gardens and flop down onto it. Its wood has been wonderfully warmed by the sun. I shut my eyes and tilt my head towards the evening rays. There aren't many better human experiences than the feeling of the sun on one's face. I can't wait to get to France next week. It's been way too long. Bloody lockdown.

After a couple of minutes of catching rays, I open my eyes. There's an abandoned Evening Standard on the bench next to me. Since COVID, the act of picking up others' left-over newspapers on benches or tubes seems far less natural, but it's lying face-up.

On the cover is a grainy photo of Honor Chapman crossing the street, head down. She has her son with her; he's in his school uniform. There are two faces inset next to her—Jackson James and that actress, Leila whatever-her-name. The headline screams HONOR DEVASTATED BY JACKSON'S LATEST FLING.

For fuck's sake. That guy is such a twat. A great entertainer, that's for sure—apparently he even does most of his own stunts—but a useless fucking husband. What the hell is he thinking? He has literally the world's most beautiful wife, and he cannot seem to keep it in his pants. Not that the papers usually come out and say that, but you can't avoid the consistent rumours about him if you move in certain circles in West London.

If I had to describe my ideal woman, physically, at least, Honor Chapman would be her. She's flawless. Just flawless. The photo shows her gazelle-like stride, and those amazing legs. She's wearing some kind of short, white sundress with a full skirt, and she looks positively girlish. Her face is hidden, her beautiful auburn hair swinging over it. The poor woman. It's so fucking depressing to think that even someone as gorgeous as her isn't entitled to love and fidelity and the fucking basics of the marriage vows they presumably made to each other.

Just seeing the story has shifted my mood. I push the paper away in disgust and, getting up, make my way through the park and out to Phillimore Gardens. Some people are so entitled that they think they have *carte blanche* to behave how they want. Surely humiliating your wife like that has got to be one of the worst things you can do to a fellow human?

When I get to my parents' place, there are a couple of guys lurking near the house with bulky long-lens cameras. Across the street, a security guard with an earpiece leans against a black Mercedes, arms crossed, staring at the cameramen in a menacing fashion. What the fuck? God knows who Mum has at the house this evening.

As I extract my set of keys, a couple of the cameramen click, and I make a run for it down to the basement entrance. It's quicker to get out of sight that way, and I have a plan: grab a few slugs of ice-cold Peroni in peace to recover my personality before pasting a smile on for Mum's friends and whatever poor person is dealing with her mother's illness.

The basement door leads straight through to a huge white kitchen which, thanks to the power of a very expensive lighting consultant, is beautifully lit. Several platters of cellophane-covered food stand on the island, ready to go. Ooh, Ottolenghi. Mum's go-to.

I resist the urge to pull off the cellophane and dig in and make a beeline for the drinks fridge. Peroni. Bingo. I crack off the lid and take a long swig. The cold, tart bubbles hit the back of my throat. Heaven. If life is about simple pleasures, this is as simple and as good as it gets.

I'm leaning against the island, resting the bottle against my cheek and contemplating facing Mum's gang of superwomen, when I hear the handle turn on the door to the loo and look up.

What happens next seems to be in slow motion. The woman who comes through the door is tall, elegant. Beautiful. And instantly recognisable. Wearing a short, white summer dress that looks as fresh as if she's just put it on, even though I know the paps saw it hours ago.

Her huge eyes widen as she clocks me, and I catch a

flash of panic—she's momentarily like a deer caught in a car's headlights—before she visibly collects herself and steps towards me, the smile on her face the same polished, professional but *dazzling* smile that I practically wept over on so many viewings of Sunrise, after so many night shifts when I was at med school.

'Hello.' She puts out her hand. Her cut-glass accent is instantly recognisable, after all these years. Iconic, one might say. 'You must be Elaine's son. Noah, isn't it? I'm Honor.'

4

NOAH

How can it be possible that she's even more beautiful in the flesh? She's *on*, I can tell; she's putting on a performance just for me, but by God does it work. I'm embarrassed to note, while I'm actually doing it, that I look behind me briefly as if this is a set-up.

There is no way I just walked through Mum's front door, thinking about Honor Chapman, and conjured her up out of Mum's loo. I didn't even know Mum knew her that well. If ever there was a reason I should have paid more attention when Mum talked about her friends, this is it.

In that split second, I decide to avoid the elephant in the room, which is the fact that, of course, I know who she is. She'll be well aware of that fact, but I don't want to embarrass her. She's here at a friend's house; I will not behave like some icky, star-struck fan. Even though I want to.

'That's me,' I say instead. 'Good to meet you, Honor. How's it going upstairs?'

She leans in towards me, and widens her smile, and it's all I can do to stand there and drink her in. Jackson James gets to come home to *this* every night. And instead he buggers off to the States and shags his co-star. What the hell is wrong with him?

'It's getting a little lively, I'll be honest. Stacey's here.' She raises an eyebrow. 'Do you know Stacey?'

'Oh, yes. I know Stacey. She's great fun.'

'She is. And she's particularly great fun this evening. She's on fire.'

'God. I'm a bit scared.' I mock-grimace. 'Maybe I won't go up there.'

She laughs, and I fucking *marvel*. Melt. The press is so hard on Honor Chapman. They're always calling her fragile and high-maintenance. And here she is, with her family's faces splashed across the front of the tabloids, and she's putting one step in front of another and smiling and making perfectly nice—heavenly, even—small-talk with a complete stranger. I'd say there's nothing fragile about that. Not that she hasn't had plenty of practice at putting on a brave face, being married to Jackson James.

'Well, it's kind of you to come,' she says now. 'Elaine mentioned she was dragging you over here to talk to me, and I'm so grateful.'

It's only now that her gaze falters, and she reaches for the glass of wine that she must have left on the island when she went to the loo, and takes a sip.

'It's *you* who needs to talk to me?' Good lord. *This would have been useful information, Mum.* 'Your—your mother is sick?'

'Yeah. We just found out this week. We got the whole bloody bombshell in one go. It's cancer. *Boom*.' She gesticulates with her hands in the air. 'Metastatic pancreatic cancer. *Boom*. Advanced. Terminal. *Boom*. There's nothing they can do, apparently. We didn't even know she was that ill

until quite recently—I mean, she's been in
didn't expect this. And now it's like she's di
front of our eyes; she's losing weight so
terrifying.'

'I'm so, so sorry.' Jesus Christ. I cannot bloody well believe she has to deal with this, on top of all the other crap she's clearly navigating at the moment. 'That is an enormous amount of information for you to process. Do you and your mum have any support?'

'Well, my sister Ally is very involved, and she lives in London too, so... But we're all still reeling, to be honest. And Mum's lost so much strength so quickly. She's at Ally's for now—in Wimbledon. And we have a nurse. But her oncologist has said we should think about a hospice now because we'll probably need one within the next few weeks.'

She puts down her glass and drops her head, rubbing a hand over her eyes. And she doesn't come back up. She stands, head bowed, shaking slightly. 'God. Sorry.' She's crying.

'Hey.' I step closer to her, puts a tentative hand on her bare arm. Make a very deliberate effort not to stroke it, for her skin is baby-soft. 'You have zero reason to apologise. This is a huge burden for anyone. Please know you're not alone. I'm happy to help in any way I can, and there are plenty of professionals like me who can support your family as you go through this. We will find a solution that represents the best fit for your mother and her priorities at this time, and one that also makes you and your sister feel supported. Okay?'

'Okay.' She lifts her head and looks at me. Her eyes are enormous and green-gold and luminous with tears, and her adorable little mouth is quivering. Being this close to her, I can see her makeup is immaculate, and that she probably doesn't need any of it. She's utterly stunning. No wonder she made it onto the Sunrise sofa at such a young age. No wonder she bagged one of the biggest action movie stars to come out of the UK. She has star quality; I can see it. I can *feel* it. The paps outside must be waiting for her—and I'd put money on that security guard being hers, too. Her presence outside makes me feel better on Honor's behalf.

She holds my gaze and lets out a shaky exhale. 'Wow, you're good at this.'

I laugh and try not to let the praise go to my head. 'I do this every day. I know for people like you and your mum, especially right now, end-of-life care feels like some sort of nightmarish parallel universe. But I promise you, there are plenty of people out there who are well-versed in this and capable of supporting you throughout this journey.'

She nods, and there's a jut of determination to her jaw. 'Will you tell me about your hospice? What's it called?'

'Of course I will. It's called the Good Vibes Hospice, and I know you won't believe this, but it's actually a lovely place, and we work very hard to make it feel as unlike a medical centre as possible, and I like to think it has a happy vibe to it. It's not all misery and death.'

'Were you raised in California, by any chance? Adopted as an adult by Elaine and Philippe?'

Her smile is dazzling. That, and the combination of the tears dancing in her eyes, is too much. It's like sunshine shining through raindrops. I almost expect a rainbow. That's the effect she has on me.

'Hey.' I keep my tone gentle. 'I'm as much of a hippy as someone raised in West London can be. It's a funny name—but the idea of calling it something like Serenity was ghastly. People are either put off or drawn in by the name. And it does what it says on the tin. Good vibes only.'

I grin at her and am relieved and gratified to find her returning my grin, and I grab a bottle of wine and another glass and steer her up the back steps to the garden, where we sit and talk for a good thirty minutes.

And once half an hour is up, I like to think that I've even slightly alleviated her fears of the unknown journey her family is facing, and at the very least, it's half an hour where her philandering fuckwit of a husband hopefully hasn't been at the forefront of her mind.

By the time I begrudgingly lead her back inside so she can join the other women and I can go pay my respects to them, we have a date. She and her sister will drop by Good Vibes tomorrow morning for a recce. Not the most obvious trappings of a good date, being that she's married, way out of my league, worried sick about her mother, and bringing her sister along—but I'll take it.

5

HONOR

I'm surprised at how reluctant I am to leave Elaine's leafy garden, and this man, and a conversation that should be horrifying, but is instead gentle, and frank, and reassuring, and eye-opening. There's something about embracing what lies ahead for Mum, and for all of us, that feels cathartic.

Since we got the news earlier this week, I've felt helpless, like everything's unravelling, and I'm totally powerless to stop it. Chatting to Noah makes me realise I still have some currency; I have the power to make Mum's last few months with us a period that may even have its own kind of quiet happiness about it.

He gestures for me to go first as we head upstairs to join the others, and I'm conscious of the fact that he leaves a few steps between us before following me up. He's a gentleman.

He's already given me the names of a few books I may want to read on palliative care, and we've set a time for me and Ally to visit the Good Vibes Hospice tomorrow. I can hear Ally scoffing at the name already, but I don't care. I trust this guy. Besides, he's Elaine and Philippe's son. He's likely to be a super-overachiever, just like his parents.

I'm surprised by how relaxed I feel after a short time in his company. It's probably the wine, and the restorative nature of Elaine's lovely garden, but it's also him. He's the absolute antithesis of Jackson, who's always on, always dominating the conversation, always wanting to *talk* and *do*.

Noah was quiet just now. Quiet, and gentle, and sensitive in the questions he asked me and the way he approached Mum's diagnosis. It's clear he's good at what he does.

I have to hand it to Elaine. She couldn't have produced a doctor son with a better bedside manner than Noah. He's gorgeous looking, too. Utterly smoking, with his light tan and his Keanu-Reeves-esque dark hair, that he kept running his fingers through when he got particularly passionate about a point he was making.

I found myself wondering, several times, how it would feel to touch that hair, to run my own fingers through it. Jackson's head has been shaven for as long as I've known him. And his smile! Jackson has the megawatt Hollywood grin perfected; his smile dazzles. Noah's warms. It's genuine and confidence-inspiring. And despite his consummate professionalism, I recognise a smile of male appreciation when I see it.

But it's not just that. Noah's calm, and calming: quietly confident and authoritative, without showing the slightest bit of ego. Some people in my life could learn from him. He has a good aura around him—a good vibe, I think, and giggle to myself. If his hospice is an extension of his own personality, I'm already sold.

When we get upstairs, the excitement and the noise level have escalated. Elaine breaks free from the other women to kiss Noah.

'I see you've met the good doctor,' she says to me, after Noah has smiled bashfully at an enthusiastic call from Stacey to go say hi, and taken his leave. 'I came down to grab the food and saw you two chatting in the garden. I thought I'd leave you to it.'

'Thank you.' I give Noah's departing back a smile. 'He's been really helpful. My sister and I are going to go and see his hospice in the morning.'

'Fantastic. I hope you'll be pleasantly surprised. I don't know how he does it, but it's such a lovely place. Flowers everywhere, cosy furniture, rugs... it's as far away from a hospital as it could be.'

'I'm looking forward to seeing it,' I say. 'Really, he's made me feel better about everything. You've done a good job with that one.'

'He's a good boy.' Elaine smiles after him fondly. 'We're very lucky. We would have welcomed him into the drinks trade, but he's always had a vocation. Now, tell me. Do you have any plans for the summer, or has this news about your mother knocked you for six?'

'The latter, unfortunately. That, and Jackson's promo schedule for this new show. Oh, and the fact that Boris keeps changing his mind about this bloody traffic light system—I'm desperate to go abroad, but I haven't quite worked out where.'

'Come and stay at Des Anges with us! Please! We'd love to have you and the kids. Philippe and I are headed out next week for the summer, and Angus and Evelyn are joining us with Eddie and Rose. And I think Noah's going to come for a long weekend, too.'

I hesitate. That does sound wonderful. Serena and Rollo break up later this week, and I'm at a loss what to do with them. Chateau des Anges is an incredible biodynamic vineyard that Elaine and Philippe's drinks company bought two or three years back; I've heard amazing things about it.

'Gosh, that's tempting. Do you seriously have space?'

Elaine laughs. 'My dear, we have oodles of space. And Rollo and Eddie must be similar in age, no?'

'They are. Eddie's maybe a year older than Rollo?'

I think. It would be great to have another kid to keep my kids entertained in the pool.

'Then it's settled. If you can get your assistant to pull together the paperwork, you should come out. Come for as long as you'd like. And—extend the invitation to Jackson, or don't. Your call.'

'I think he'll struggle to get away from work.' That's the diplomatic answer to give. I need some space from my bloody husband while I work out what to do about this latest woman of his.

Elaine's kind nod tells me she gets it. 'That's fine. You and the kids come, then. The more the merrier.'

When we rejoin the rest of the group, Elaine says, 'Evelyn, I think I've persuaded Honor to come with Serena and Rollo.'

It doesn't escape my notice that Noah grins widely at this information. He's very sweet.

'I can be manny while I'm there. Especially in the pool.' He sticks his hand up. 'As long as there are floaties.'

'You and Angus can tag-team,' Evelyn says. 'Angus is firmly on kid duty. I wanted to bring our nanny—Rose is still pretty full-on, especially now she's mobile—but he says he won't hear of it. He wants "family time". It's his funeral. I'll be stuck to my sun lounger, drinking my body weight in your delicious rosé, Elaine. Honor, you can be my drinking buddy.'

'Oh my God.' I moan despite herself. 'It sounds like heaven. Count me in.'

My imagination drifts to a sun lounger by a gorgeous pool in the idyllic Provencal countryside. Tuning out the raucous shouts of ecstatic children and falling headfirst into a trashy novel. Sublime. I can already feel the sun on my skin, smell the coconut scent of suncream. It's been far too long. The kids and I need this. Badly. But before that, I have a mountain to climb.

6

HONOR

'You'd better have some freebies for me. You owe me big time.'

My sister Ally drums her hands on the wooden tabletop. We're having breakfast at the Cowshed spa in Clarendon Cross before walking up to Avondale Park and braving the hospice. Despite all of Noah's reassurance last night, I'm seriously spooked by the idea of walking into a place that's basically a waiting room for death. I can tell Ally feels the same under her bravado.

'I do. Guilt presents.' I haul a large, glossy Honor Chapman Cosmetics bag off the floor and onto her lap. 'I wasn't sure how many freebies I'd need to make up for the fact that you're putting up our terminally ill mother and her nurse.'

'Many, many freebies is the answer to that.' Ally's face is already buried in the carrier bag as if it's a horse-bag. 'Oh my Goooooood. You brought me the new tinted moisturiser. Thank you.' She emerges from the bag and holds up a box in our signature rose-gold.

'It's not moisturiser. It's iridescent primer. You're

welcome. We're launching it exclusively in Selfridge's next week. I figured death-watch earned you a pre-launch goodie or two.'

Ally blows me a kiss. 'Thank yoooou. Thank you.'

'I'm lucky you're so easily pleased. All I have to do is bring you freebies. You have to look after Mum. How's it going?'

'It's going. The nurse doesn't have a huge amount to do at this point. She's mainly keeping Mum company and prepping her meals when we're all out.'

'Still. It's a big ask for you guys.'

Ally is a professor of Twentieth Century English Literature at King's College. She has two children, Ralph and Dottie, who are a couple of years younger than Serena and Rollo, and is married to Ted, who's one of the most genuinely decent people I've had the good fortune to meet. They live in Wimbledon, not far from where we grew up. Mum's been staying with them for the past month, and I feel gut-wrenchingly guilty about that fact every day.

It should have been me and Jackson taking Mum in. But Mum put her foot down, said she didn't feel comfortable being ill in our huge house—she actually called it a mausoleum—and that she'd lived in Wimbledon Village her whole adult life and didn't want to stray too far (it will be interesting having to pitch a move to Good Vibes to her, if we like it).

The principal source of my guilt is the relief I feel that we haven't had to bring the spectre of illness and death into our beautiful home. Sickness scares the hell out of me. Mum's always been an incredibly strong woman—well, until Dad passed a couple of years ago, anyway—and seeing her like she is at the moment is extremely upsetting.

There's a part of me, I'm guiltily aware, that wants to stay the hell away from this new, sick version of Mum, no matter how awful that sounds to my own ears. And now Ally, whose house is far smaller than ours, has Mum staying, and this nurse staying, and the burden it will all put on my sister will be enormous. This Good Vibes place had better be a viable option, because, right now, it's our only option.

'It is what it is.' Ally shrugs. 'Yeah, it's a pain at the moment, and it's been weird and upsetting for the kids to see Grandma like this, but life isn't all surface glamour. Sometimes you have to get stuck into the real stuff, y'know? And we do have limited time left with her, Duck Face.'

And that is the crux of the matter. I'm so scared of the realness of life that I do everything possible to avoid scratching the glossy surface of this lifestyle I've built: I've hired fixers to sweep my marital problems under the carpet, and publicists to paint a shiny picture of my family, and stylists and image consultants to ensure that the version of myself I portray to the public is flawless. And the more I build up that veneer, layer by lustrous layer, the higher the stakes get, and the less well equipped I am to deal with anything real.

And somewhere, in a part of my mind I don't allow myself to wander to, I know that this refusal to dig deep and grasp the most profound parts of life with both hands is costing me a real understanding of the human experience. I know this because my therapist may have mentioned it once, or twice, or a million times. Meanwhile, my sister is facing up to what needs to be done, fearlessly, while holding down a professorship and a family of her own.

'I know I need to get stuck in,' I tell Ally now. 'I promise, if we move Mum to this place, I'll do a lot more of the heavy lifting.'

My phone lights up and I look down. It's a WhatsApp from Di.

'For fuck's sake.'

'What?' Ally pops a large piece of apple and bran muffin in her mouth. It looks delectable. I'm drinking green tea.

'Di says there are some paps outside. I'm afraid walking's out of the question. D'you mind if we drive up there?'

'Your life is so fucked up. Honestly, I don't know how you handle it. But that's fine, Duck Face.'

She's called me Duck Face ever since we saw *Four Weddings and a Funeral* for the first time. Ally reckons that my face whenever I look in the mirror is as smug as Duck Face's is when she sees her bridal wreath before her own (aborted) wedding. It's not, obviously, but unfortunately, the more something pisses me off, the more tightly a grasp my little sister holds on it, and the name has stuck. For years and years.

'It's part of the deal,' I say now, looking wearily around. The Cowshed is a tiny spa that's part of the fabric of this corner of London. It sits on the apex of two pretty streets, so there are windows all along two sides of the triangular room. There's just room on the ground floor for some obscenely comfortable terry-covered armchairs, where the mani-pedis take place, a large oval wooden table, where we're sitting now, and a tiny kitchenette that manages to conjure up all manner of home-cooked goodies for which its owner, Soho House, has become so well-known.

'So who's this guy?' Ally asks. 'The mysterious doctor?' She brushes some hair out of her eyes. My sister is beautiful, though far lower-maintenance than me. She's wearing boyfriend jeans, Birkenstocks and a pretty white peasant top that I suspect is a recent haul from her insatiable H&M habit. Her hair is longer and blonder than mine, thanks to flawless highlights. Her hair is the only high-maintenance thing about her.

'Nothing mysterious about him. He's the son of my friend Elaine. I hadn't met him before. I knew her son was a doctor, but I didn't realise he ran a hospice—I suppose I zoned out that information because it wasn't relevant at the time. Anyway, he's very nice. Very—impressive. And right now, I have no bloody clue what we're supposed to do, so I'll take all the hand-holding I can get. Right?'

'Definitely.' Ally wipes her mouth with a napkin, which seems pointless, because she then rams more muffin in. 'So,' she says with her mouth full. 'Talk to me about Dick Face. What lines is he feeding you this time?'

'Duck Face and Dick Face. No wonder you're a shining star in the King's College English Department.'

'Stop deflecting. Sorry'—this as a crumb shoots out of Ally's mouth in my direction. 'Tell me you've confronted him about all this bullshit.'

'I've danced around it.' I lower my voice and glare at my sister to do the same. 'Believe me, I'm livid about all this.' I gesture at the window, where the paps are presumably circling.

'You're livid the *press* knows, or you're livid Jackson is shagging that mythical creature?'

'Come on. You know we have an arrangement.'

'I know, and I still think it's messed up, but don't you ever worry that he'll fall for one of them? I mean, shooting a TV show during lockdown must have been pretty intense for them, being in, like, a little bubble together.'

'I am worried about that.' I look up from my teacup. 'I'm going to have it out with him. He's around this evening, so I'll ask him what's going on.'

'You guys are so weird.' Ally shudders. 'God, the idea of

having to have a chat like that with Ted... It gives me the heebie jeebies.'

'I get that it's—unorthodox. But you've got to understand, what Jackson and I have is as much a business as a relationship. We've both worked ridiculously hard to get to this place. He has needs that he goes to other women for, and I get the rest of him. And he's a great dad, when he's around, and we're happy, in our own way. It works for us, basically.'

'But you have to share your husband with other women.'

'I have to share my husband with the *world*. He's public property—everyone wants a bit of him, and it's been that way for as long as I've known him. Look, your stance comes from the fact that you blindly accept monogamy to be the default acceptable state for a relationship, despite the fact that your students must argue this point with you all day long. There's nothing to say people have to be monogamous in a marriage, except for the weight of centuries of social and cultural norms.'

I sit back and fold my arms, but Ally doesn't take the bait.

'You're monogamous.'

'Yes, yes, I am, but that's because I get my kicks elsewhere: from watching my company grow and my kids grow and being around amazing, smart, stimulating people. I don't need any more men in my life. I have quite enough on my plate as it is.'

Ally raises her eyebrows. 'Fair enough, but have you ever had the chat with Jackson? Is he on board with you playing away if you wanted to?'

My sister always manages to make me feel defensive, mainly because she never shies away from asking me the exact things I hope she won't ask.

'Not explicitly, no.'

'What do you think he would say if you *took a lover*?' The last three words are in a French accent.

'You're ridiculous. I'm not taking a lover. And—I'm sure his nose would be out of joint, initially, because I'm not sure being cuckolded goes with his alpha male reputation, but then I'm sure he'd realise it was just his ego getting in the way and he'd come around.'

'Hmm.' Ally's going to take far more convincing than that. 'That I would like to see.' She must see the exhaustion on my face, because she puts an affectionate hand on my arm. 'Let's go and pump this doctor for all the information we can get. Right, shall we face these dickheads? Maybe I can put my arm around you and pretend to be your lover. That'll distract them from your Dick Face husband.'

7

HONOR

Thankfully, there's a parking spot right outside the Good Vibes Hospice. Di helps us out of the car and we stand together in front of the glossy red door.

Ally leans in. 'I'm a bit scared.'

My heart lurches. Ally will always be my amazing little sister, who I love so much. I put an arm around her shoulders and squeeze before letting go. 'I know, sweetie. It's shit, and it feels really wrong that we should even be considering a place like this for Mum. But Noah promised me it's not scary or depressing, so let's hope he was telling the truth.'

We ring the doorbell at eleven sharp, and when it swings open, Noah himself is there. I wasn't expecting that. He stands with one arm up on the door and shoots us—but if I'm honest, mainly me—a wide grin. I also wasn't expecting what he's wearing: a very faded, soft-looking t-shirt sporting a cracked image of Homer Simpson, and some knackered jeans. The sleeve of the t-shirt rides up his raised arm, exposing a tanned bicep. Nothing like Jackson's, of course, but still. It's a gratifying sight.

I feel unaccountably flustered and clear my throat. I'm aware of Ally looking from Noah to me and back again.

'I didn't realise hospice owners wore jeans and answered doors,' I say archly to cover my sudden discomfort.

He sweeps his free arm open and steps back. 'Come in, come in. There's no job too humble for me here. And white coats are scary and serious, and we don't do scary or serious here. My man Homer has better vibes than a white coat.'

'So I see.' I adjust my posture and sweep through the door. 'This is my sister, Ally. Ally, this is Doctor Noah Thierry.'

'Noah, please. How do you do, Ally?'

He shakes Ally's hand and then goes to kiss me on both cheeks. He kissed me goodbye last night, but somehow I wasn't expecting a kiss this morning. As he brushes my cheek with his, I catch a sniff of something citrusy. Verbena. Shampoo, maybe. He doesn't strike me as a cologne kind of guy.

'It's good to see you again,' he says quietly, somewhere near my ear, and then straightens up. 'Thank you both for coming. It's not an easy step to take, but I hope we can make you feel better about everything you're facing. D'you fancy a quick tour first, before we sit down and have a chat?'

Ally and I exchange glances.

'Sounds good,' Ally says. She's smirking. I know that smirk.

'Okay then. Let's do this. Welcome to Good Vibes.'

We're standing in a large, square hallway with a wide wooden staircase in front of them. It has a stairlift attached to it, but that's the only sign we're not in a private residence. Noah leads us into an airy sitting room. The two sash windows are thrown wide open and there's a hotch-potch of furniture: bookshelves, cosy sofas, tonnes of throw pillows, and a few pretty lamps dotted around. Against one wall stands a large console with a kettle, a Nespresso machine and a tray of mugs. It's a delightful room, if you can forget the purpose it really serves.

'If Soho House did death,' Ally quips.

'That's exactly the look we went for.' Noah looks bashful. 'We actually got one of their ex-designers to pull this place together. When we brainstormed on how we wanted this to feel, one of our team joked that he'd like to retire to Soho Farmhouse when he's old, and have their converted milk floats bring him a bacon sandwich every morning and a vodka martini every evening when he's confined to his cabin. It got us thinking that we should make it as comfy and tasteful as possible. Some relatives end up spending a lot of time here.'

I flinch at the reminder that I could end up stuck in this place for most of my waking hours quite soon. Noah seems to catch my expression.

'Come and see the kitchen.'

He leads us across the hall and into a charming kitchen with a communal wooden table. Two men are standing at the island, prepping food. They give us a smile and a wave.

'Nick and Ty, our chefs,' Noah says. 'We take nutrition seriously here. Our guests may be out of time for treatment, but an anti-inflammatory diet can really prolong life and avoid unnecessary suffering. Also, food is one of the main pleasures in life for most of us, so as long as our guests can enjoy it, we'll spoil them.

'All our meat is pastured; the vast majority of our produce is organic. We prepare and serve a lot of bone broths, too. But it's not too virtuous. There's tea and home-made cake or scones every afternoon. It's become a bit of a tradition. You'd be amazed how many of our guests have visitors around three o'clock.'

He winks at us and puts his hands in his pockets. My first impressions are good. I have no idea what the medical credentials of this place are, but I can appreciate that it's as far from my preconceived idea of how a hospice would look and feel as possible.

'Let's take a look upstairs,' he continues. 'We've got eight rooms; two of them are free at present. They're all nice, big rooms, and they're all ensuite.'

He skips up the shallow staircase, and I find myself checking out his arse. Absentmindedly, yes, but I'm definitely checking it out. It's not my fault; he has a very, very nice arse. Delectable, even. The jeans curve around and under it, the fabric pulling taut as he climbs the stairs, providing quite enough definition to be tantalising.

Ally hits me on the arm. She opens her eyes as wide as she can and presses her lips together in an exaggerated fashion. I know that facial expression. It means: *If I open my mouth I am likely to say something inappropriately lascivious.*

I shake my head in what I hope is a stern manner. We're here to scope out the place where Mum may die, for God's sake. Ally needs to act her age. She doesn't have to know I'm admiring the good doctor's fine rear view, too. He's definitely more Ally's type: all bohemian and altruistic. I tend more towards the high-wattage alpha male. Case in point: my husband.

Noah shows us the two available rooms. Most of the other rooms have their doors closed or kept slightly ajar, and I look fixedly ahead, not wanting any surprise glimpses of dying 'guests'. Being upstairs brings home the real point of this place.

The room at the front will be perfect for Mum—if this is

the right next step for her. Moving her somewhere, out of the family, into a place where she'll be waiting to die, feels like giving in without even a fight. Even though the doctors have been very clear that there's nothing to fight for.

The room is square, with what look like original floorboards, their chestnut colour warm and lustrous in the morning light. It must be east facing. That would be good. Mum's been sleeping badly, and it strikes me that facing the morning might be easier after a bad night if the sun is shining in. And before she got sick, Mum was a morning person.

'It doesn't look like a hospital room.' Ally is moving about the room, peering behind the curtains, opening the wardrobe and pressing down on the bed. 'Nice bed.'

'It's not a hospital room. We've tried hard to make it homely. Our team is all highly trained and very experienced, but the priority here is to make our guests feel as comfortable as possible—not just physically, but emotionally.'

Noah shows us down the hall, past a neat line of wheelchairs, to the nurses' station. He introduces us to two nurses, who are also two of the smiliest human beings I've ever met. Thank God for people like these, who dedicate their lives to making other people's lives better. I could never imagine having that sense of vocation.

'Would you like to have a coffee and a chat about how this might work?' he asks. 'You don't have to decide anything right now, of course, but I'm sure you have a lot of questions.'

Ally and I exchange a look.

'That would be good.' Ally brushes some hair out of her eyes. 'It's all a bit overwhelming.'

'I know it is.' Noah puts a hand fleetingly on her arm

and I catch the ghost of another smirk on my sister's face. I roll my eyes internally.

Noah leads us back downstairs to the sunny living room. 'Have a seat in here and I'll grab the iPad. Then I'll get you both sorted with a cuppa.'

He's barely out of the door when Ally spins around.

'Ok, I want to divorce Ted and marry this guy and have his babies, but he is so into you it's quite pathetic.'

'Don't be ridiculous!' I hiss, looking around in a panic. He could be back at any minute.

'I'm not being ridiculous. It's actually quite sweet. You know in *Something's Gotta Give*, when hot doctor Keanu totally ignores Frances McDormand and whatever the daughter's name is—'

'Marin. Amanda Peet.'

'Exactly. And he just stares and stares at Diane Keaton—'

'Erica Barry. Please. She's a famous playwright, don't you know?'

'Erica *Barry*. How could I forget? And the others are laughing, because it's so obvious that he has eyes for *no one except Erica*. That's exactly what's going on here. Come to think of it, Dr Noah has more than a bit of a Keanu vibe going on…'

She's so right. He really does. 'He really doesn't.'

'Just saying. Doc's got it *bad*. And you're not as old as Diane Keaton.'

'Can we focus on the task at hand, please? Finding the right place for our beloved mother to die?' I wheel out my favourite snippy tone.

'You're such a superior pain in the arse. Loosen up a little.' Ally winks. 'This is a shitty situation; take your fun where you can get it.'

'And you're an immature pain in the arse. Let's get Mum sorted and then I can free up my headspace to focus on my useless fucking husband.'

The last part of that comes out somewhat more loudly than I mean it to and coincides with Noah walking back into the room with an iPad. His eyes widen, and out of the corner of my eye I see Ally let out a silent whistle. For God's sake.

'My apologies.' I fix my signature smile on my face: polite, fake, and brooking no arguments. 'Let's get to it.'

8

NOAH

I make three espressos, glad for the opportunity to turn my back on the awkward scene I just interrupted. Hearing Honor Chapman referring to her famous and infamous spouse as *my useless fucking husband* has given me far more of a thrill than it should have. At least she's fighting back against Jackson James' outrageous shenanigans. She's feistier than the press gives her credit for. Contempt seems a healthier reaction than heartbreak.

By the time the three of us sit down, the two women on the sofa and me on a nearby cocktail chair, the tension has eased. I hand Honor her espresso cup and saucer, forcing myself to make the clear, friendly eye contact any doctor would make with a patient's family member.

I've been trying to control my glances at her since she walked in here in the ridiculous and jaw-droppingly gorgeous little dress she's wearing today. It's a pale, sea-foam green that sets off her huge, green Disney eyes and her pale auburn hair perfectly. It's made of some super-light, silky fabric with an abundance of frothy ruffles. She's wearing high, strappy sandals, and between the dress and sandals lie acres of pale, satiny leg.

She crosses her legs daintily as she settles down on the sofa with her coffee, and I catch a couple of perfect little freckles on the side of her thigh and hastily avert my gaze. I've grown up in privilege, seen and even dated women in these circles, but I've never quite had the same impression of otherworldliness from any of them that I have from Honor. How does she even achieve this, every morning, before she presumably does the school run? Nature has blessed her, that's for sure, but I'm not naïve enough to think she wakes up like this.

Although, if she has to deal with potentially being splashed across the front pages every day, it makes sense that she wants to make an effort, portray a certain image to the world. The entire process must be exhausting.

I shift into professional mode. These two women, and their mother, have already begun understanding and grieving the imminence of death, and it's my job to make the process as smooth and as meaningful as is possible.

'I know this place is a lot to take in,' I say. 'Do you have any initial thoughts?'

'It's much—happier—than I expected,' Ally says. 'Less scary. It feels very calm and warm.'

'Calm and warm is a good start. I'm glad you feel that way.' I smile at her. It's easier to focus on the job at hand when I'm talking to Ally. She's normal. Very attractive—but a normal woman. Not like the mythical goddess sitting next to her, the goddess who's been the object of my most prolonged and intense celebrity crush ever. 'I understand your mother's been staying with you and your family these past few weeks?'

'Yeah.' Ally rubs her eyes with her hand. 'And it's been

seriously weird. I mean, it's fine, because she's my mum and that's what you do for family, right? But it's a strain. We don't really have the space, and the kids are finding it a bit freaky, having Grandma there, super sick and confined to her bed most of the time, and all the medical equipment and oxygen tanks that are suddenly around, and having a nurse in the house, too...

'And I know Mum is uncomfortable about it too, because she's the one who's been pushing us to find somewhere more—permanent. She says she doesn't feel comfortable taking over the house like this, and she'd rather be somewhere that's more her own, where she's not imposing. Which is silly, but...'

She trails off, and I nod. This guilt among family members when it comes to transferring dying patients to a hospice or hospital is so common, and so understandable.

'I get it,' I tell Ally now. 'Having the spectre of illness and death hanging over your home, which has been a safe space for your family, is very unsettling, and even upsetting. Especially if you have children. One of the biggest advantages to a hospice is that you and your mum have an entire team focused on making this final part of her life a human experience. It's not about medicine now. It's about us taking the burden off you—the burden of caregiving and ensuring your mum is comfortable and as pain-free as possible.

'And by doing that, we free you and your family up to do what you should be doing—spending meaningful, high-quality time with your mum. Talking about her wishes for the remainder of her life as well as after her death. Seeing loved ones. Reminiscing about happy times. All of these things are so important, and I promise you, the time your mum has left with you doesn't have to be filled with pain and grief. It can be special, happy. That's what we're here for. That's *precisely* why we created this place.'

I pause to give them time to process. They're both staring at me. Ally looks to be on the verge of tears.

'That sounds... amazing,' she tells me shakily. 'Like, heavenly. I feel so guilty that we can't look after Mum properly, and when I think about what lies ahead for us all, I imagine this awful, horrifying descent into death with lots of pain and suffering for Mum—it sounds like it's just going to get worse and worse, from what I've heard.'

I lean forward, put down my cup.

'Not at all. Honestly. Often, it can be the treatment stage that's the most traumatic: the endless cycle of hope and crashing disappointment, and that mentality of always having to be fighting whatever illness it is—particularly for cancer patients. But the benefit of the palliative phase is that it can bring with it acceptance, and with that comes a sense of peace. Don't feel guilty about *anything*, you hear me? You are not qualified for this. We are. Offload it.

'The one thing your mum doesn't have is time. Use that time doing what you're qualified to do, which is to be her daughters, whom she loves. Delegate the rest to us. It's no exaggeration to say that many of the most beautiful moments of human connection I've ever had the privilege to witness have been here, or on palliative care wards. I promise you, we will find a way to give your mother some peace, and I hope you will find some peace through this process, too.'

My gaze flits from one to the other while I speak. Tears are now running down Ally's cheek. Honor shifts to rummage in her handbag, pulling out a tissue, which she gives to Ally. It's perfectly reasonable for Ally to be upset; she's been shouldering the bulk of the burden so far.

I hold my hands up. 'Listen. I don't mean to give you a hard sell. You should check out some other facilities too, before you make your decision. I'm happy to suggest some names, if you'd like to check out a few places. I just want you to know that you aren't alone, and you absolutely should not need to shoulder this burden without proper help.'

The two women look at each other again, and Honor gives a tiny nod of her head.

'I think this place sounds perfect,' she says. 'You've said all the right things. Right now, we're so overwhelmed, and so worried about what lies ahead for Mum. The idea that we can salvage something out of all this and ensure that the next few months aren't a total bloody nightmare is—heavenly, as Ally said.'

A weight leaves my chest. Good Vibes can help this family; it really can. I categorically do not allow myself to think about the fact that I'll doubtless be seeing far more of Honor too.

'That's great news,' I say brightly. 'Can I ask how your mum is finding everything at the moment?'

We discuss their mother, Stephanie's, latest conversations with her oncologists, her prognosis (which is three to six months), the shocking speed of her decline and weight loss so far, and the fact that the recent diagnosis and prognosis have completely taken the wind out of her sails.

'She's usually so feisty,' Ally says. 'Like, seriously feisty. But it's like she's just given up.'

'That's common. Also, remember her body is being ravaged. She's exhausted. The silver lining is that she doesn't have to fight when she's here. Once she's at Good Vibes, the small things will become the big things. Little things are so important to letting our guests feel that they are truly seen and human and *alive*, rather than just written off. Hence the tea and cake. We have musicians visit weekly.

'And we'll ask you and your mum, if she's up to it, to complete a long and tedious questionnaire when she arrives. It means that if pedicures are what she needs to feel her best, we'll know about it, and we'll take care of it. Or if she likes a blow-dry. Or whether she's a side-sleeper or a back-sleeper. And exactly how she likes her tea. And in these tiny ways, we will honour and celebrate the very essence of what makes your mum your mum, for as long as we have with her.'

'God.' Ally has her tissue to her eyes. 'It sounds bloody amazing. Thank you, Dr Noah. I'm so happy Honor here found you.'

My eyes flick to Honor as I reply. 'I've got you. We've got this. Okay?' God knows, I mean it, and not just in a professional sense. I will use whatever tools are at my disposal to help this incredible woman through the pain that lies ahead for her and her family. If she'll allow me, being a source of support for Honor Chapman is my new mission.

9

HONOR

I eventually make it into the office. It's gone midday, and I'm filled with frustration at the vastly different directions my life is pulling me in lately. Thank God for Di and the car. It would be far more time efficient to take the tube into our offices in Soho, but obviously that's out of the question. I haven't been on public transport for years.

So I sit in the car, and put up the glass screen, and pick at some sashimi Di's picked up for me, and dictate yet more interview questions for Harper's Bazaar into my phone, and have a catch-up call with Lydia, my executive assistant.

The afternoon passes in a tightly scheduled flurry where there is no margin for error. I approve sample packaging for a new concealer we're launching later in the year, sit down with my Finance Director to go through the numbers for the first half of the year—things are really picking up, now that lockdown has finally eased in the UK—and sign off on the proposed media spend and split for the upcoming illuminating primer launch.

It was inefficient to come in, but since people have started filling up the office again, I get in there whenever humanly possible. The office has a wonderful pulse about it, thanks to the young and insanely enthusiastic team I've built around me, that being at home on Zoom just doesn't deliver.

On the way home, I do a video interview with a new senior candidate for the marketing team, which means that by the time Di delivers me back home to The Boltons in South Kensington, I've had almost no opportunity to think about what I'm going to say to Jackson. The press is still running a loop of stories on us both. There were shots of me arriving at Elaine's house last night in this morning's papers, juxtaposed with photos of Jackson and Leila cosying up on their press junket up north yesterday.

I arrive home to a scene of domestic bliss, and for a moment I have a wobble, an out-of-body experience where my brain can't quite process whether what I'm looking at is real or a carefully crafted scene. So much of our family life is curated at worst, fake at best. But no, this is real. My husband is sitting at the vast white marble island that dominates the kitchen, his shaven head bent close to Rollo's curly mop.

'Count it out in fives,' he tells Rollo. 'Or use your key numbers.' Rollo was diagnosed with dyslexia a couple of years back, and since then Jackson's publicly embraced his own long battle with dyslexia to the point that he's now an ambassador of the British Dyslexia Association. He's also endlessly patient with Rollo, in a way that I often fail to be, because he understands far better how the little guy's mind works.

I pause a moment before interrupting this gorgeous little tableau. I'm suddenly nervous in the pit of my stomach. God knows, we've had enough arguments over the years, but I never relish confrontation.

'Hi, boys,' I say finally, swinging my tote bag onto a bar stool and approaching them.

'Mummy!' Rollo swings around in his stool and jumps off at the same time as Jackson pushes his back and stands up.

'There's my gorgeous girl,' he says, and throws his arms open. I stumble into them. The reality of him is always so impactful, such a relief. He wraps those immense, rock-hard arms around my upper back and squeezes me as Rollo wraps his reed-thin arms around my waist in delight and I close my eyes.

Home. Jackson either has zero shame or is the world's best actor, because right now he's acting like he has nothing to be nervous about or guilty for, as if his face hasn't been plastered all over the papers next to that of his twenty-something co-star.

It's definitely that he has no shame. He has such an extraordinarily well-cultivated sense of entitlement that he quite honestly believes he can move through life doing whatever (and whomever) the fuck he wants. It must be wonderful to have such all-encompassing self confidence.

I shift my head so I can bury my nose between Jackson's pecs and inhale as hard as I can while edging one arm around his back. My other hand is on the back of Rollo's curly head, pulling him into me. Jackson smells like he always does: great, and expensive, and masculine. Excitement and home. Refined and untamed.

And I have that moment, as my nose brushes the fresh cotton of his polo shirt, that I always have. It's equal parts relief and smugness and wonder that I have him, still. That at the end of the day, he always comes home to Rollo and Serena and me. So it's with a lighter, fonder tone than I've intended that I whisper *we need to have a talk* before disentangling myself so I can stoop down to hug my beautiful, astonishing little boy, who elicits feelings in me that are completely uncomplicated: pure adoration.

Shortly afterwards, while our housekeeper gives Rollo his supper and Di goes over to Serena's school to pick her up from a netball fixture, I head upstairs with Jackson to our bedroom. My body and mind are tired and I need a shower and a change of clothes into something more comfortable. Time to shed the armour I've been wearing all day.

I love this room—it's my retreat, with its lacquered wood floors and stunning bay window and huge white bed. There's a massive Rococo nude on the wall that Jackson bought me a few years ago at Christie's. He got into a mega bidding war, but it was worth it. It's glorious.

'Unzip me?' My tone is practical, not coquettish. I turn my back to Jackson and dip my head, and he brushes my hair over one shoulder and pulls down my zip, kissing the nape of the neck.

'Hi, beautiful.' He slaps me on the arse. 'You're all good.'

I turn around, rolling my bare feet over the soft white rug. Those sandals bloody kill me. But they're worth it.

I pull the dress off and step out of it, throw it on the bed. Jackson's taken off his polo shirt, and he stands before me in just a pair of beige linen trousers. He is... a knockout. He always makes me catch my breath, though I've done enough work on myself to know that that caught breath is seventy-five percent appreciation and desire, and twenty-five percent knowledge of how many other women would *kill* to be in my shoes in those moments.

That's why it's so much more complicated with him than Ally or anyone else will ever understand. That he is so universally desired is a turn-on. That he has other women, and yet he always comes home to me, is a turn-on, if I'm completely honest with myself. Jackson is what he is. He's never going to be the most profound guy out there; he's no tortured genius. He's a very masculine man who has a lot to give and has very healthy sexual appetites in return. He loves women. He loves sex.

And he loves the thrill of the chase, a thrill which, by definition, I can't really give him. We can play games, of course, but I can't give him that thrill on a grand scale. I get that. And given that sex is way, way more important to him than to me, I've made peace with it.

What I do not like, what is not acceptable, is being made a fool of. The irony of his infidelity is that it adds a frisson to our marriage. It makes it less comfortable, and therefore less predictable. He's never one hundred percent sure that I won't have changed the locks when he returns from his philandering, and I'm never one hundred percent sure that he'll come back. It keeps things fresh. Pathetic, but true.

He comes towards me, grinning that grin that has earned his studios billions of dollars over the years. He's a sight for sore eyes—perfectly defined pecs above an abdomen that tapers right into those linen trousers. The caps of his shoulders are perfection, as are the sculpted curves of his arms. Those arms slide around my waist and he unclips my bra.

'Nice lingerie.' He brushes his lips down the side of my neck. 'New?'

'No. Jackson. Stop. I'm not doing this. I want to talk about the fact that you're screwing your co-star. According to the daily press, anyway.'

'Let's talk about it in the shower.'

He releases me and drops his pants and boxers, kicking them away. Slides my thong over my hips and down my legs. Kisses my stomach lightly. I roll my eyes and tense at the inconvenient flicker of desire that hits me. For God's sake. I have no intention of sleeping with my husband. It's the last thing he deserves.

'Eau de nil.' He flicks the little lace thong across the room.

I laugh. 'How the hell do you know that colour?'

'I know that colour. I'm good at colours. It's the same as your dress. It matches your eyes.'

'You are very good. And it does match my eyes; that's why I wear it.'

'It works.' He kisses me lightly. 'Let's get you in the shower.'

He leads me into the bathroom and turns on the twin rain dance shower heads. A torrent of water hits the marble. Jackson tests the temperature and pulls me in. It's just about tepid, which is as warm as I can handle in this weather. I step under the full flow of the water and tilt my head back. That feels *great*. Refreshing. Life-affirming.

Jackson gets behind me and wraps his arms around me. He's already hard. That man is relentless. I lean back against him and remind myself to be angry with him, even while my traitorous hips press into him.

'Jackson.'

'Hmm?'

'Are you screwing Leila? Tell me straight.'

His hand strokes up and down her stomach. 'I am. We were in a tiny bubble for so long, in Utah. What else was I supposed to do?'

'I wouldn't expect anything else, but are you still screwing her? While she's in the UK?'

A slight hesitation. 'Yeah.'

'Did you use protection?'

'Babe! Always! You know that.'

'Is it serious? Should I be worried?'

'No, babe. It's—it's always intense, y'know? Filming with someone, especially when we couldn't interact with the outside world, and I couldn't see you. So there's a... habit, I suppose. A bit of a hangover from filming. But it's not serious. It's not like—you're my person.'

I know what he was about to say. *It's not like* Jenna. That schoolteacher he fell hard for a couple of years ago. The one woman, apart from me, who he let get under his skin.

'Okay.' I exhale. 'So why the hell is the press all over this? What about our arrangement? And why aren't Mara and Alex dealing with it?'

'Precisely because the press has nothing. There's nothing to talk about. If they had something concrete, you know Mara and Alex would make it go away.'

Mara would cajole the news outlet in question and threaten to withhold the very generous access they have to the Jackson family. Alex would wave carrots (cheques) and sticks (NDAs) and threaten and cajole and bully as needed. They're a formidable team.

'This is to be expected, babe,' he continues. 'We're doing a tonne of press ahead of the launch. Of course they're going to speculate.'

'Can't you be a bit less... cosy? You're all over her like a rash.'

His voice in my ear is almost apologetic. 'You know how it is, babe. It's good publicity, if they think the leads have chemistry off-screen too.'

And there it is. The truth I have no choice but to accept. Mara's not challenging the press because, without a shadow of a doubt, Jackson and the studio will have given her a very clear mandate: don't interfere with coverage that whips up speculation as to the off-screen nature of the leads' chemistry.

'For God's sake.' I pull out of Jackson's hold and put my hands over my face while the water thunders down over my head. 'I get it, but it's so bloody humiliating, Jackson.'

'I know, babe. And I'm so sorry. Let's do some public appearances together, yeah? Present a united front. It's really important to me that everyone out there knows I love you, and that we're a family. And'—his voice drops further and his mouth finds my ear again—'it's even more important to me that *you* know I love you. Jesus Christ, you are so fucking beautiful.'

He comes behind me again, and gently pulls my head back so it's leaning against his chest. One hand finds my breast and massages it, slowly, slowly, while the other one slides equally slowly down, over my stomach and between my legs. And despite myself, I widen my stance to let him in, telling myself I deserve this. God knows, I need a release after the past few days, and I definitely require a fix of attention from my husband. And so I succumb to the heaven of his magic hands on me.

And it's not until later, when he's bounced back downstairs and I'm towel-drying my hair, that I realise he hasn't even asked me how Mum is.

10

HONOR

We move Mum into The Good Vibes Hospice the following Monday. Di takes us, driving so slowly over the million speed bumps we pass between Wimbledon and Notting Hill that it breaks my heart a little. We've sandwiched Mum and her oxygen tank in the middle of the backseat between me and Ally. Each of us has one of her hands in ours.

'This is one of the oddest journeys I've ever taken.' Mum's head lolls back against the headrest and she sighs.

'I know, Mum.' I squeeze her hand. This woman fading away before our eyes is not Mum. This is not who Stephanie Chapman is. She's an academic, an award-winning writer of several books, a woman who broke glass ceilings before they even had a name, and one with the ability to be a total bitch when circumstances (usually a man who made the mistake of underestimating her) demand it. At least, that's who she was.

'It's got to be as odd as following your father's hearse to the crematorium.'

'Jesus, Mum.' Ally lets out a humourless half laugh. 'You're not dead and buried yet.'

'I know that, Alison. But it just feels... ominous. Portentous. *Final.*'

I squeeze her hand again. 'Don't be a drama queen. This isn't the end of the road for you. Good Vibes is a lovely place where highly trained people will make you as comfortable as possible.'

Mum sniffs. 'Comfortable. That's a ghastly phrase. What are they going to do—give me a hot toddy and then put a pillow over my face when I've passed out?'

'Mother.' Ally rolls her eyes. 'What Duck Face said. Drama queen.'

'I don't think euthanasia's their business model.' I keep my tone light. 'They're more about mani-pedis and string quartets.'

'That I can manage. And martinis, I hope. As long as they're not as hippy as their name.'

'Not hippy at all,' Ally tells her. 'It's very impressive. The delectable Dr Noah runs a tight ship. *And* he's madly in lust, or in love, with Duck Face. For some unknown reason.'

'You should have married a doctor.' Even in her weakened state, Mum can pull off a theatrical sigh.

'They all have God complexes, don't they?'

'Seriously?' Ally leans around Mum to look at me. 'Newsflash: you're married to Jackson *James*. I would have thought God complexes were your kink.'

And we both lurch forward in alarm as Mum lets out a huge honk of laughter and rapidly clutches her abdomen.

NOAH

When Honor's sister—Ally—comes to the door of Good Vibes to tell me they've arrived, I leap into action. One of the nurses, Will, grabs a wheelchair, and we go to meet the car. The security guard I clocked outside Mum's house last week helps Honor out of the car and she exits it like the A-lister she is: feet out first, encased in some painful looking heels, ankles neatly together. I make a supreme effort to drag my gaze up her endless legs to her face as she appears. She's in a silky sleeveless top and matching shorts, and I have the oddest flashback to Julia Roberts at the polo in *Pretty Woman*. Honor's channelling the same effect: ultra-feminine, super classy and hot as hell.

I grin and hold my hand out to her, but she turns around and sticks her head back in the car, the security guard hovering by her side. I quickly avert my gaze from this unexpected glimpse of her shapely arse in those silky shorts, and turn jerkily to Ally.

'Was the journey okay?'

'It was, surprisingly. Mum was a bit morose when we left the house, but once we started taking the piss out of Honor's husband, Jackson, she got surprisingly chipper.'

'Ah. Excellent.' I'm stuck for words. There it is again: a clue that Jackson James is a figure of fun for the Chapman women rather than a screen idol made flesh. 'Well, it's good that she's cheered up,' I manage. 'Will, see if they need help transferring Mrs Chapman, will you?'

Will scoots forward with the wheelchair and Honor backs away from the car to make room for him. In the end, he and the security guard assist the older woman in her surprisingly elegant exit. She's skeletal, but beautifully groomed, with silver hair in a bob and a colourful silk scarf around her neck despite the warmth of the day. It's impressive she's made it here in one piece in her own—or her daughter's—car. Most of our guests require an ambulance transfer.

It's important not to fluster guests at these stressful moments of transition. I wait until Honor's mother is comfortable in her wheelchair, Will at the handles, before I stroll over, a broad grin on my face, and extend my hand.

'Mrs Chapman. It's a pleasure to meet you. I'm Dr Noah Thierry, but please call me Noah. I hope you'll be very comfortable here at Good Vibes.'

She fixes me with her steely gaze, and I immediately see where Honor gets her flintiness from.

'I don't like that word. Comfortable. It suggests you're intending to drug me up to the eyeballs.'

'I wouldn't dream of it.' This is all par for the course.

'I hope you allow alcohol, though.'

I pretend to look horrified. 'Of course. God, what kind of hell-hole do you think I run?'

'Excellent.' There's a twist of amusement at her mouth. 'My poison is a very dry vodka martini.'

'Great choice. I may join you on occasion, if you're partial.'

She twinkles at me, and I can see how beautiful she must have been a couple of decades ago. Honor has her bone structure.

'He's a keeper,' she announces, keeping her eyes on me. 'You were right, girls. He's delectable.'

My splutter comes at the same time as Honor's look of abject horror and Ally's hiss of *Jesus Christ*. Delectable. Interesting. I go to take the wheelchair off Will.

'I look after the feisty ones myself,' I tell her, as I wheel her up the ramp.

Half an hour later, we have her settled into her room, though she's refused to get into bed yet. Honor fusses around with what are apparently her own silk-covered pillows and puts a pale pink quilt on the bed. This is good. Things like this are important.

When Stephanie (as she's commanded me to call her) is tucked up in an armchair by the window, I call on Elena to come in. I've already explained that I won't be the doctor assigned to Stephanie because I'm in a supervisory capacity at the hospice and don't take on my own patients. It's true, but it's also so I can retain an arms-length relationship with Stephanie and her daughters.

I'm well aware that Honor's not only married, but that she shares her marital bed with one of the finest male specimens on the planet. So I'd be smoking crack to think that anything could ever happen between us. Still, the combination of my years of pining over her when she was on Sunrise and the strength of my reaction to her these past few occasions we've met is enough to trigger serious alarm bells. I cannot ethically care for her mother if I have feelings for her.

Elena will be a good match for Stephanie. She's warm and empathetic and has a steely core that she may need with this trouble-maker. I've known Elena for years, since we were residents together on a palliative care ward—a residency that prompted us both to pursue a lifetime career of end-of-life care.

We may or may not have history, in the shape of the occasional night together when we were both lonely and frustrated and privy to the unspoken codes of junior doctors that dictated you shag each other because you all understand the difficulties of the job, and because none of you has any time to actually go out on the pull.

Elena's made it clear in the past that she'd like to take things up a notch between us. Like me, she's in her thirties and unattached. But I've made it equally clear that my feelings for her aren't sufficient to take that leap. She seems to have accepted my stance and, most importantly, we're a great team at work, with a common vision for how we want to mould the future of palliative care.

I leave Elena to it and head down to my office at the back of the ground floor. About half an hour later, there's a tap at the door. It's Honor standing in the doorway.

'Am I interrupting?'

'Of course not.' *Never.*

She takes a tentative step in, hovering just inside the door frame as I jump up and usher her to the free chair. The office is tiny; she's less than a metre away from me when she's sitting down beside my desk, one bare arm resting on the desktop, two bare legs crossed right next to me. I swallow. She's brought the most incredible floral scent with her into this little room, which would be stuffy if I didn't have the sash window wide open.

'I just wanted to say thank you before I go.' She leans forward and drops her phone in her bag. Straightens up and looks at me. 'I need to head into the office. Ally's going to stay here and keep Mum company for a bit.'

'Is your mother doing okay?'

'She seems to be handling it pretty well. I think having you greet us helped. You've got her hot under the collar. She's been behaving more like a One Direction fan than a woman who's arrived at the place where she'll die.'

'Excellent. Do I get to be Harry?'

She raises her eyebrows. 'If he's the one who floats your boat.'

'His success rate floats my boat. Unfortunately, my success rate with older women is much better than with women my own age.'

I grin self-deprecatingly and she smiles back. Narrows her eyes. Assessing me.

'Not unlike Mr Styles. But something tells me you do just fine for yourself.'

'If you're generous enough to assume that, I won't dissuade you. At least, thanks to Stephanie, I have a martini date for this evening.'

'Don't let her get you drunk. She's an enabler. But thank you. She feels like herself today, which'—she drums her fingers on the desk—'none of us were expecting. It's been far easier on all of us than we expected, to be honest.'

Her smile is open and I drink her in. That her hair is pulled off her face in a low bun isn't helping with the Julia Roberts comparisons. Her skin is improbably dewy and youthful looking. Her extraordinary beauty has always led to the press dubbing her decorative, but I remember this woman interviewing world leaders on that sofa, and not giving an inch. She may be decorative, but she's far from fluffy. She shifts. Uncrosses and recrosses her glossy legs. It's getting harder not to look.

'I'm really glad you've had a good start,' I say now. 'It won't be a totally smooth ride, but we've got a good team here to help you through the ups and downs. And you noticing that she's being herself here is the biggest reassurance you could give me right now. That's a wonderful sign. We really don't want any of our guests to feel like they're on a conveyor belt to death. This should be a place where they can relax and embrace who they are.'

'Hashtag live your best end-of-life? I think you're missing a t-shirt opportunity there.'

She's funny. And stunning. And married to a celebrity god. Jesus, Noah. Get a grip.

'Stephanie would look great in that t-shirt,' I quip.

'She'd certainly rock it. I like the questionnaire, by the way. We're working through it with Elena.'

'The goals of care?'

'Yes, but also the questions about her values. It's a brilliant way to approach this period in... I guess, a mindful way. Like, how does she want to be remembered? And what are the things that are most important to her from here on in, and what can she live without? It's a helpful way to focus in.'

'It is. The thing I've found about palliative care is that this stage is about letting go of all the stuff that doesn't serve you. Your family's already relinquished the physical care and logistics just by coming here, and now you and Stephanie hopefully have the headspace to relinquish some other stuff, too.'

'Yeah.' She bows her head, avoiding eye contact. 'Can I ask you and the team another favour?'

'Anything.'

'Would you mind just being careful what newspapers you give her, please? I saw you have a table of papers outside the bedrooms. There's a lot of shit hitting the fan about my husband in the tabloids right now, and I don't want Mum to see that kind of stuff. It'll just upset her. We're dealing with it, but I don't know how long it'll be before the press gets bored with us and move on.'

Jesus. I stare at the top of her head for a moment. For her to have to deal with this crap, on top of everything else, makes my blood boil. It's clear she's uncomfortable having to bring it up with me. I grit my jaw and only realise I haven't answered when she looks up at me.

'Of course,' I say quickly. 'Consider it dealt with—I'll let the others know.'

'Thanks.' She gives me a weak smile. 'I'm looking forward to getting away from all this.'

'You coming to France, then?'

'Yep. Ally's going to hold the fort here—she's a university professor, so she has the summer off. The kids deserve a bit of fun, and I need to lie by a pool for a few days and drink rosé and turn off my phone.'

I swallow as a crystal-clear mental image of Honor lying by the Chateau des Anges pool in a bikini hits me.

France is looking up.

11

HONOR

The thing I can't get over is the smell. The smell of France is like crack after far too long stuck in the UK. As soon as Di, the children and I step out of our hire car at the entrance to Chateau des Anges, the scent of foreign soil and vines and vegetation hits me so powerfully that I inhale like a sniffer dog.

We've driven up a gloriously straight, cypress-lined driveway that intersects pleasingly regular lines of vines on either side. The sea is somewhere over to the left, but a pine wood obstructs the view.

The anticipation hit me squarely in the stomach as soon as we turned off the road and through the massive wrought-iron gates into the vineyard. The latter part of the journey from Nice was heavenly, as we came off the autoroute and wove through medieval perched villages that glowed gold in the afternoon sunlight, and ancient *bastides* with verdant gardens. And all the while, the Mediterranean sparkled in the distance.

But nothing has prepared me for how downright gorgeous the chateau is. Elaine and Philippe have had it for less than three years, and I've seen some photos, but this place is divine, steeped in architectural charm.

It's been two years since I was last in France. We managed to escape to our place in Ibiza last summer, but lockdown has stopped us from getting anywhere else, and now it's as though a part of my soul is gradually unfurling, coming back to life.

I disentangle Rollo from his iPad and headphones as I help him out of the back seat of the car. Di is already unloading our suitcases—too many for a four-day trip, but never mind—and Serena has her head buried in her *Harry Potter* book.

'*Bienvenus*!' Elaine appears in an open doorway set into the wall in front of us, her husband Philippe following her out. They're both charming, gracious. They'll be delightful hosts. They fawn over the kids and kiss me, and I notice for the first time that Noah takes after his father. The height, mainly. And the dark, Gallic good looks, although Philippe has gone elegantly grey.

On the other side of the doorway is a charming courtyard, a tinkling fountain at its centre. Elaine points to the open front door across the courtyard.

'Serena and Rollo—if you run straight through there and out the other side, you'll find everyone at the pool. Go say hi!'

The children scamper away, bubbling over with excitement at finally being here, on holiday, after a long day of travel and a long year of being stuck in the UK. I know how they feel.

Elaine ushers me through the grandiose doorway into an incredible square hallway. It's blessedly cool and has that mix of austerity and magnificence the French do so well: bleached, ancient flagstones and plastered walls providing a blank canvas for an oversized chandelier and ornate, curved staircase.

'Oh my God. This is to die for.' I don't normally gush—I'm harder and harder to impress, these days, but this chateau has such natural style and such a sense of place. I couldn't be anywhere else but France, and it's been far, far too long.

The best part: the wall of French doors on the opposite side of the hall, all thrown open to showcase a vast terrace and a vista dominated by the Mediterranean, in all its blue, effervescent glory. There's no pine forest here to block the view. It's *magnificent*.

The breeze carries the children's whoops of delight into the hallway.

'We have a full house now.' Elaine gestures to the French doors and Honor steps out onto the terrace. 'Noah arrived on Wednesday, and Angus and Evelyn yesterday. Eddie's been beautifully behaved, but he'll be thrilled Rollo's here. He's been asking when you're arriving every half an hour since breakfast.'

'Oh, Lord,' I say. 'At least they'll keep each other entertained, so we can all sit back and relax.' I'm distracted by the sheer gorgeousness that lies around us. To my right, a cluster of low rattan sofas and tables under a woven bamboo shade. And straight ahead of me: heaven. Broad steps down to another terrace, with multiple loungers and a couple of white-curtained daybeds, and a huge, turquoise pool. Rollo already has his top off. He insisted on wearing swimming trunks as shorts on the flight.

I'm used to making an entrance, but it's just old, dear friends here. No sign of Noah. I follow Elaine lightly down the steps. Philippe has hung back. He's sweet, but a man of few words. I suspect he'd love to have the house to himself and bury himself in a book.

Evelyn squeals and waves from a day-bed. She's sleek and stunning, as usual, in a red one-piece, with beautiful little Rose in her arms. She heads in my direction, Angus behind her in a pair of shorts.

'You're here, and we can party!' She throws her arm around my neck and hugs me, Rose gurgling between us.

'I'm not sure I'm ever the life and soul of the party, but God, am I happy to be here! I'm feeling more sociable already.'

I take Rose from Evelyn. She's delicious. Velvet soft baby skin, clad only in a pair of frilly white swim-pants over her nappy. She gives me the benefit of her tiny front teeth with a huge grin and instantly latches onto my pendant earring with a little fist.

'No, you don't, monkey.' Evelyn laughingly detaches her fist and holds it.

'She's heaven. Good enough to eat. Hi, Angus.'

Angus is looking tanned and well. He's extremely attractive, in a rustic kind of way, with the kindest, crinkly eyes that melt when he looks at his wife and their daughter.

'Well done for making it.' He kisses my cheeks. 'The journey wasn't too painful, I hope?'

'It was fine, actually. The kids were so excited to be on a plane. Even I found it exciting. I've really missed travelling. Ooh!'

The shriek comes as Eddie and Rollo take a run at the pool and cannonball in, sending a huge splash my way. Serena is out of her sundress and down to her swimsuit, and hot on their heels.

A flash of movement catches my eye, and I turn to see

Noah exiting the cabana at the far end of the pool and walking towards us. There must be showers over there, because he's soaking wet and combing his dark hair back off his face with his hands. *Holy shit.* He's far enough away that I can take him in properly through my sunglasses without him or anyone else being able to see exactly what I'm looking at.

He's beautiful. And he's been working on his tan. Those French genes mean he just has to *look* at the sun to turn bronze. His swim shorts sit low on his hips and show off his lean, rangy figure and a dark, wet happy trail. He's far leaner in build than Jackson, who's completely ripped, and his body has an easy grace when he moves. And then there's the body hair. Jackson's had to wax religiously for as long as I've known him, and I'm used to it, but the light coating of dark hair on Noah's chest and stomach is mesmerising. He's grinning at me, and when he gets close enough to put a damp hand carefully on my bare arm, it gives me the delicious ghost of a shiver.

'Sorry.' The grin widens. 'And welcome to the Cote d'Azur.'

'Thank you. I'm not sure why you don't relocate out here. Forget the hospice. This place is incredible.'

'It is. Sadly, it's a recent purchase. If they'd bought it when I was at med school, I doubt I would have qualified.'

'How has the trip been so far?'

'Magical,' Evelyn interjects. 'But we've missed you. Elaine and I have missed having long, rosé-fuelled gossips with you after lunch. And Noah's been a very gracious gooseberry, but now you can keep him company.'

She means it innocently, but Noah's smile turns more bashful.

'It's good to have someone here to rescue me from being

thrashed relentlessly by Angus at backgammon. How was your mum when you left her?'

'She was on good form, thanks.' I set my heavy tote bag down on the table next to me and rub my shoulder. 'No thanks to the big boss buggering off and leaving his team and his patients to fend for themselves.'

'I hate to admit it, but I've surrounded myself with a hugely competent team who are probably far happier when I'm not around, getting in the way. Which works for me.' He gestures around the pool area. 'Now, what do you need? Shower? Change? Dip in the pool? Although maybe not while those lunatics are in there... glass of rosé? I'd offer to show you to your room, but I know Mum's excited to give you a full tour.'

12

HONOR

The Cote d'Azur sinks into my bones and works its alchemy on me in no time. I check my phone as little as possible and leave Lydia to filter my emails. Give myself over to recalibrating to this delicious, indulgent way of life.

That first night, we dine in a characteristically French style—at leisure, and with appreciation. There are drinks on the terrace first: delightful sparkling rosé from Chateau des Anges' own vines, with olives from the olive groves on the property, and crostini topped with quintessential Provencal tapenade, and rolled up anchovies speared with cocktail sticks.

It's my favourite time of day: that, and first thing in the morning. Dawn and dusk are the times when the sky is at its most magical and the temperature is manageable in this part of the world in high summer. Showering and dressing for dinner after an indulgent day by the pool feels decadent, as does taking my place on a shady sofa on the terrace.

Elaine insists I sit facing the sea to drink in the view. I'm cool in a laser-cut Cult Gaia sundress, and all is good with the world as I sip my drink. Especially because my dear friends are around me, the children's whoops carry across from the well-shaded *pétanque* court, and Noah is sitting a couple of feet away, stretched out with a glass of pastis and a lazy grin on his far-too-handsome face.

It's not a set-up between the two of us; of course it isn't. There's no way on earth Elaine would have invited me out here for Noah; there's no way she'd entertain the mere idea of her golden boy getting it on with a married woman whose daily life is tabloid fodder.

And yet, this little group of six feels balanced. Elaine and Philippe, married for decades and revelling in having their friends around them in their favourite place. Evelyn and Angus, still completely in their honeymoon period, their new family providing them with so much happiness. And me and Noah. It feels natural with him. Natural, but charged.

The only way I can explain it is that I'm conscious of him at all moments. I keep seeking him out. If I'm in the pool and he gets in, the water feels warmer. When he seeks me out for a game of backgammon or to see if I'd like a drink, it's strangely thrilling. And when he sat down next to me on the sofa this evening, I did a tiny internal air punch.

And the smiles. The smiles he gives me are like gifts: warm, and generous, and radiating appreciation. I've had smiles like that from men my whole adult life, but I usually shut them down with my well-honed frostiness. Not Noah. Not these smiles.

It's silly. I know that. I'm a long-time married woman and it's natural I should get some cheap thrills from the attention of a good-looking, slightly younger guy. I don't have my husband to myself. It makes sense that the farce playing out in the British tabloids and the US celebrity sites right now is making me defiant. Itchy. Distracted.

And yet, this sense of supreme well-being continues. It continues through the next morning, when Noah and I meet Evelyn and Angus on the clay tennis court to play an early, single set of mixed doubles, in the short window before the heat builds.

It continues as I watch his form on the court. That easy elegance translates through to his tennis style, and it's heaven to watch.

It continues when, after we whip their arses six-four, Noah throws a lazy arm around my shoulders as he leads me off the court, and leans his head into mine as he tells me: *Well played, partner.*

It continues when I busy myself with making some espressos in the butler's pantry after breakfast, and he walks in. I turn to look behind me and clock the look on his face, which is definitely checking out my arse, before he collects himself.

It continues every time he says my name. When any of the others say my name, it's nothing, but when it comes from Noah's lips it feels loaded, and the sound of it whips through my abdomen like something delicious and forbidden.

It continues through the long, lazy lunch chef Gui serves up of *pissaladière* and crisp salads and cold meats and cheeses so ripe they could walk off the platters, as the carafes of palest-pink rosé dotting the long trestle table miraculously empty and refill themselves and the adult guests groan and tug at the waistbands of our clothes.

And it continues until, as I lie in the blessed shade of a day-bed by the pool, Rollo fast asleep and curled into me, my mobile goes. It's Mara, our publicist. I reject the call.

Mara calls straight back. I sigh and, disentangling myself from Rollo, sit up. Keep my voice to a whisper.

'Hi.'

Mara's walking. There's traffic in the background, and she's out of breath.

'Have you seen TMZ?'

A warning pang hits me in the stomach, an unwelcome contraction of muscles, as if my body knows better than I do what's coming.

'No. Why?'

A sigh. 'They've just released an exclusive with a former server from Chateau Marmont, who claims to have evidence Jackson and Leila shared a room there.'

Shit shit shit. 'What's she saying?'

'It's all hearsay. She doesn't have photos, or anything. But the hotel hasn't been able to stop her blabbing. Said she cleared away some room service one morning, and they were in bed together. The *Daily Mail* just called me for a comment because they're going to run it.'

'Does Jackson know?'

'Yeah. That's why I'm calling you. I didn't want you to be blindsided.'

'I see.' There's nothing else to say. Mara won't try to hush this up because Jackson doesn't want her to. Because, unlike all the other times we've bribed and pleaded with and threatened the press because Jackson wanted to protect his 'family man' image, this time it serves him to let the press speculate. Because it will be gold-dust for *Vet*, when it launches.

I end the call and stumble off the daybed and up to the house. The force of the mid-afternoon sunlight is blinding. I hear my name. It's Evelyn behind me. Rose is in her arms, grizzling and swiping at her hot face with her tiny hands.

'I'm going up to give Rose a bottle in the shade. You okay?'

'It's Jackson.' I slide my sunglasses down over my nose for a second to look at Evelyn. 'Some server from Marmont has gone public with her story that he and Leila Sherazi—the actress he's starring with in *Vet*—have been sharing a room at the Chateau.'

'Oh, Jesus.' Evelyn is no stranger to the havoc the tabloids can wreak.'Are you guys going to quash it?'

'Apparently not. Because it's good for publicity.'

Evelyn gasps. 'You are shitting me. That's not cool.'

I follow Evelyn into the kitchen and hold Rose while Evelyn prepares a bottle of formula. She's divine: sweet-smelling and gummy and gorgeous. She reaches out for her mama and rewards Evelyn with an enormous grin when she takes her back.

We collapse in the wonderfully cool *salon* off the main hall. Evelyn settles Rose in the crook of her arm and pulls off her sunhat before popping the bottle's teat in her mouth. She tilts her tiny head back and sucks hungrily, taking noisy, drunken gulps as her little hands try to grab the bottle and her eyes roll back in her head.

'She'll be out like a light after this.' Evelyn fondles one of Rose's perfect little feet.

'She's so beautiful, Ev. Angus strikes me as the happiest man in the world, surrounded by his gorgeous women.' Seeing my friend this loved-up and contented makes me smile, despite the shit currently hitting the fan in my own life.

'He's amazing. I'm so lucky. And he's equally wonderful with Eddie and Rose. And his own boys, of course. We're one big, messy, happy family, and I wouldn't have it any other way.' Evelyn runs her lips over Rose's downy head. I remember that feeling. The scent of talc and baby shampoo. The impossible softness. Nothing would persuade me to go through the experience of having a baby again, but there were definitely moments to treasure.

'You're lucky. You had a shitty time of it with Seb, but it's worked out for all of you. I'm so happy.'

'Thank you, dear friend.' Evelyn murmurs the words into the top of Rose's head. 'But what about you? What are you going to do—what do you even want?'

'I don't know.' I pick at a microscopic chip in my nail polish. 'I'm so used to this weird, fucked-up existence being our lives that I don't really spend much time wondering what the alternative could be, if that doesn't sound crazy.'

'It doesn't. You get sucked in, don't you? By the money, and the profile, and the adrenalin rush... you've told yourself you want this for so long that you can't actually remember if it's fact, or just a story you've made up for yourself. And you're in so deep, you can't see a way out.'

'Too true.' It is true. Morally questionable, but true.

We're silent for a minute.

'Can I ask you a question?' Evelyn looks at me from under her lashes.

'Anything.'

'Have you ever cheated? Or considered it, even?'

Only this week. And last week.

'No.' It feels like a simpler answer. 'I don't have the time for an affair. Or the energy.'

'All I would say'—Evelyn seems to be choosing her words carefully—'is that no one would blame you. If you don't want out of your marriage, maybe it's time to level the playing field.'

NOAH

I pad through my bedroom, a towel around my waist, the water droplets from my shower cooling my skin. Beyond the open window, the early evening light is golden. I peer outside. The vines are gilded, their shadows growing long. It's one of those tranquil French evenings whose perfection defies belief.

I flick the TV on as I saunter to my wardrobe for a clean shirt, and scroll to Sky News.

Speculation is escalating over the nature of the relationship between Jackson James and his latest co-star, Leila Sherazi, the reporter intones.

I grab a shirt and back up. There's a photo of Jackson and Leila smiling together at a recent event, before the screen switches to a photo of what looks like a hotel, and a scrolling banner: *BREAKING NEWS. SERVER CONFIRMS JAMES AND SHERAZI SHARED A BED AT CHATEAU MARMONT.*

What the fuck?

The voiceover continues. *Jackson and Leila have been spotted cosying up at several events now, prompting questions over whether they're as close as their characters on upcoming HBO series,* Vet. *Today's statement, by a server at the world-famous Chateau Marmont, comes as little surprise to insiders who have been reporting for some time that the stars' on-screen chemistry is just as strong off-screen. This is bound to be a blow for Jackson's wife, Honor Chapman, who cannot be reached for comment.*

'Because she is France, hiding from scumbags like you, you fuckwit,' I sneer aloud as the screen shows footage of Honor walking swiftly down a London street, head bowed, sunglasses firmly on. I recognise that dress; this must have been shot that day I met her.

I turn off the TV and throw the remote angrily on the bed. The woman on that screen is a living, sentient creature and she happens to be the most exquisite human being I've ever seen. Why Jackson James sees fit to humiliate her in front of the global press, I'm unclear. And I'm even more unclear on why the fuck she lets him.

13

HONOR

That evening, Noah's not his usual, relaxed self. Something's off. He drinks quickly during cocktail hour on the terrace. He's more silent than usual, less ready with the easy conversation he made last night. No good vibes from him this evening. He looks amazing, though, an open-necked white linen shirt and pale pink shorts showcasing his tan. He's like an ice cream. Good enough to eat.

I fiddle with the thin shoulder strap on my Missoni dress and take a swig of champagne. The dress is a new purchase, part of an enormous shipment from Matches when things began to open up in the UK and I got shopping accordingly. Missoni has worked its knitting magic with this: rows of its signature chevron in metallic hues that undulate from copper, to rose gold, to gold, to silver, to icy blue, to turquoise. It fits me like a sheath and ends at mid-calf. It needs no accessories, and very little in the way of underwear, except for a tiny nude thong. Nothing else will fit under it.

Angus is regaling Elaine and Philippe with some

amusing tale involving Evelyn's first attempt at hand-milking a cow. He's a great story-teller—very droll—but I can't quite focus on the story. Instead, I turn my head to Noah. He's sitting where he sat last night, and he's looking at me, but the expression on his face is intense, unsmiling.

'Are you okay?' My voice is a whisper.

'I could ask you the same question.' His gaze flicks to tumbler he's circling in his hand and back again to me.

'Oh?'

'I saw the news about your husband.'

I keep my voice light. 'I didn't have you pegged as a *Daily Mail* reader.'

'What? I think everyone's running it. I saw it on Sky News when I was getting changed.'

'Oh, really? Shit.'

He edges closer to me. 'I'm so sorry. If you want to... I don't know, talk, I'm here.'

That this man is sitting here, pitying me, makes me a little nauseous.

'I'm fine, honestly. It's under control. I'd just rather forget about it and enjoy my evening.'

'No problem. As long as you're okay.' He nods and scoots away from me to his original position, and I can't shake the feeling I said the wrong thing.

A guffaw from Philippe breaks the tension as Angus reaches the climax of his story (I've heard it before; the cow takes a huge dump right in front of Evelyn) and the moment is gone.

Much wine is drunk over dinner. Much glorious, incredible food is served up, and the others tuck in. I take it relatively easy, given the various stresses compromising my appetite and the unforgiving nature of my dress, but I swoon over the mouth-watering bream and the fragrant ratatouille Chef Gui serves up.

Afterwards, we disperse. I suspect my and Noah's personality failures dampened the atmosphere at the table, and I feel bad about it. The guilt jostles for position with my humiliation and frustration over Jackson having chosen the publicity of his new show over respect for his wife. And children. If he thinks this media circus won't affect his kids, he's naïve at best.

Elaine and Philippe have retired to bed. Angus and Evelyn are upstairs with their kids—Rose has grizzled on and off over the baby monitor all evening, and Eddie came down towards the end of dinner, adorable, tow-headed, and clearly having not received the memo from himself that he's utterly exhausted. I'm not sure where Noah's got to, but he made a pretty quick exit after dinner.

I'm restless and definitely not ready to lie on my bed and try to avoid the news apps on the phone. After I've ascertained that Serena and Rollo are in the deepest of sleeps, the drone of the air con providing the perfect white noise, I head back downstairs and pour myself a glass of rosé in the kitchen. Go to put the bottle back in the fridge and think better of it. Keep hold of it. Maybe I'll just lie by the pool for a while and try to wind down.

But, as I walk through the hallway and across the terrace, the strains of some beautiful melody, and the purest voice, reach me, and as I head down the steps, Noah comes into sight at the side of the pool. He has his back to me and his legs in the water. A glass of wine next to him, and a portable speaker playing the music.

'Oh, I'm sorry.' I freeze. 'I didn't mean to disturb your peace.'

He turns around and scrambles to his feet. '*You're* not disturbing my peace.'

There's that voice again, the voice that he's been using with me all evening, as if I should know exactly what he means when he speaks to me.

'I was just going to—' I point at the nearest daybed. 'Chill out. Get some headspace.'

'Go for it.'

A pause.

'Will you join me?' God, Honor. Not *would you like to join me*, but *will you join me?* Needy, much?

His eyebrows shoot up. 'Of course.'

He squats to grab his glass and phone and the speaker and gets on the bed beside me. He sits down near the edge, like he's scared to come closer, but he hasn't taken his eyes off me. I look away, out to the inky blackness that is the sea. The nothingness is punctuated only by the lights of various super-yachts in the distance. It's cooler down here, as the breeze from the sea dances in. The foreground is better lit, by lights dotted around the low wall of the pool area, and the pool itself is illuminated in breathtaking turquoise.

'Who's this singing?' I break the moment. The voice is incredible: a woman singing in French, with just a piano in accompaniment.

'It's Barbara Pravi. She's pretty big over here.'

'Her voice gives me goosebumps.' I settle in a mermaid pose, my legs folded to one side, resting on my arm.

'She got France second place in the Eurovision this year.'

'No way. She doesn't sound very Eurovision-y.'

He laughs. 'She's not. But she was mesmerising. Her performance was very Piaf. Look it up on YouTube—the song was called *Voilà*.'

'This song sounds so sad. Yearning.' The melancholy piano chords, the quiet desperation building in the singer's voice, somehow reflect how I'm feeling at that precise moment. Like I'm mourning something: I'm not sure what.

'It is. It's called *Louis*. She's singing about a former lover, and from the sound of things, she's definitely not over him.'

'Oh.' Hearing the word *lover* from his lips gives me a small thrill. 'What's she saying?'

'She's saying,'—he closes his eyes briefly as he listens—'I'd give my soul for your skin. See, my heart ignites at the heat of your words.'

He opens his eyes again and looks straight at me. Unsmiling.

'Oh.' I've already said that. But *Jesus Christ*, could I have asked him to translate a more loaded couple of lines? There's an instant flush of heat up my neck and on my cheeks. 'Wow, that's—the French certainly have a way with words.'

My chat could not be more lame. Seriously, get a grip, Honor. But he's still looking at me, and I take a hurried, panicky sip of my wine and stare back out at the blackness. The air hums with thousands of cicadas; it's a solid wall of noise, and it's wonderful.

We're silent for a few moments, and then the song finishes and a lighter, more upbeat one comes on, and I realise I've been holding my breath. I set down my glass and, reaching behind me, stack a couple of the huge cushions on the bed. Lower my head so I'm in a semi-reclining position and stare at the top of the daybed's canopy.

'This spot is positively medicinal.' I sigh, more deeply than I mean to, and close my eyes.

'It's intoxicating, isn't it?' I can hear a smile in his voice.

'Yeah.'

'Look. Can I ask you something that's none of my business? You're free to tell me where to go.'

I have an uncomfortably clear idea of where this is going.

'Okay...?'

He shifts his weight on the bed next to me. 'Why the *fuck* do you let your husband get away with the stunts he's pulling at the moment?'

His vehemence takes me by surprise. I turn my head and open my eyes. He's raking one hand through his hair and staring down at me.

'You mean why do I not fight his cheating, or why do I not fight the papers for exposing it this time?'

He's taken aback; the skin between his eyebrows creases into a V.

'The former, I suppose. I—'

I make a split-second decision to trust him. To open up; not to patronise him with the practised lines I feed most people.

'Jackson's slept around for years. I don't expect you to understand, but it is what it is. The articles right now are the tip of the iceberg. And that iceberg is kept well out of sight thanks to a load of relationships and bribes and injunctions and deals and fixers that are so tawdry, you really don't want to know more about them.'

Silence.

'The difference with the current shit-show is that it's 'good' publicity for his upcoming show. The public loves nothing more than an on-screen-off-screen romance. So

Jackson and our publicist have no intention of quashing the speculation. For once, it's serving him.'

The shock on his face is sweet. He's a little boy who just found out Father Christmas doesn't exist.

'So… your marriage is a sham? Or it's real?'

'It's real, all right. It's just—unorthodox. The rest of the world seems to consider my husband public property, and I've come to think of him the same way.'

'But you're not heartbroken? Humiliated, when he does this to you?'

'You sound like my sister. Humiliated, yes. Of course I am. Heartbroken, not so much. As I said, it is what it is. But honestly, I'm tired of justifying our arrangement to people. I don't mean to be rude, but it's exhausting. I've been over this a million times in my head, and with Jackson, and I really am okay with it. I'm just not okay with him parading around with this woman Leila and adding fuel to the fire.'

'So it's an open marriage, basically… at his end, anyway.'

'Yes.' I narrow my eyes. Where is he going with this?

'But not at your end.'

'Not that it's any of your business, but no.'

He holds up his hand. 'That seems unfair. It is just *such. A fucking. Waste.*'

His tone makes me freeze. 'Not really. I have enough on my plate.'

'Honor. You should consider levelling the playing field. You really should.'

'Wow. You're the third person to suggest that to me. First Ally, then Evelyn, this afternoon, in fact. Do I have *victim* scrawled across my forehead, or *needs to get laid*?'

'You have neither, and you know that.' He scoots around onto his stomach and edges closer to me, resting up on his elbows, looking down at me. 'But—and I say this objectively

—you are the most beautiful woman I have ever seen. *Ever.* On screen, or in the flesh. And the idea that that wanker is making a public fool of you, and you're *allowing* it, makes my fucking blood boil. I mean, what the hell is wrong with him? So, yes. You should have an affair. Find out what it is you're missing, that your husband is enjoying so much.'

His face is so close to me, suspended above me, his sleek dark hair hanging down. He brushes it off his face and stares at my mouth, and my lips part in response as I stare right back at his. *You are the most beautiful woman I have ever seen. Ever.* For all his coolness, that makes it sound like he's pretty invested in this.

He licks his lips. My heart is beating right out of its cage at his scent, his proximity, and the fact that he's looking at me as if I'm supper.

'Are you putting yourself forward for the job?' I mean it to come out jokingly, but it sounds serious.

'I am. There's a shortlist of one. Just so you know.'

'Right.' I swallow. It's been so long since I've done this: flirted with anyone who wasn't Jackson, attempted the dance of expressing my interest, all the while protecting myself from rejection. 'And what do you think I'm missing out on, precisely?'

He smiles, slowly, and I'm mesmerised by the ripe curves of his lips. He takes a piece of my hair between his fingers and twirls it. The side of his hand brushes my shoulder.

'Do you want me to tell you? Or show you?'

This is one of those moments. Those forks in the road that, afterwards, define what went before and what comes after. In this slip of a moment, I'm weightless, suspended between reality and possibility.

I make my choice.

'I want you to do both.' *I want you to undo me. I've begun to get a glimpse of what I'm missing, and I suspect that glimpse is about to become a revelation.*

A wider grin, only for me. God, he's gorgeous.

'That I can definitely do. Close your eyes.'

Jesus fuck. I shoot him a *you'd better not betray my trust* look, and close them.

14

HONOR

There's nothing for a moment, only stillness, and cicadas, and the scent of him mingling with the scent of France.

Then the shift of his weight on the bed, and soft rustling noises that tell me he's pulling the daybed's curtains closed around us. At least he's a gentleman on some level.

He lies back down. When he speaks again, his mouth is closer to my ear than before.

'You're missing *this*. Anticipation. The fun of wondering about all the magical possibilities that await you.'

His hand slides onto my stomach and I narrowly escape gasping, because the heat of it through my dress is nothing compared to the heat that pools inside me when I feel that hand, slowly, gently stroking my stomach back and forth.

'Right now, you've got a lot of shit going down. Your Mum, all this stuff with your husband... you're also a mother—an amazing mother, from what I can see—and you run a huge empire. I'm sure you have a very glamorous, exciting life, but a lot of it's responsibility? Right? Duty?

'What if that existence also included the certain knowledge that you have a man—a very adoring man—on hand, who spends an unhealthy part of his time thinking about what to do for you? How to make sure you feel as beautiful and sexy as you truly are, all the time?'

His hand changes direction, starts stroking up and down. Up to my ribcage, down to the top of my thong. His mouth comes closer to my ear.

'What if you had a man who was in danger of neglecting his job because he was too busy dreaming up new and wonderful ways to make you come?'

My eyes fly open as his fingers tighten on my stomach. His face is right next to mine, and he grins at my reaction, which must be absolutely priceless. Jackson talks dirty to me, but it's *Jackson*, and it's all part of his never-ending banter.

This is different. This is Noah, the mild-mannered (until this evening), good-natured doctor who I've been pining for these past few weeks, and lusting after shamefully. This is a side of him I could never have predicted, and I'm so turned on just by his hand on my stomach and his voice in my ear that I can't quite believe it.

He nods at me. 'Close your eyes.' His voice is soft. 'I'm just getting started.'

Oh, God. I smirk at him and turn my head away and settle on my back. Closing my eyes. Inhaling him. Willing him to keep going. Loving the fact that I have no idea where he's taking this. Loving even more the fact that presumably that's precisely his plan: to demonstrate this. The wonder. The anticipation. The *delicious* anticipation.

'I'm sure my proposal needs more specifics for you to consider it. Well, let's take this morning, when I came across you in the butler's kitchen, making coffee. I was checking you out. I know you noticed. Damn right I was checking you out, in that little backless swimming costume and those tiny hot pants.'

'I checked you out, too.' I whisper it.

'I know you did, gorgeous. But if we were involved, I wouldn't have had to leave it there.'

His lips graze my ear; his voice gets quieter and deeper.

'I would have come up behind you, and slipped those little straps down off your shoulders, and slid down the top of your swimming costume, and I would have pulled and sucked on those beautiful nipples of yours while the others were outside, waiting for you to bring their refills. Oblivious. And I think you like the idea of that, because they're hardening right now.'

My head is spinning with the visual he's given me. I can see it, clear as day: him, pressing up behind me in the pantry and pulling down my swimming costume and putting his hands and tongue on my breasts. His fingers fiddle with the shoestring strap of my dress, and for an endless, tortuous moment, I'm not sure if he'll *show* me, like I've asked him to. I lie there, frozen.

Okay. He may be onto something with this anticipation business.

He slides the strap down my shoulder and runs a fingertip over the fabric covering my nipple.

I buck.

He does it again, rubbing in a circle. The fine metallic knit of the dress against my nipple adds to the heavenly friction, and I moan, softly.

'Oh, God.' His lips are still by my ear. 'That sound. I can't tell you what you do to me, Honor.'

He pulls the other shoulder strap down and tugs the neckline of the dress below my breasts. His sharp inhale matches mine. I can't believe I'm letting him do this. I can't believe how much I want it.

'Jesus.' He shifts beside me. 'You are so *fucking* beautiful.' And then his mouth is on the nipple nearest him and he's licking and sucking and teasing it with the very edges of his teeth. I'm really moaning now, but I can't help it, because not only is the sensation unbearably wonderful, but this is right up there with the hottest moments of my life. And he hasn't even kissed me yet.

'*Noah*.' I put my hand on the back of his head. 'Please. I need you.'

A little growl from him. 'When you say my name like that...'

His mouth comes up to meet mine and I pull him in as close as I can, and there should really be a symphony playing right now to match the immense relief of our mouths clashing together. Lips against lips. The soft slide. Tongues testing and tasting and curling. Teeth nipping, breath hot. His hand in my hair, fingers splayed on the back of my head before they trace down my back. The linen of his shirt perfectly rough against my bare breasts. The hard ridge of his erection against my hip.

He pulls his mouth away and holds me, forehead to forehead, nose to nose, as we attempt to catch our breath. Then, his hand at the back of my head, he lowers me back down onto the cushion, hovers over me.

'Impressive pitch.' I try for casual, but the way he's looking at me, with rapt, dreamy eyes, makes casual difficult. 'I think I'm sold.'

'You *think*?'

His face is amused as he swings a leg over and straddles me.

'Oh, baby, I'm not finished yet.'

'No?'

His hands move in my hair. Smoothing it off my face. Combing it out. He leans forward and kisses me on the lips. Mouth open. Tongue gently teasing mine. Sits back up.

'Nope. Close your eyes. I haven't told you yet what I'd do to you in the pool if we were having an affair.'

Oh, Jesus. I close my eyes and squirm in anticipation. He mentioned certain knowledge, didn't he? It appears the good doctor knows exactly what he's talking about. The *wonder* of not knowing what he'll do next, combined with the *certain knowledge* that it will be off-the-charts good, is hot as hell.

His palms make contact with my nipples.

Just a soft swipe, and then nothing. I try to arch my back but he has me pinned beneath him. The top half of my dress is around my middle.

He makes contact again.

And again.

He's palming my breasts in a circular motion and applying more and more pressure before he switches to his fingertips, pinching and rolling and pulling. The ache he's creating is building and building and going straight between my legs, where I've already soaked through my totally ineffectual thong.

He speaks again, the struggle he's having with his self-control evident from the raspiness of his voice. His fingers continue their torture.

'If we were in the pool, and the others were around, I'd lead you over to the near side, so it looked as though we were having a nice chat.'

He lifts off me and edges my dress downwards. Oh, God. I raise my hips to let him. I half expect him to pull my thong down too, but he leaves it. When he's got rid of the dress, he's back on top of me, his erection hard against my pelvic bone.

'You'd be more dressed than this. You'd be in that swimming costume, or that little white bikini you wore on your first day here.'

His hands glide up over my hips, my stomach, my breasts. And back down. Up. And down.

His breathing is harder, and I can't resist the urge to open my eyes and enjoy the effect I'm having on him.

He shakes his head in mock disapproval.

'You are… a sight for sore fucking eyes. I can't tell you what I want to do to do. I want to do everything. Be everywhere. Taste everywhere. Now, close your eyes, please, baby, because I'm running out of self-control.'

He runs his tongue over his lower lip and I'm struck by the fact that I haven't experienced real, red hot desire for a long time. Not like this. Not like the burn I feel all over my body when I see Noah on top of me, his face a study in intent, his ice cream-coloured shorts bulging and his unruly hair falling over his eyes. And the fact that he's still fully dressed and I'm pretty much naked is even hotter. The contrast seems to be doing it for him too.

I close my eyes again, for him, but mainly for myself. It makes my other senses sing; it makes the tension and the expectation churning inside me all the more potent.

'I'm having a hard time staying on track.' His laugh is a shudder. 'As I was saying.'

A fingertip glides down between my breasts, over my belly-button, and teases the top of my thong. He takes his weight off me and edges my legs apart with the other hand. Further apart. Further. I let him, gladly, sliding my feet upwards so my legs are slightly bent. He kneels back between them, his fingers brushing my inner thighs.

'If we were having a friendly chat in the pool, I'd have to be very careful. But you'd have to be more careful not to react when I did this.'

One hand reaches the top, and he grazes my soaking thong and the surrounding flesh with his knuckles. The tickle is too much, and I gasp and jolt and push into his hand.

'That's definitely what I would call a reaction, baby. But we're only practising, so I'll let you off. Besides, you wanting me to touch you is the most incredible thing I've ever seen.'

He pushes the thin fabric of my thong aside and his fingers stroke, stroke, stroke. They dip inside me and begin a leisurely wander around my wetness, avoiding the one spot I'm desperate for him to touch. It's clear that's by design, and it's infuriating. I grind into his fingers.

'I'd make you come like this, with my hand inside your bikini bottoms.' His finger finally moves north and I begin the heady process of unravelling before he pulls it away.

'But I don't think you're going to be capable of being very discreet. So instead'—he rears up again and pulls off my thong, before settling back between my legs—'I'd have to wait till we had the pool to ourselves. Like, at this time of night. And I'd sit you up on the side and I'd spread your beautiful legs as far open as I could, and I'd make you come like this.'

His hands move my knees further apart, and I let them fall to the sides. And finally, finally, he delivers the killer part of the pitch. His tongue on me, taut and circling with deadly focus, exactly where I need it. A couple of fingers from one hand inside me as I push against him. His thumb massaging just south of his tongue. And his other hand stroking up my stomach to find my breast, and rubbing, rolling, squeezing, tweaking.

And I'm good for nothing. Nothing. My hands find his hair and claw at it, my back arches, and my mouth opens into an O at the relentless build of heat and pressure under his tongue and fingers.

'Harder.' I moan the word. 'Harder—*please*, Noah.'

He ramps everything up. Fingers squeezing. Tongue pushing. And I explode around him, shuddering and convulsing and thrashing my head from side to side until I'm too sensitive to bear any more of his ministrations, and I tug him up to me. Pulling him into my arms. Tasting myself on his mouth. Sighing into him and listening to the words that stream out of his mouth and into mine. Telling me I'm so beautiful. He's never tasted anything better. He's addicted. *I'm* his addiction.

And as waves of post-orgasmic bliss wash over me, I know: I'm pretty addicted too.

15

NOAH

The world is a joyful, wondrous place when I wake the next morning. The sky is a perfect, cerulean blue through the open curtains. I'm alone, but that can't be helped. Honor couldn't risk a night with me in case her children came looking for her.

Honor. I cross my arms behind my head. Last night was the most extraordinary explosion of desire and connection. I've wanted to do all those things and more to her in a very real way ever since I met her in Mum's kitchen, and in a much more abstract way ever since I watched her, glazed-eyed, on morning TV after my night shifts.

But the proposal I made to her wasn't premeditated. It was born out of so much pent-up frustration and outrage over the way she allowed that fucking husband of hers to treat her. I never seriously thought she'd go for something like that—not until I had her on the bed, anyway. Not until she settled herself on the pillow, and looked up at me, and showed me that the looks I'd seen her giving me—for the heated looks of the past few weeks had seemed very much mutual to me—were based on a real interest.

I also never, in my wildest fantasies, thought she'd be so receptive, so quickly ignited. Like the proposition itself, the dirty running commentary I delivered was inspired by the reactions I had to her lying there, in the moment, as well as my idle fantasies while observing her over the past couple of days.

I thought I'd have to tread carefully. Warm her up slowly. Take care not to scare her while suggesting ways I could help her through her husband's infidelity. Suggesting being the operative word. Not telling. Certainly not *showing*. But she got into the fantasy as quickly as I did, and the reality of being with her was far fucking hotter than any of the fantasies I'd talked her through.

Her body is... flawless. So beautiful, as I told her, with those small, high breasts and that pale skin of her stomach. Last night plays out in searing flashes. Her face beneath me as I rolled her nipples between my fingers. Eyelashes fluttering. Mouth open. Jaw tightening. Licking down her stomach. Tasting her. The tension of her around my fingers. The spasms of her body as she came in my mouth.

By the time I made my way back up to kiss her, I was on the brink of release myself. But last night was for her. It wasn't about me getting off; it was about showing her what she was missing by sitting at home while her husband humped his way through life.

But when she kissed me, relaxed and cat-like and smiling against my lips, she asked me if there was the remotest chance of my having a condom in my shorts pocket.

'Afraid not.' I laugh-groaned and rubbed her nose with mine. 'Anyway, this is your night. I'm fine.'

'You don't feel like you're fine.' She put a hand on my

arse and pulled me closer in towards her nakedness, wrapping her legs around me, and I nearly lost it then and there.

'Don't worry about me.' This was requiring a stupendous effort. I was so close. I kissed her again, revelling in the feeling of her arms and legs around me.

'Are you kidding me? This is a two-way thing, Noah. I'm not in the market for a sex slave. I *want* to. I've been drooling over that happy trail of yours since I got here. You are. Absolutely. Gorgeous.'

She manoeuvred herself up and guided me onto my back.

Now I was in her position, lying back against the cushions, gazing up at her as she grinned down at me, her hair brushing my face and neck as she kissed me.

Watching her bite her lip as she unbuttoned my shirt.

Inhaling sharply as she kissed her way down my happy trail and, miracle of miracles, unbuttoned my shorts.

And then, universes collided as she brushed her lips against the cotton of my boxers, the fabric barely containing my erection, and, tugging down the waistband, took me in that mouth. Her mouth. Her exquisite, supple mouth that had formed the basis of all my fantasies. A reality that surpassed all of them, because holy fucking shit, the reality of her was beyond my wildest dreams.

~

The trestle table in the shady area of the terrace groans with food. A massive platter spills over with nectarine and cantaloupe melon, both of which are abundant in Provence at this time of year. Fresh baguettes in their paper sleeves wait on the heavy wooden breadboard. And there are cured meats, and soft cheese, and local honey. Life is good.

Mum and Dad are already sipping coffee, as are Evelyn and Angus. Angus has lovely little Baby Rose next to him in a plastic highchair. They've wisely left her naked, aside from her nappy. Her tiny torso is streaked with sticky trails which look to be nectarine, given the number of crushed, pulpy segments abandoned on the tray of the highchair. She has one squished in one plump little paw; in the other is a half-chewed crust of bread. Eddie's focus is wholly on the bowl of hot chocolate that he's tipping with two hands, his face buried in it to the extent that there's chocolate on his nose.

But there are three seats empty. Honor and her kids aren't down yet. There's a weird stab of apprehension: that she may regret last night, that she may regret giving herself over to me so freely. I, on the other hand, have never regretted anything less.

'Morning, morning.'

I rake my hand through my damp hair and take my seat.

'You've woken up on the right side of the bed. Good.'

Mum's expression is pinched. She wasn't thrilled about my personality failure last night. She definitely has nothing to worry about on that front today.

I nod at Angus and Evelyn and give them a chipper smile. Lean over to high-five Eddie, before sliding into my chair. Christ, I'm ravenous.

I slice off a big chunk of baguette and tear it. Miraculous. The outside is perfectly crispy, and the inside comes apart in my hands. Slather it in Gui's strawberry compote and take a huge bite. I've just leant back in my chair, eyes shut in foodie ecstasy, when the slap of bare feet hits the ground behind me and Rollo appears over my shoulder.

'G'day, mate.' Rollo's going through an Aussie phase.

Honor says he's been watching too much of an Australian TV show on Netflix.

'G'day.' I twist in my chair, ostensibly to ruffle Rollo's curls, but really to see if Honor's turned up yet. And she has. And she's glorious. Damp hair slicked off her face in a ponytail. She's wearing the same black swimming costume and denim cutoffs as yesterday. The little beauty. She's skittish; her eyes dart around the table, landing on me for a split second before focusing on Evelyn, who gets a genuine smile.

'Morning, Honor,' I say cheerfully, patting the seat next to me. I'm causing mischief, but I also want to put her at ease. 'Have a seat. Did you sleep well?'

She narrows her eyes at me. 'Very well, thank you. I'm just—uh—I'll just go get myself a coffee. Anyone else?'

She practically runs into the house before anyone can answer.

'I should have asked her to refill the cafetiere,' Evelyn says.

'I'll do it.' I jump up and grab it; follow Honor into the house.

When I get into the little butler's pantry off the kitchen, she has her back to me and she's busying herself with the Nespresso machine. That black swimming costume shows off most of her flawless back, and her cutoffs hug her delicious little arse perfectly. Knowing that things have shifted between us, that I can (hopefully) go to her, is the most extraordinary feeling.

'Hey.' I keep my voice soft and she jerks her head around. The look she gives me is a mix of fear and desire. She flicks her gaze down my body and back up again and licks her lips.

'Hi.' She turns back to the coffee machine.

I cross the small space and put the cafetiere down so I

can slide my hands over her shoulders and down her arms from behind her. I bury my nose in her damp, fragrant hair and kiss the side of her head.

'You okay? Any regrets?'

She sags back into me and turns her face to mine.

'No. Definitely not. I just... haven't done the morning after thing in a long time. I don't even know how to act.'

'I know. It's okay. It's just me. You're good.'

I bend my head so I can kiss those beautiful lips gently, and thread my arms around her waist, pulling her into me. My cock stirs in appreciation against her arse, and she makes a little noise in her throat.

I stroke her stomach through the thick knit of her swimming costume.

'This is a very sexy swimming costume.'

I drop a kiss on her shoulder, then another. Nudge the strap with my nose.

'And we're in the butler's pantry. Remember what I said I wanted to do to you in here?'

She laughs nervously. 'It was pretty memorable.'

'I'm very tempted, as you can feel. But I don't want to make you uncomfortable.' My hand moves higher on her stomach and I trace the underside of her breasts with my thumb through the swimming costume. She grabs my other hand, which is still on her stomach, and holds onto it.

'Can I tempt you upstairs after breakfast?' I mumble into her neck. 'Any chance you can excuse yourself for an hour to deal with some "pressing work stuff"?'

She twists around and leans into me, slipping her arms tentatively around my neck, her lips brushing softly against mine. I wrap my arms around the exquisite, silky skin of her back and squeeze her as I lose myself in kissing her.

'It's a date,' she says a few minutes later.

16

HONOR

Noah's bedroom smells of him. Which is a very good thing. And he's made his bed perfectly. Which, for some reason, tugs at my heartstrings. He's a good boy, tidying his duvet and fluffing up his pillows before breakfast—even if he had an ulterior motive for making the bed look inviting.

He pokes his head out of the open door to what's presumably his ensuite bathroom, toothbrush in his mouth. Grins and holds up a finger before disappearing back inside. He's still in his shorts and t-shirt. That's a relief. I'm definitely hooked. Definitely. But it's one thing to have an evening of passion that's more spontaneous and uninhibited than I've ever had before, and it's another to show up to this guy's booty call, stone-cold sober and in the relentless, dazzling daylight of a Cote d'Azur morning.

I passed out last night and then woke at five, and I've been awake ever since, my gut churning with an emotionally exhausting mix of guilt, self-judgement, smugness, desire, excitement and bewilderment. After a decade of being firmly camped out on the moral high ground, I put myself on an equal footing with Jackson last night before I could say *I'm coming.*

Waking up to this knowledge was the most bizarre feeling. It's exactly like that gut-churning anxiety and excitement I used to get at uni, or in my early days at ITV, when I'd snogged someone the previous night and then had no idea how to react, or behave, or think. The difference is, last night I got naked with a man who was not my husband! And my kids were upstairs in bed! And we were outside—anyone could have come down to the pool and found us starkers!

My mind has been pumping out exclamation marks ever since. When I came down to breakfast (again, with my *children*!), the turmoil in my stomach got worse, especially as soon as I saw him grinning at me, and I ran for the hills. And when he came into the butler's pantry, I didn't know whether to be more scared that he'd give me the cold shoulder or make good on his promise and pull down my swimming costume there and then.

But of course, he behaved like the perfect gentleman (apart from the boob graze). He held me, and reassured me, and made me feel desirable without going full-on predator. And he looked gorgeous. And smelt amazing. And my stomach's been flip-flopping in a *really* good way since then. Right through breakfast, trying to avoid his unhelpfully suggestive grins as I swatted away his bare foot under the table. Every time I snuck a peek at him, it was as if I got to see him in a new light, now that the veil had been lifted.

I took in the curve of his jaw and knew how it felt to run my mouth along his stubble. He licked some jam off his lips (he was really going for it with that jam) and I was jealous of his tongue. Ridiculous! He rested his elbows on the table as Angus regaled them with some anecdote (who knows what about; I wasn't listening) and I knew exactly how the jut of that bicep and the hairy tautness of that forearm would feel under my fingers when I got him to myself.

He's done in the bathroom. He hangs from the doorframe for a moment, back-lit against the sunlight, and his t-shirt rides up. That flat stomach. That happy trail I kissed my way down last night before surprising both of us by letting him have his full release in my mouth. Admittedly, a small part of my motivation was not wanting to get my new Missoni dress ruined. I didn't want Di having any awkward conversations with our dry cleaner.

But I enjoyed the whole thing more than I expected. Far more. I *loved* being in the moment with him, showing him that I was far less uptight than he would probably have guessed. Loved the exhilarating sense of power that came with being the instrument of his desire. Loved the slick hardness of him in my mouth, the look of disbelief and adoration on his face when I glanced up and nodded at him, signalling that I wasn't going to pull away. Loved the fervour with which those fingers twisted in my hair. I loved the whole fucking thing.

So when he walks towards me, his hands up in front of him as if he's approaching some unstable gun-wielder, it makes me smile. But his answering smile is as lazy and inviting as ever.

'Is it creepy that I made you come up here? We can go for a walk, if you like. I just wanted to get you to myself. We don't have to do anything if you don't want to.'

'It's pretty creepy. Lucky you're very hot.'

I slide a hand around the back of his neck and lean in. The smile lines bracketing his mouth are the sexiest thing ever. I press my lips to one corner of his mouth, then slide them over his lips and find his tongue with mine. He's minty and perfect, and our kiss is slow but heated. This must be what happiness is: standing in a sun-filled room in the South of France, your body pressed against that of a man whose hands are doing laps of your bare back, punctuated with squeezes at each end to the nape of your neck and the curve of your arse. His mouth and tongue showing you you're tantalising and delicious and addictive. Just in case his steady hardening against the front of your shorts isn't a clear enough sign.

He pulls away enough to pull off his t-shirt, and my insides do a little dance. Are all women hard-wired to find the sight of a man pulling off a t-shirt panty-meltingly perfect? It must be relentless subliminal brainwashing from formative years filled with Levi's ads and Athena posters and Baywatch on a Saturday evening. Put a puppy or a baby in his arms right now and I wouldn't know my own name. My lips part of their own accord.

'Wow.' He laughs. 'Hungry eyes.'

'Famished.' My hands slide down the glorious curves of his shoulders. Biceps. Forearms. Yup. Exactly how I knew they'd feel at breakfast.

He leans his forehead to mine before taking my shoulders and turning me gently away from him. Brushes my ponytail aside and kisses my neck. Slides his hands around my waist, to the flies of my cutoffs.

'May I?'

'Yes.' My throat is tightening by the second. The anticipation has kicked in again.

My eyelids drift shut as he fumbles with the button and zip, before his fingertips push the shorts down and brush down my thighs. Back up my thighs, to the sides of my high-legged swimming costume.

'Jesus.' It sounds more like a whispered prayer than blasphemy as he lowers his mouth to my shoulder and his hands coast over my waist and hips. My heart-rate is ratcheting up. His featherlight strokes are working my nervous system into anticipatory bliss.

I turn, slowly. Take his rapt face in my hands and kiss him. Slowly. Deeply.

'Last night was ridiculous but… I'm enjoying every second of this,' he tells me. 'You, in the light of day—you're even more beautiful like this.'

His hands go to the straps of my swimming costume, his eyes searching my face for permission. He peels the straps off my shoulders, down my arms, the costume sitting at my waist. His face is a picture. He stares at my breasts and runs a hand over his face. The level of awe reflected on his beautiful features tightens my chest. And my nipples.

I help him out, pushing my swimming costume the rest of the way down and stepping out of it. His gaze drops to my landing strip—which is impeccable, if I do say so myself—and he lets out a shuddery groan.

'Oh, God. Oh, God.'

Then he's fumbling blindly with the drawstring on his swim shorts, tugging them down and doing an unintentionally comedic dance to get them off from around his ankles. I giggle.

'Sorry.' He laughingly kicks them away and puts his arms around me. 'Not my smoothest moment. You have me acting like a spotty fucking adolescent who's never seen a naked woman before.'

'You feel like a fully grown man to me.' I press myself against him and cup his arse for good measure. It's slightly, softly hairy and utterly glorious. I didn't get a good handful of it last night.

And then we're on the bed, and my legs are around him, and the sensation of his skin and hair and muscle against mine is sublime. He disentangles my limbs from his and crouches above me on all fours. Admiring. Absorbing. His hair brushing my face as he leans in to kiss me. His hand sweeping over my breasts, across my stomach.

He groans. 'Jesus Christ. Where do I start?'

I shift on the bed. The sheets are crisp beneath me, and the light breeze coming through the open windows dances on my skin, reinforcing the fact that I'm gloriously naked and exposed for this man. Every nerve ending on my skin is awake.

'I said it last night, and I meant it.' He parts my legs and sits back on his heels, his hands brushing my skin. His thumbs making a trail up and down my inner thighs. His eyes flickering over my body. 'You are the most beautiful woman I have *ever* seen.'

His thumbs move north and I open my legs further. My pulse is beating in parts of my body that are nowhere near my heart. The blood builds between my legs. From arousal comes courage.

'Show me.'

He grins at me. I'm not the only one who's famished.

'I will, baby. I promise. I'm going to show you how beautiful you are. But I may need some help. I don't have enough hands.'

He runs his hands firmly up over my stomach. Fingers tracing my breasts. When they hit my nipples and squeeze, I convulse. *That*. That feeling. Is. Everything.

He takes his time. His hands on my nipples. Rolling. Pressing. Chafing. It's simultaneously heavenly and torturous. I could explode just from this, but it's not going to hit the spot the way I need. I squirm on the bed.

'Noah. I need you inside me. Please, for the love of God, say you have condoms.'

'I do.' He kisses me. Slow. Tongue taut. 'But I want to make you come first. Unless you can come just from my being inside you?'

'Not usually,' I admit. Vaginal orgasms are as intriguing, and as improbable, as unicorns.

'Not a problem. Give me your hands.'

He puts my hands on my breasts. 'I need you to touch yourself for me. Do what I've been doing, okay?'

His hands move downwards, and he slips a couple of fingers inside me. Oh, God. He's finally given me a body part. I push into his hand, but he doesn't move it. Instead, he grins and raises his eyebrows at me.

'Go on. I need you working your magic at that end.'

'Dick.' I make a face at him, but he's unmoved.

'Come on. Team effort. Don't be shy.'

Desire and frustration overtake self-consciousness. I move my fingers, rolling my aching nipples between them like pebbles. As soon as I do, he pulls his fingers out and pushes them back in, hard. The sense of relief at both ends of my body is so massive, I close my eyes and moan. When I open them, he's watching me, and wetting his lips, and shaking his head.

'You're going to kill me. I may not survive this. The most beautiful woman in the world, touching herself.'

My breath comes faster.

'Make it worth my while.'

'I will. I fucking will.'

And he crouches down. Puts his mouth on me. Holds me open with his hand, his tongue hitting all the most sensitive parts of me. His long fingers pushing into me, like they did last night. There's no way I can hold out for long. The heat builds and swells and pulses through my entire body and crescendos in an almighty rush between my legs, and the heavenly torment turns to blissful, unreal release as my entire body surges against him.

'Quick.' I'm delirious. 'Quick. Where's your condom?'

He kisses my inner thigh and scoots up to grab one off the bedside table. My legs hang open. Shaking, useless. He rips the foil and I stare at the delectable sight of him rolling the condom over his very hard, very gorgeous, very large dick. He runs a hand over it and I smirk. The Cote d'Azur knows how to put on a good show.

'Come here.' I hold up a hand and curl it around his neck.

He crouches back down, framing my shoulders with his elbows. He's shaking as he edges into me, and I take. No lube necessary today. Definitely not.

He reaches down and hooks an arm behind one of my knees, pulling it up. Edges in further. And the sensation of being filled up is glorious. Far better than his fingers. The aftershocks of my orgasm are still coming, the friction as he moves inside me rounding out that sensation to a state of perfect fulfilment. I may not come like this, but I can sure as hell revel in the perfection of his hard, rhythmical thrusts as he drives into me, sending a wall of pressure up through my entire abdomen, pushing the air out of my lungs. This. This. This.

I kiss him—deep drives of my tongue that mirror the effect he's having on my insides, and I can feel him near his own orgasm. When he does slow and still inside me, and shudder, he releases a long groan into my mouth before thrusting through his climax, and I move with him. Hold him in my arms as he shakes. My chest is tight with exhaustion and emotion and overwhelm.

He pulls up and out of my embrace and I whimper.

He kisses me softly on the mouth. 'Give me a sec.'

I ogle his arse shamelessly as he heads into the bathroom to deal with the condom, my head propped up on one elbow.

He strolls back in, grinning, before hopping back on the bed and folding me into his arms. He wraps his top leg around me. His hand is on the back of my head; my nose against his chest. I inhale him as my breathing slows. If that was just sex, we're both in trouble.

17

NOAH

Honor lets me take her for lunch. Not Club Cinquant-Cinq, like I would have liked, because it's far too conspicuous, but Villa Marie, a beautiful boutique hotel in nearby Ramatuelle. The best way to pitch it to Mum is to be casual.

'D'you mind watching Serena and Rollo for a couple of hours?' I ask her. 'Honor mentioned she wants to check out Villa Marie for a possible work thing next summer, and I thought I'd accompany her over, maybe grab a spot of lunch.'

It works a treat, and here we are, sitting under a cheery tomato-red parasol at a charming table at the edge of the terrace. The view is spectacular: across the hotel's lush tropical gardens and the surrounding pine forest to Pampelonne Beach and the sparkling Mediterranean sea. Although we're well shaded here, Honor is wearing the biggest sunhat I've ever seen, with a huge, floppy brim that appears to be getting the better of her. I squat down further in my seat so I can meet her eyes.

'Is that the kissing equivalent of a chastity belt?'

'Ha ha. It's so I can be incognito.'

'Nothing about you says incognito.' She's in a white, backless linen jumpsuit, her hair pulled back under the offending hat. She's painted her mouth a bright tomato red that matches our parasol and seat cushions, and I'm itching to kiss it. Even among the wealthy, polished and chic French clientele here, she stands out. It's a huge thrill to have managed to sneak Honor Chapman out of the house and off for a public, if incognito, lunch date.

'You're sweet.' She blows me a kiss. 'But if it stops you from being able to get close to my mouth in public, then it's multitasking effectively.'

'Are you totally incognito today, or do you have an alter-ego when you go out in disguise?'

'Hmm.' She pouts at me and adopts a ridiculous French accent. 'I zink today I am Gabrielle. My first and second 'usbands both died, and I 'ave taken a young lover. 'E is very sexy.'

'Jesus. That sounds suspicious. Remind me never to marry you, Gabrielle. But I'm very happy to be your young lover.' I brush my white-chino-clad leg—when in the South of France—against hers under the table. 'I wish we could get a room here. I can't get enough of your skin. If I could just have you wrapped around me, naked, for another hour or two, I'd happily join your first two husbands in heaven.'

That white jumpsuit is something else. Its little shoulder straps kiss her glossy shoulders. I'd give a kidney right now to bury my nose in her collarbone and tug her jumpsuit down and off. God. I discreetly rearrange myself under the starched white tablecloth before leaning in.

'I have a confession to make.'

She adjusts the brim of her hat so she can see me better and narrows her eyes at me.

'What?'

'Well, I have two confessions, really. One, I'm getting hard right now, just imagining taking that jumpsuit off.'

Her perfect red lips curl up.

'And two. You might run a mile when you hear this, but I feel awkward not telling you that I have fantasised about you a lot. A lot.'

'Since you met me, you mean?'

'Um.' Heat is rushing to my face. 'Well, yes. Obviously. But also before. Years ago, when you were on TV.'

'Seriously?'

I can't look at her. I fiddle with the heavy knives at his place setting. 'I did so many night shifts when I was a resident. And I used to find it impossible to unwind when I got home. I was always overtired and wired. So I developed a bit of a routine. Come home, eat a couple of bowls of Weetabix on the sofa while I watched you on Sunrise, and then I'd head off to bed, think about you, and I'd, er, bang one out, and then I'd sleep like a baby.'

'*What?!*' She leans in further, drops her voice. 'Look at me, Noah. You mean you jacked off over me? What exactly do you mean by *think about you*?'

I laugh nervously and do her the courtesy of reestablishing eye contact. This was possibly a huge mistake. She could well be offended, or seriously creeped out. 'I think that should stay between me and my dick, if you don't mind.'

'I do mind. You can't leave it there.' She lowers her face to mine. 'So baby Noah, gorgeous, sexy junior doctor Noah, gets home from a night of saving lives and *watches me* and gets himself off on it? *Tell me what you thought about.*'

'Ah. Um. It was a long time ago.'

'Don't give me that. Shoot. Pun intended.'

Good Lord. I'd forgotten who I was dealing with: a master interviewer, someone trained to extract information from her victims. I'm falling prey to the precise skill-set that used to turn me on.

'Okay. Ah.' I discreetly wipe the sweat from the back of my neck with a napkin. 'I'm definitely not showing off my most evolved self, all right? It was everything, really. Those shift dresses you always wore, especially the sleeveless ones. You always looked so elegant and put together. And you never lost your cool. You had—have—this cut-glass accent and you were always so charming but composed. No one ever cracked you. You were badass. Especially when you were interviewing politicians. That was always my favourite thing. You wiped the floor with them. And it was very sexy.'

'Interesting. So.'

She reaches around the side of the table furthest from the rest of the diners for my hand, and I take it, run my thumb pad over her delicate fingers.

'That's what does it for you? Me breaking politicians' balls?'

I exhale. I'm not sure if the churning in my stomach is worry or desire. 'Kind of. I liked the challenge you represented.'

Her lips purse. 'Elaborate.'

This is a very poor decision on my part. Shit.

'I used to fantasise about being there with you, on set. And when you were done, we'd go back to your dressing room, and...'

'I'd break your balls?'

'I'd help you channel all that adrenalin. Help you wind down. Ideally on your sofa.'

'How would I be?'

'You'd be completely amped up at the beginning, and

then purring like a kitten at the end. In my arms. And your sexy little shift dress would definitely be on the floor.'

'I can live with that.' She pauses for a drink of her rosé. 'I just have one question. Would you be in a white coat?'

'Scrubs, probably.'

'Oh, *God*. Baby Dr Noah in scrubs. I can't even. Will you wear them for me sometime? In real life? And do you have a stethoscope?'

'I don't use them at Good Vibes, if I can help it. I don't want to scare our guests. But I have plenty of old pairs at my flat.'

'Done. I'll wear a slinky shift dress that says *I regularly break politicians' balls before breakfast*.'

I grin at her. Her insinuation that this thing may have legs after we get back to London and reality later in the week makes the muscles around my heart loosen up in relief.

I take a sip of my wine. 'Would you believe, I even have a perfectly good sofa?'

Honor's security guard, Di, gets us back home in one piece, giggling and buzzed from the rosé. Clearly, Honor has no secrets from her. I've been nursing a semi all through lunch; I resort to covering my lap with Honor's ridiculous hat in the car. Honor is pressed up against me and I allow myself to imagine how it would be if we had the chateau to ourselves this trip: how miraculous it would be to lie naked with her on one of the daybeds and have the sun warm our skin.

Di drops us in front of the door to the courtyard before taking off to put the car in the garage. The shrieks of hilarity from the pool area hit us before they're even across the courtyard. I brush my fingers against Honor's.

'Sounds like nobody's missed us.'

Then comes a booming voice that neither of us can mistake.

'Jump, Rollo! Cannonball! CANNONBALL!'

Honor stops still in the courtyard. I turn to her as if she holds the answers, but her face is frozen in utter horror.

'Shit,' she says. 'It's fucking Jackson.'

18

HONOR

Fucking Jackson.

It's all over. Just like that. I knew this fledgling *thing* I had going on with Noah was precarious, transient, but I thought I had a couple more days of staying in this fantasy. Two more days away from the real world: away from the relentlessness of the press, and responsibility, and image, and my *husband*.

Sure, we've just been joking, fantasising, about hooking up at Noah's flat when we're back, but it's not the same. It's not the same as being here, at Des Anges, in this idyllic, sun-kissed bubble. Hours ago, his delicious weight was bearing down on me in his airy bedroom. Minutes ago, my hand was on his thigh in the car. My fingers clasping his. My head nestled into the crook of his neck.

And now, as we stare in the direction of Jackson's unmistakable voice, he looks as stricken as I feel. It's like we've both been the butt of this cosmic joke. The gods must be having a laugh that I thought I could pull off a little affair—the kind Jackson makes look so easy—and not have it come back to bite me in the arse. Immediately.

I'm furious Jackson's shown up. I made it clear to him that this was a break for me and the kids, but he's overruled me. As usual. And alongside the fury and the desolation—that heavy dropping sensation in my stomach—comes guilt. I got involved with Noah, and by doing so I've embroiled him in the particular brand of toxicity that is my and Jackson's family life.

'I'm so sorry.' I whisper it. 'I'm so sorry, Noah. I had no idea—'

'Hey.' He brushes his fingers down my arm. 'Of course you didn't. You have nothing to apologise for. Are you all right?'

I nod.

'Okay, then.' He squares his shoulders. 'Let's go say hi. This should be interesting.'

Jackson's in the pool with the kids when we emerge onto the terrace. As soon as he spots us, he vaults out of it one-armed. Of course he does. I've lived with this man for years, but it's too easy to see him through Noah's eyes, and I'm aware of his quiet *holy fuck* amid Rollo and Serena's excited yells.

It's so unfair to put Noah through this. He sleeps with someone, and that woman's husband, who happens to be one of the most famous action movie stars on the entire planet, shows up to surprise them. It's brutal.

Jackson walks towards us, all rippling muscles and waxed chest and sky-blue shorts clinging far more than they should, shining the full wattage of his billion-dollar grin on me, and my body betrays me with a flip of my stomach. This reaction to him is far too deeply embedded in my subconscious: the thrill of being Jackson James' Chosen One (most of the time).

'Hi, gorgeous.' He stoops and kisses me on the lips, and

it's a good job he's soaking, because it gives me an excuse to keep my distance.

'This is a surprise.' My tone is light, but anyone with more emotional intelligence than Jackson could surely pick up on its *froideur*.

'I know, right? My FOMO kicked in. Couldn't bear the idea of my people being out here without me. This place is heaven.'

It's amazing how much power he has to withstand said FOMO when he's fucking his co-star in the middle of a lengthy US-based shooting season.

'It certainly is,' I say evenly. 'Jackson, meet Noah.'

I won't provide context. The only context that's relevant is the stuff that Jackson absolutely does not need to know.

'Mate.' Jackson pumps his hand. 'I've heard great things about your hospice. Good to put a face to the name.'

To his credit, Noah doesn't flinch from coming face-to-face with an A-list celebrity he's currently cuckolding.

'Good to meet you, Jackson. Glad you could make it out here.'

My lips twitch.

'Excuse me. I need a swim.' Noah heads off towards the cabana and, over the next few minutes, as Jackson grabs a lounger and chatters on about his flight, I'm only aware of Noah. Emerging from the cabana in his swim shorts. Executing a perfect dive and shooting down the length of the pool underwater. And when he's done swimming, he grabs a towel and heads straight for the house without a glance in our direction.

Noah keeps a low profile for the rest of the afternoon, and it makes me seriously antsy. I'd almost prefer the excruciating awkwardness of watching him chat to Jackson. He makes an appearance with a book, which he proceeds to read on a shady day bed at the far end of the pool while Angus and Jackson get stuck into a long backgammon tournament punctuated with endless rosé.

It's irritating to admit, but Jackson's arrival has had a boosting effect on the atmosphere at Des Anges. I preferred the low key vibe we had going on before he showed up—I needed a break from Jackson's high-octane personality—but he's perked most of the others up.

He and Angus know each other reasonably well already, mainly through me and Evelyn. Elaine is skittishly pleased to see him and welcomes her uninvited guest into her home with characteristic grace. And all the kids are thrilled. Unfortunately, his A-list credentials and his undeniable (and finely honed) charm give most people a major kick, and our friends are not immune. It's just me and, presumably, Noah who are put out by this unexpected turn of events.

By the time pre-dinner drinks roll around, Noah is showered and changed and on impeccable form. His tan continues to build, and he looks hot as hell in a pale pink polo and white shorts that showcase his dark, perfectly hairy, Mediterranean skin. Noah, the human ice-cream. Yet again. I can't get enough.

No one on that terrace would suspect for a moment that there is anything between us, or that Noah has any beef with my husband. He's relaxed and full of smiles as he engages Jackson in an animated conversation around his upcoming show, *Vet*. It's based on a series of blockbuster books, all of which Noah's read, and he appears fascinated by Jackson's inside scoop on which aspects of the books they've stayed true to and which they've sacrificed.

I suspect that irrespective of his relationship with me, Noah is secretly pumped to be hanging out with Jackson James. Jackson's a man's man as much as he's a ladies' man. A national treasure. Noah's only human. It's impossible to be immune to the full power of Jackson's attention.

Although I'm grateful and relieved Noah's putting on a good show, I'm antsy. Desperate for a moment with him. I get nothing but a few crumbs all evening.

'Another glass of champagne, Honor?' he asks casually, brushing my bare shoulder with his fingers as he rounds the back of my chair. When I look up, only I see the heat in his eyes, and I'm pretty sure my eyes reflect that heat right back at him, judging by the tiny, knowing smirk on his face.

Hmm. This aspect of having an affair I can handle. The secret glances. The subtle touches. The forbidden nature of it certainly gives me a definite frisson.

What I haven't thought through sufficiently is juggling these two guys—especially under one roof. That was most definitely not the plan. I've been working on the assumption that I can neatly pigeonhole my married life and my relationship (or dalliance, or whatever it its) with Noah in London. After all, Jackson will be back on the road again with his beloved Leila from next week.

But here in Provence, I'm facing the discomfort not just of logistics (I'm not having sex with two guys under one roof!) but of my emotions. My reaction to Jackson tells me my husband still does it for me. Of course he does. Every human being with a pulse has a reaction to Jackson James. But I'm also in this bubble with Noah that's enchanting, and not just because of its sparkling newness and intoxicatingly forbidden nature.

No, it's enchanting because of the way he makes me feel. As though I'm this incredible, perfect being, to be seen, and treasured, and adored. Not that one-way adoration is particularly sexy. That's just a power imbalance. What's really irresistible about our liaison is that I'm equally drawn to him.

I may not have the history of years of crushing Noah does (and masturbating; I giggle to myself at the image of Baby Dr Noah crushing *hard* over me after his night shifts), I'm as in the moment as he is. I'm crushing equally hard over his skin, with that tan and that body hair, over his laughter lines that bracket that beautiful mouth, over the silkiness of his hair when I claw at it.

And most of all, over the heat in his dark eyes when he kisses me. When he moved inside me this morning. That heat, and the way it makes me feel the entire way through my core, tells me this liaison is rapidly becoming at risk of escalating into something far more than an easy little fling.

One could even say I'm becoming an addict. A Dr Noah addict.

It's too much. My head and my heart are too full of unfamiliar turmoil and emotions. As soon as supper is over, I practically sprint to bed. With any luck, I'll be asleep before Jackson materialises. If I'm not, I'll damn well pretend to be.

One night down; two more to go.

19

NOAH

An insistent rapping on my bedroom door brings me abruptly to consciousness the next morning. I sit bolt upright and rub my eye with the heel of my hand.

'Come in.'

It's Honor. She peeks around the door before stepping into the room and closing it behind her. She's in a tiny romper suit, hair pulled back. A leggy, gorgeous vision. One visitation I was *not* expecting.

'Hey. What are you—where's Jackson?'

'He's gone for a run. He'll be a while.' She takes a few tentative steps forward. 'Is this okay? I wasn't sure—but I wanted to see you.'

'Of course it's okay!' Is she kidding? I spent far too much time poolside yesterday and in bed last night contemplating the uncomfortable question of why I was so devastated when her husband showed up. I swing my legs out of bed and make for the bathroom. 'Give me a sec.'

Her eyes widen at the sight of my nakedness, and she bites her lip and nods. It doesn't do my ego any harm.

I've never brushed my teeth so quickly. I wrap a towel around my waist—if she's just here to talk, I don't want her to feel pressured—and head back through to my room. She's standing by the window, looking out at the hazy sunrise over the vines. I trail my fingers lightly down her back and run my lips over her glossy shoulder before coming to face her.

Her mouth curves into a tentative smile.

'Hi.'

'Hi, yourself. How are you holding up?'

She exhales shakily. 'Fine, I suppose. I don't know—it's awkward. I didn't expect things to get tricky so quickly.' She fiddles with the draw-string at the waist of her romper.

'I know you didn't. You seem to be handling it well.'

'I just feel so awful—I never meant to put you in this position, Noah. I didn't sleep with him, you know. Last night. I haven't touched him.'

'*Hey*. Look at me.' My hands go to her jaw and tip it up. 'Baby. You don't owe me any explanations. Or justifications. Okay? I'm a big boy. I knew what I was getting into.' I take a deep breath, because what I need to say to her next is surprisingly difficult. The sentence catches in my throat. 'You're allowed to sleep with your husband. You're *married*. It's part of the gig for me; I know that.'

She dips her head and wraps her arms around me tightly so I can't see her face. Whispers against my neck. 'I didn't want to, though. I didn't want him to touch me. At all. All I could think about was you, but I was worried I'd pissed you off, that you'd want to run for the hills.'

This situation we're in is so bizarre. On the one hand, it's a game. We've been playing make-believe out here in dreamland. On the other, the very circumstances of her being married mean we have to be far more open, honest, with each other than I would usually be with a woman I've only been involved with for a day or two.

The extent of her vulnerability is eye-opening. She has no idea that of the three of us, she's the one in the driving seat. She also has no idea her words thrill me to my core. *All I could think about was you.* Whatever this is between us, it's escalated from flirtation and desire to need and raw, intense human connection. I draw back.

'I'm going to keep making you look me in the eye till I know you're hearing what I say. I'm not pissed off with you, baby. This is the deal. *You* are in control here. You call the shots. Your husband has been fucking around for years. You're levelling the playing field; you're taking the pleasure and attention you're owed. And I'm just...' I grin at her, tuck a lock of hair behind her ear. 'I'm just along for the ride. At your service.'

'Okay.' She exhales. 'I'm not very good at this, am I?'

'There's no rule book. Whatever issues you have with Jackson, those are between you and him. But if guilt is part of what's making you keep your distance from your husband, don't let it. I imagine Jackson sleeps easy at night. No guilt there. I told you the other night, this is supposed to make your life better. Not harder. I don't want to be a pain in your delectable backside.'

She leans into me as I stroke said backside and kisses me, and I focus on doing exactly what I promised. Making her feel better. Fantastic. Gorgeous and desirable. Because she's all of those things. It's a pinch-me moment as I stand here with this woman, the woman who's been the object of my fantasies for so many years.

Because the reality of her is so much better. The pillowy softness of her lips as they move against mine, the emotion in her huge green-gold eyes, and the sensation of her slim body in my arms, pressing up against my bare chest, is nothing short of magic. The fact that I get to do this to *Honor Chapman* is ridiculous, but it's increasingly difficult to square the wonder of the woman in my arms with my old celebrity crush.

All I know is, right at this moment, there's nowhere I'd rather be. And judging by the delicious little moans she makes as I ramp up the intensity of our kiss, my hands smoothing greedily over the skin of her arms and back, she's as committed to whatever *this* is as I am.

20

NOAH

Jackson has upgraded my return flight, so I'm in business class with the James family. It's a generous move, but it adds to the pain I've had to endure for the past forty-eight hours. Thankfully, in a few hours I'll be home in Westbourne Grove without feeling like a third wheel in Jackson and Honor's marriage.

I considered changing my flight back, but the amount of paperwork I've had to submit for my bloody Day Two PCR test prevents any attempts at spontaneity. So here I am with Di, sitting right behind Jackson and Honor at the front of BA's spanking new cabin. I feel uncomfortably like part of their entourage. Excellent.

We managed to find a rhythm for the rest of the holiday that assuaged Honor's worry on my behalf and her bizarre, but real, fear that her family entanglements had put me off her.

Even so, the past couple of days have been a combination of my working hard to give Honor space while making a genuine effort with Jackson (surprisingly easy, given the guy has bucket loads of charm and hilarious anecdotes and is pretty fucking impressive when he's not cheating on his wife) and seizing the occasional opportune moment to show Honor I'm still wild about her.

There have been fleeting, hot-as-hell kisses in the butler's pantry at breakfast. Surreptitious gropes and brushes of limbs in the pool. Innuendos and light flirtations and even a moment in the cabana when we 'coincided' by the showers, the mere memory of which makes my trousers tighten.

The flight itself is fine. I'm directly behind Honor, by the window, and if I squeeze my hand between her seat back and the wall of the cabin, I can graze the soft, bare skin of her arm without Jackson seeing anything at all. She covers my fingers with hers, and I close my eyes and lay my forehead against the back of her seat. God only knows what toxic fucking entanglement I've got myself into.

Di's eyes are mainly trained on the aisle. Once or twice she intercepts random members of the public from further down the plane who try to get surreptitious phone shots of Honor and Jackson, and even the kids, on their way back from the front loos. How they handle this bullshit constantly, I do not know.

As we stand to retrieve our overhead baggage, Honor dons oversized sunglasses and her enormous hat. I'm not sure how that thing fit in the overhead compartment. Jackson pulls his baseball cap further down over his eyes and makes sure the kids are wearing theirs, too.

'You may want to keep your distance from us when we get through customs,' he tells me. 'Or stick a cap on, if you've got one. The paps are expecting us.'

I know this already. Honor briefed me yesterday evening. Apparently, their publicist thinks their arrival back in the UK *en famille* is a golden opportunity to present a united front. It seems to me the James family's publicist is hedging her bets. Keep speculation about Jackson and his co-star alive in the papers, but throw the press a few money shots of him and his family looking sun-kissed and relaxed on the way home from an idyllic holiday.

If only they knew the truth: that Honor, the long-suffering wife in the eyes of the world, has finally started enjoying herself and sampling some physical delights outside of her marriage. Thinking of it sends a warm glow through me. It's something I've been able to give her: a secret she gets to hold on to all by herself. The press is oblivious. And I hope it goes a tiny way towards insulating her from all the bullshit the tabloids throw at her.

'Got it.' I nod and exchange a brief look with Honor. Her smile is tight, the apology it holds clear.

'Will it really be that much of a circus?' I ask Di.

'Wait and see.' She smacks her gum. 'It'll be a fucking shit show. But that's what Jackson wanted. This time.'

Di's been acting as a buffer between them and the public the whole time they've been travelling. It's clear why they normally fly private. The French have largely left them alone (I suspect the French know exactly who they are but are way too cool to publicly crush on anyone) but numerous British holidaymakers approached them with excited faces and phones at Nice Airport.

We thank the cabin crew, all of whom are still bright-eyed and giggling from their interactions with Jackson and Honor. I can empathise. They're not the only ones who are star struck.

Baggage collection is eye-opening. The James-Chapman family doesn't travel light. Jackson, Di and Jackson's body-guard pile trolleys with case after case of sleek, cappuccino-coloured Louis Vuitton luggage that's far too precious to have entrusted to the Heathrow baggage system.

'We should probably say our goodbyes here.' Honor glances towards the frosted doors standing between us and whatever circus awaits us. 'That way, you can make yourself scarce.'

'Yeah, mate. Run for the hills, that's what I say. You don't want any of this bullshit.' Jackson bro-hugs me, and as I feebly bang his enormous back with my fist, I can't help but feel the irony of his choice of words. It's utterly unconscious, and probably excellent, advice. I should run for the bloody hills. Unfortunately, Honor's cast a spell on me and I'm no more capable of running, or even walking, away from her than I am of choosing not to breathe.

'Of course. Good idea. I'll hang back here.'

I lean over and duck beneath the brim of Honor's hat to kiss her on both cheeks. Quick. Casual. No reaction to the musky, floral scent of her perfume—the scent that's lingered on my own skin over the past few days.

'I'll see you soon. At the hospice.' I nod and take a step back.

'I'll be there tomorrow. I'm keen to see Mum.' Her voice is artificially bright and she darts her head around, but Jackson's larking around with Rollo and Di's scanning the room.

'Of course. See you then, perhaps. Good luck out there.' I jerk my head towards the doors.

'Thanks.' She throws me a weak smile and pulls the brim of her huge hat further over her face before grabbing Rollo and Serena by the hand. She's reapplied her scarlet lipstick on the flight, and her floaty white sundress is pristine. She's a knockout. A creature from another world. And in this moment, as she prepares to face paparazzi mayhem with her beyond-famous husband standing next to her, I feel as far away from her as I could possibly be.

That feeling intensifies as their little entourage heads for the doors, and as they walk through them, camera flashes and shouts assault them. It's feeding time at the fucking zoo, and they're the prey. I keep a safe distance and walk out behind them.

The press is a solid, writhing bank, and the noise is deafening.

Jackson! Over 'ere, mate!

Where's your girlfriend, eh? Where's Leila? She on holiday too?

You 'ave a nice trip, Honor? Where you been, then? Family holiday, was it? France? Nice.

Like your dress. Nice 'at, Honor.

Jackson, you playing the family man this week?

Honor, what d'you make of the rumours of your husband and Leila?

Jackson's bodyguard leads the way, and Di brings up the rear. They should use those trolleys as battering rams. They could do some serious damage with that many cases. Honor holds her children by the hand, her head dipped. Hopefully, the brim of her hat is affording her some privacy.

I can't believe these cretins are yelling this kind of stuff at them in front of their children. How anyone can actively seek out this level of fame and media intrusion is beyond me. How Honor can tolerate this in the name of building her family's brand is a fucking mystery. Not tolerate: cultivate. It's beyond comprehension.

The paps peel away from the Arrivals doors to pursue their targets and I duck gratefully away towards the anonymity of the lifts to the Underground.

21

HONOR

The airport was a shit-show. Over the years, I've acclimatised to the intrusion of the paparazzi, but I dread them most when the press has a particularly juicy scandal to hold over us. And given our success at keeping most of Jackson's sex life definitively out of the public domain, this scandal is journalistic crack.

Those guys shouted questions at us that my children should not hear. Dickheads. They went over Rollo's head, to a certain extent, but Serena was upset in the car, and Jackson had to explain to her that the press was once again making up silly stories about his work to sell newspapers.

She seemed to have bought it for now, but she was extra clingy to both of us yesterday evening. Poor little thing. Allowing the press access to a carefully curated edit of our family life is one thing, but exposing Serena and Rollo to that kind of highly stressful, conflict-ridden situation is the part of our fame I wrestle with the most. It's at times like this that the sensation of having made a Faustian pact haunts me.

Worse, I couldn't help but see the whole farce unfold

through Noah's eyes yesterday. He's a normal guy—over-achieving, but normal—for whom a charade like that at the airport is just insane. It must have felt to him like travelling with a circus. He's obviously fully aware of our level of fame, and of the downsides of his getting involved with someone whose personal life is apparently fair game for the public. But I can't help but worry that having a front-row seat to how events played out yesterday will have been a massive turnoff for him.

I respond, as always, by overzealously tackling the things I can control. I'm up at five-thirty the following morning to work off my French carb consumption in our basement gym. Rider, my ex-military PT, subjects me to a punishing routine of combat HIIT which leaves me collapsed on my gym mat, begging for mercy.

Next, it's a shower and blow-dry before I pack on as many hydrating and resurfacing treatments as I think my skin can take. The flight and the wine consumption of the past few days have taken their toll—my skin is patchier and less plump than normal. Two years ago, Honor Chapman Cosmetics expanded into Honor Chapman Skincare, and this is the area that really fascinates me.

My love of cosmetics was born out of years learning at the hands of makeup artists when I was on TV, but makeup is the ultimate example of managing symptoms, not causation. Yes, it's fun to play and to change up my look—I adore makeup—but the more success a woman has treating the underlying condition of her skin, the less makeup she'll need.

My skincare range is based on the concept of modular building blocks that help women (and the growing number of men who use them) feel confident enough to reduce the amount of makeup they "need" as a crutch to leave the house each day. It's growing far faster than our cosmetics line, and it could even be a candidate for a spin-off at some point. A dedicated menswear line is also in the works—with Jackson as the proposed face of the brand, naturally.

I sit at the kitchen island and work away as Carmen processes the kids for camp, my various facial acids working away equally hard before I put my clothes and makeup on.

Because today, I'm going to need whatever tools are at my disposal.

Today, I need to remind Noah why I'm worth every second of the hassle of sneaking around with someone who's deemed public property.

Today, I'm going to give him the Honor Chapman of his med school crush.

~

I can't wait to see him. It's ridiculous, and immature, and enormous fun to be sitting in the car as it edges towards Notting Hill. That stomach-churning mix of excitement and lust and will-he-won't-he is so high-school, and yet that's exactly how I feel.

Last night, I lay in bed next to Jackson and replayed every heady, decadent moment from the south of France. Chateau des Anges is now burnt on my brain as the backdrop for the most magical thing to have happened to me in years. I arrived there exhausted and under attack, and I left wrapped in the cloak of my delicious secret: a beautiful, talented and thoroughly lovely man wanted me and was extremely skilled at showing me just how much. But since we parted ways in the shit-show that was Heathrow yesterday, I've begun to doubt myself. To doubt his commitment.

'Excited to see lover-boy?' Di asks from the front.

'Fuck off.' I make a face that Di returns in the mirror. Thank God for Di. If I didn't have someone to confide in, I'd die. It's very likely I'll break and tell Ally the first chance I get.

'I approve of him. I never thought you'd have it in you, but hats off to you for taking up with someone *normal*. He's gorgeous.'

'What kind of person did you think I'd take up with?'

'I don't know—an ageing playboy, perhaps, who'd wow you with his huge yacht in Cap Ferrat.'

'Please. Give me more credit than that.' I gaze out the window as we roll through Hyde Park. It's been such a wet summer that the grass is weirdly green. It should be totally scorched by now.

'It suits you, you know.'

'What does?'

'Sex with someone other than Jackson. You have this... soft look about you. It's good. Whatever Dr McDreamy is doing with those magic doctor's hands of his, he's obviously doing it right.'

'It's categorically none of your business what he's doing. But Noah has many magical body parts, I'll have you know.' I grin out the window, but Di catches it.

'Oooh! Look at that smug smirk! You lucky bitch. Honestly, your therapist should have told you to do this years ago. You'd have saved a shitload of time and money.'

'True.'

'Seriously, Honor. Enjoy yourself. How many tissues have I wasted on you over the years? It's good to see you taking something for yourself for once, instead of moping around and waiting for whatever scraps Jackson can be arsed to throw you.'

'You'd definitely have more fun driving Jackson, that's for sure.'

'No kidding. The things Ty must have witnessed in the back of that car.' She glances in the mirror. 'Sorry.'

'No, you're right. There's a reason the BMW has wipe-clean seats.'

'See? You're making jokes! Let me know if you and McDreamy need a ride later. Like, to his shag-pad? I have the Dettol wipes right here.' She waves a pack.

'You're revolting. I'm off to visit my dying mother, remember?'

'Of course you are. You always were a good multi-tasker. Give my love to Steph.' A pause. 'And Noah. You look gorgeous. Go get him.'

A nurse lets me into the hospice and I nod to Di, who'll wait in the car. I smooth down the inevitable car creases on the front of my dress. I've gone for an upgrade (an expensive Astrid Carmichael upgrade) on the type of dress I wore most days on TV: an impeccably fitted, sleeveless sheath in palest pink wool crepe. It skims me perfectly everywhere, exuding good taste but leaving little room for doubt as to what lies beneath.

I've even blow-dried my hair differently. It's not tonged like usual, but more of a Park Avenue Princess blow-dry: exactly how I used to wear it on TV (minus a *lot* of hair spray). Noah may not pick up that detail, but he will recognise the general vibe. If TV presenter Honor is who he's lusted after (and wanked over), TV presenter Honor is who he'll get.

I step through the threshold, and there he is, right in front of me.

Oh, God.

He's with a small gaggle of guys in suits in the hallway, and Noah himself is wearing a white shirt, suit trousers and a tie. Because this is Noah, his top button's undone and he's rolled his sleeves up. His heavenly French tan glows against the white fabric and I stare at him like a starving woman as he clocks me. I'm not the only person who's dressed up today. I want to pull that tie loose and bite that bottom lip. Now. He's utter perfection. The only thing missing is a stethoscope slung around his neck.

He runs a hand through his dark hair and shoots me the most enormous grin. I suspect it's involuntary; he tries to rein it in in front of his buddies but he seems incapable of lessening the wattage.

'Honor. Good morning.'

His tone is more formal than the smile on his face. Two can play at that game. The other guys turn around and I catch their double-take: a classic reaction I'm well used to. I smoothly slide my oversized sunglasses up onto my head and adjust my dusky pink Birkin on my arm. Smile blandly at him. My mouth is definitely twitching.

'Noah. How nice to see you again.'

Every guy in that hallway is staring shamelessly at me right now. It's usually creepy, but at this moment it's perfection. There's nothing more heady to a man than knowing he gets to have what every other man wants. These guys are doing my job for me: convincing Noah I'm a prize worth enduring a little (or a lot) of hassle for.

'Are you'—Noah clears his throat—'visiting your mother?'

'I am.' I raise my eyebrows at him. 'See you later, perhaps. If your meeting is over when I'm done.'

And off I sashay up the stairs, knowing that every pair of eyes in that hallway will be on my arse just now, and that Noah will be making the glorious discovery that my dress has a zip running *all* the way down the back.

22

HONOR

Mum looks like a tiny bird, propped up against her pillows in bed with her nasal cannula in place. It's an instant, and sobering, reality check after my fun little flirtation with Noah downstairs. This is why I'm here. To care for my dying mother. Not to pick up guys.

I kiss her forehead and inhale the botanical scent of Honor Chapman Skincare. Trust Mum to keep up her skincare routine on her deathbed. She probably has the nurses applying anti-ageing serums and giving her facial massages. Somehow, the knowledge that she still gives some shits is reassuring. It means she's hanging on for now.

I pull up a chair next to the bed. 'How are you feeling, Mum?'

She flutters her eyes closed and considers. She's always given thoughtful answers to the most perfunctory questions.

'Physically or mentally?'

'Both, I suppose.' I take her hand, slide my thumb across the thin layer of skin. It's bruised by the multitude of cannulas she's endured in recent weeks.

'Well. Physically, I seem to be "going downhill", as they say. I don't have much appetite. Except for fruit and cake. The cake here is very good.'

'Right. What does Elena say about that?'

'She says not to stress; just to listen to my body. They're giving me drips to keep me hydrated when they need to.'

'Good. You in pain?'

'They're managing it. I'm fine.' Mum taps the discreet morphine button next to her and sinks deeper into her pillows. 'The morphine is giving me terrible constipation, though. They had to give me an enema yesterday.'

'Oh, Jesus.' The gritty, messy side of illness is not my strong suit. Thank Christ Mum's now being looked after by trained professionals in a place that's properly equipped to deal with all this crap (literally). 'You poor thing. It adds insult to injury, doesn't it?'

'It was very liberating, actually. I don't know why they get such a bad rap. I feel so much better.' She pats her stomach.

'Excellent. Moving on. And mentally? How are you finding being here?' I don't want to exhaust Mum with too many questions, but this has been a huge move for her.

'It's... less odd than I expected. If I allow myself to dwell too much on being in a *hospice*—well, it's terrifying. But if I merely accept that I'm spending time in this delightful place, I'm all right. Just about. The pace is pleasant—restful, but with enough little treats thrown in to keep my spirits up. Elena's a good girl. She pops in a lot. But I miss Noah.' She winks at me. 'On which note, tell me about France.'

'Only if you're sure you have the energy?'

'Darling. We both know I'll never get to France again. I'll be leaving this place feet-first. Now, humour me and paint me a picture.'

'If you're sure.' I reach into my Birkin and pull out my iPad. 'I took so many photos and videos for you. You'd love the house. Elaine's taste is just as exquisite as you'd imagine.'

And so I walk Mum through the footage. A video tour I took of the house; the view from my room; the vista that runs from Elaine and Pierre's beautiful terrace down to the pool and beyond it to the sparkling, intoxicating Mediterranean sea.

There are endless videos of the kids pulling stunts in the pool. Diving competitions and synchronised swimming and basketball with an inflatable ball and a floating inflatable hoop.

'Why on earth is Jackson there?' Mum points with a shaky finger.

'He came to surprise us. It was sweet, really. Rollo was thrilled.'

'Did he let anyone else get a word in once he'd showed up?'

'He was fine, Mum.' Guilt makes me magnanimous towards my husband. 'Everyone seemed pleased to see him. He definitely got the party started.'

There are no incriminating photos of Noah on any of my devices, just a few shots of him in group photos. My favourite is one of him and me on the sofa, the night he seduced me. Serena took it before dinner, so he and I were both still in foul moods over Jackson's media coverage at that point in the evening, but I have on my Missoni dress, and his arm rests along the back of the sofa in my direction. He's tanned, and brooding, and so fucking hot.

I've looked at that photo a million times since we got back yesterday, casting myself back to that moment of oblivion before he undressed me on the daybed and changed everything. I'd give anything, right now, to be back there.

'Do you think Noah had a good break?' Mum asks. 'We missed him around here. He's so delightful—like a ray of sunshine.'

Noah had a great break, and almost as many orgasms as me, before my husband showed up and ruined it all.

'I think so. He seemed pretty switched off from work. And he was great with the kids.'

At that precise moment there's a soft rap on the open door, and Mum comes to life as if someone's stuck an epi-pen in her.

'Noah!'

My head spins around. Noah stands in the door frame, one arm up against the frame in the same sexy stance he adopted when Ally and I first came for our recce. He shoots me a panty-melting grin.

'Ladies. I hope I'm not interrupting. Just thought I'd check in and see how you're doing, Stephanie.'

Mum wipes a strand of hair off her face and smiles coquettishly. Dear Lord. Is no one immune to this man's charms?

'We were just talking about you, dear. Honor was showing me some photos of your holiday. Did you have fun? Come in! Come in.'

He sticks his hands in his pockets and saunters into the room. I hope naked lust is not written all over my face.

'It was very special, thank you.' A fleeting, but smoking, glance at me. 'It's a wonderful part of the world.'

'And your parents are incredibly generous hosts.' I smooth my dress over my thighs.

'They do a good job; I'll give them that. Though sitting on a few hectares of grapes helps. But are you being well looked after, Stephanie? You haven't drunk us dry, I hope, while I've been away?'

He stands next to me as he chats through things with Mum. He's so close I can feel the heat of his body. He laughs, and banters, and reassures, and I drink it all in. I have to get this man to myself within minutes.

When he's excused himself and headed back downstairs, Mum turns to me, mouth pursed.

'You should have married someone like him.'

I sigh. 'Tell me about it.'

NOAH

Paying my respects to Stephanie was a pathetic ruse to see Honor. I've been knocked sideways since she came in. I was winding up a tour of the facility with some private equity folk when she walked through that door and took the breath out of everyone's lungs. I knew exactly what she was doing with that casual smile and that fucking incredible dress, and boy was I there for it.

When she'd sashayed upstairs after giving me (and everyone else) the full benefit of her easy-access rear zip, the finance guys turned back to me.

'Holy fuck,' one of them said. 'That's Honor fucking Chapman.'

'It is.' My tone was stiff. They'd better not say anything disrespectful about her here, on my turf, while she's here to visit her mother.

'She is *smoking*. Jesus! God, she gets better with age. Did you say her mum was here?'

'I can't discuss our guests, I'm afraid. Now, let me send

the prospectus over to you by email and you can shoot back any questions you may have.'

'The zip on that dress,' another one huffs out. 'Asking for trouble.'

I get them the hell out of there and retreat to my office, sinking deeply into my chair. I put my head in my hands. Jesus Christ. I'd spent less than twenty-four hours with Honor before the reminders that I was playing with fire started to shoot like bullets.

Her famous husband arriving. Not just famous, but A-list famous and in possession of one of the most infamous and desired (by men and women) bodies on the planet. Jackson's a regular on the cover of *Men's Health* and *GQ*, for God's sake. He's a sex symbol, and I've had the balls to move in on his wife.

And then came the airport shenanigans. If I was under any delusion I could embark on an affair with one of the most photographed women in the world, the James family's welcome at Heathrow Terminal Five was a rude awakening. Honor and Jackson couldn't even sit on a plane without their security having to bat away unwanted attention and surreptitious photo attempts from fellow passengers.

The paparazzi were another level of intrusion, though. I've seen them often enough on TV, but I've never been close to them, never seen someone I care about as the target of their relentless, crass, and obtrusive attention.

This couple is watched. The Heathrow photos are splashed across every front page today. They live their lives in a bloody goldfish bowl. They've made sacrifices and taken decisions to achieve this level of fame that I can't compute. I should be running for the hills. Whatever fucked-up marriage Honor and Jackson have created for themselves, I should want no part in it.

But then I see her. *Her*. Honor, in all her insanely beautiful and surprisingly fragile glory. This morning she's my old fantasy come to life, dressed to kill as if she's about to sit back on that ITV sofa and devour a politician for breakfast. She saw she had the eyes of every guy in that hallway and she lapped it up. That little performance was perfection.

But I've also known her lying naked in my arms, the walls she builds around herself destroyed, and those, her most vulnerable moments, awaken the strongest emotions in me. That's when I find her most captivating.

Who am I kidding? She's captivating every. Single. Moment. And no matter how much celebrity bullshit surrounds her, I'm already incapable of walking away. What she sees in me is anyone's guess. I'm particularly unsure after a couple of days observing Jackson James by the pool in all his Action Man glory. I keep myself in decent shape, but I can't begin to compete with Jackson on that front.

No, Honor wants—needs, even—something else from me, and I'm walking a tightrope that's going to grow narrower the further I let myself get involved. Adoration, yes. I promised to adore her and tend to her when I made my initial "pitch". I'm pretty sure it's my obvious appetite for her that's allowed her to relax and succumb to me so easily.

But I have the sense that I can't allow our dynamic to get too one-sided. Honor has people crawling all over her, all the time. Everyone wants a piece of her. The last thing she needs is another fawning minion.

When I took control that night by the pool, she was putty in my hands. I was adoring, yes, but I also took charge, and it seemed to me she submitted gladly. Perhaps she's sick of running the show. Perhaps she likes it when I take over and bring her along for the ride.

So, while I may feel like falling at her feet and worshipping this heaven-sent woman like a lovesick idiot, lovesick idiots are ten-a-penny in Honor Chapman's world. I'm better off holding myself back, however I can, and keeping her interested. Restoring the power balance. And, as an extra benefit, protecting my heart.

23

HONOR

I leave Mum with promises to visit again tomorrow. I feel guilty to be leaving so early when I don't have a work commitment until lunchtime, but Ally is on her way. And I have to see Noah. Alone.

I put my head around his office door. His back is to me, facing his laptop with his head in his hands.

'Hey.' I knock lightly.

He's up out of his chair in an instant, pulling me in and slamming the door closed behind me before pushing me up against it. His mouth is on mine immediately; he relieves me of my Birkin and drops it to the floor before his hands fill themselves up with me. One of them twists around my neck and fists my hair, and the other moves slickly over my dress before cupping my arse, hard.

The force of his kiss opens my mouth, and I gasp as his tongue enters me. Finding mine and claiming his territory. This is no polite greeting; he's kissing me like a starving man, like he can't help himself, like he's hardly aware of what he's doing. And he's hard. He grinds against me, pushing me into the door, and I moan at the heavenly feeling of being surrounded by him, consumed by him.

I claw at his gorgeous hair and tilt my head and draw him in as close as I can. I try to slide one leg up his calf, but the pencil skirt on this dress is too tight.

His hands move. They caress my arse and dip into my waist and graze over my breasts and fondle the zip at the back of my dress.

'This dress.' His voice is hoarse, and he pushes his erection harder against me. 'Are you trying to kill me? It's so fucking sexy, I can't even…' He groans and drops his face to the crook of my neck. Begins to kiss and lick it, and I roll my head back in ecstasy.

'I wore it for you,' I say breathlessly. 'I give you Honor Chapman, TV presenter.'

'Fuck.' He groans again. His hands bracket my hips. 'Can I take it off?'

'Noah. I am not having sex with you in this broom-cupboard of an office, surrounded by people who are *dying*. Even though a horrifyingly large part of me wants to.'

He lets out an anguished laugh. 'Fair enough, gorgeous. Can I drag you to my flat? Or can I just have a sneak peek? Just a little unzip… I need to know what you've got on under that dress. I *need* to undo it.'

He's breathing heavily into my shoulder, and he rolls his hips against me again. Jesus Christ. I run my hands down over the crisp cotton of his shirt and clamp my hands on his arse. The lustrous wool of his suit trousers drapes over it in a manner that's sheer perfection. I really need to get this man naked. I really need him to get me naked. I need to be on a bed with him, with zero barriers between us.

I push him away with difficulty. His lips are swollen and

his eyes are hooded. He's heaven. 'How far away do you live?'

'Ten minutes. Ledbury Road.' He fondles a piece of my hair and grins a heart-stopping grin. 'I've even got scrubs there.'

My heart comes to life again. 'Stethoscope?'

He's still grinning. 'Definitely, Madam.'

Oh God. 'I like the suit.' I finger the tie. 'Junior doctor is sexy, but suited-up consultant is sexier. But dig out the stethoscope.' I lean forward and purr into his ear. 'I'm going to need a *lot* of help, Doctor.'

24

HONOR

Di drives me to Ledbury Road, and Noah goes ahead on his bike. He'll get there more quickly on two wheels. Di's grinning from ear to ear in the rear-view mirror.

'This is my true calling. Delivering you like a pizza to your smoking hot doctor for a mid-morning booty call. You lucky, lucky bitch.'

'I'm sorry getting me to meetings on time and helping me run my global empire hasn't been professionally fulfilling for you all these years.' I examine myself in my hand mirror. I'm flushed already, pupils dilated. I'll do. Noah seemed to like what he saw in there.

Noah is under instructions to buzz me in rather than meeting me at the front door. God knows which filthy rags have their guys trailing me today. I ring his bell and he buzzes me straight in. I make for the first floor, heart thumping at the significance of being here, in this unfamiliar building, for one sole purpose.

He's standing at the door to his flat and my entire

nervous system signals *danger*. His arm is slung up on the door frame in my favourite stance, and around his neck lies a stethoscope. He rakes his eyes up and down my body and flashes me a smile. It's not his usual Noah smile; it's professional and a little arrogant. Only his eyes give him away. They're shining with admiration, and desire, and excitement.

'Ms Chapman? I'm Dr Thierry. Come in, please.'

So we're in character already. Whew. I'm sweating. Gone is the famished Noah of a quarter of an hour ago, and in his place is a slick stranger. This is hot beyond belief. I've done a little light role play with Jackson in the past, but nothing like this. But I spent years in front of the camera. I can do this.

'Thank you, Doctor.' I sweep past him imperiously, the corners of my mouth twitching.

He has a seriously nice flat. I wasn't sure what I was expecting, but the living room in front of me is immaculate. Whoever did this interior is a professional with an excellent eye for colour.

The door shuts behind me with a definitive click. Noah grazes his fingers up my back before coming around to face me. His gaze sweeps over my face and he gives me a beautiful Noah smile before whispering *you okay?*

I'm more than okay. I nod, and his tone turns professional again.

'Excellent. Come through to my consulting room, why don't you.'

I follow him down a corridor to his bedroom. My relentless aesthetic sense hones in on the fabulous duck-egg-blue walls complemented by hints of raspberry in the soft furnishings, while my nervous system clocks the huge wooden bed and ratchets my heart rate up a notch.

'So.' He eyes me and pulls the stethoscope off his shoulders, weighing it in his hands. 'What seems to be the problem, Ms Chapman?'

He's inches away, and he's so gorgeous, and while his tone is even, he's staring at me like he wants to devour me.

I raise my chin. 'I've been feeling very... tense recently. Uptight. I need some help to relax.'

He raises his eyebrows. 'I see.'

I warm to my theme. 'I'm a TV presenter, you see. A morning news anchor. I interview powerful men every day, but I have no outlet for my stress. I thought a doctor might be able to help me find a—release.'

His eyes widen. 'I'm confident I can help you with that. I'll need to remove your dress so I can conduct a thorough physical examination.'

I swallow. 'That will be fine.'

Noah circles me like a lion stalking its prey before stopping behind me and gathering my hair over one shoulder. And then the zip lowers, down, down, as air hits my skin. It drags over my arse and Noah blows out slowly and utters a barely audible *fuck*.

I smile to myself. He'll have spotted the cappuccino-coloured lace backs of my bra and thong, then.

He gets the dress open the entire way and runs his hands lightly over my bare waist and down my hips before guiding the dress off over my shoulders. He chucks it on the bed, and seconds later, the shock of cold metal hits my shoulder blade.

'Deep breath in,' Noah orders against my ear. I obey, of course.

'Good.' He repeats the process on the other side before removing the stethoscope. A moment later, it's on the inside of my thigh, heading north, and I gasp.

'Encouraging pulse here.' His voice beneath me is a

drawl as he slides the instrument right up so it's almost grazing the strip of lace that is my thong. He brushes a knuckle over the fabric and I whimper and widen my stance. I'm still in my heels, and my legs are already trembling. Really trembling. A delicious slick of anticipation rolls over me—he's seriously in character, and it's incredibly hot.

He pulls the metal away and then he's in front of me, checking out my La Perla with hungry eyes. The stethoscope's earpieces are in his ears and he slides the metal part across one breast, teasing the lace edge of my bra cup.

'Quite an elevated heart rate,' he murmurs. He holds the lace away from my breast and slips the metal disc into my cup so it hits my nipple. Heavenly cold. I gasp and clutch his gorgeous, hairy forearm.

'Noah.'

'You have to let me do my job, Ms Chapman.' He allows me the ghost of a smile, but his beautiful brown eyes tell me everything I need to know. He's as into this as I am. 'We're going to test your body's responsiveness next. Close your eyes, please.'

This man can do anything he wants to me. I'm putty in his hands—I have an inkling I'll nail the responsiveness test. My nipples are crying out for his touch and my pulse is raging between my legs—he was correct on that front.

I close my eyes. There's a soft thud as the stethoscope presumably hits the bed.

'First your mouth.' His hands slide around my neck, under my hair, and he fists it as he kisses me roughly, his tongue invading me, thrusting against mine. I wrap my arms around his neck and kiss him back as deeply as I can. He uses his hands to angle my head to the side and sucks my tongue before allowing his hands a little trip around my body. They slide down my back and glide over my arse cheeks, where he kneads them forcefully, pushing me against his heavenly erection.

He pulls away, breathing heavily. 'Good. Then your breasts.'

He unclips the back of my bra. The relief of it falling away is enormous. He brushes one nipple with a finger, then the other. Red-hot sensation zings straight to my groin.

I gasp. 'Noah!'

'Call me Doctor, please. They seem responsive.' His voice is strangled. His lips close around one nipple and he sucks, while his fingers roll the rock-hard bead of my other nipple. He pinches hard, and my head rolls back. I grip his shoulders through his shirt. Between my heels and this head rush he's giving me, there's a good chance I'll lose my balance otherwise.

'Doctor.' The physical sensations Noah is arousing in me are all-consuming enough, but when I focus on the kink of this being a medical examination, it almost blows my mind. I'm naked aside from a scrap of soaking wet lace between my legs and a pair of heels, and this fully dressed, highly skilled professional is doing an excellent job of taking full advantage of me.

The good doctor continues to pay close attention to my breasts with both his mouth and his hands for the next few moments, as I grow more and more aroused. There's an orgasm building through my entire abdomen, and there's a good risk I come like this. I widen my legs and wiggle my arse, praying he'll show me mercy.

He releases my breasts and puts his mouth next to my ear. 'Are you ready for the internal part of your examination?'

'Yes. I am.' I'm practically sobbing with frustration.

'Good girl.'

And then, thank fuck, Noah hooks his fingers around the sides of my thong and slides it down my legs. I step out of it.

'Sit right on the edge of the bed for me.'

I open my eyes and sit down.

'Open your legs.' Beautiful Noah kneels before me and taps the inside of my knee. I open my legs and he gazes down at the very core of me. Shuts his eyes for a moment and bites his lip. At least he's in as much torment as I am. I lean forward to kiss him, but he pushes me gently on the shoulder.

'Lie back and put your feet on my shoulders. This is the most important part of your examination, Ms Chapman.'

Where the hell is he getting all this from? Did he put in a few years at RADA as well as med school? The guy is incredible, and far kinkier than I would have guessed. To be honest, *I'm* far kinkier than I would have guessed. I'll take whatever he's offering right now. I lie back on the bed and lift my arms decadently above my head, raising my legs one at a time so my feet sit on his shoulders, the starch of his shirt crisp under my arches. I'm throbbing everywhere. This good doctor seriously needs to put me out of my misery.

His hands glide up my calves and thighs, his thumbs pressing into my inner thighs. He stops right at the top before, thank God, sliding a finger inside me. Then a second. I'm so wet they slip right in. We both produce a guttural groan in unison. The sensation of being filled up is heaven, but I need more. I arch and push into his hand.

'Very responsive,' Noah murmurs. He lowers his head towards me and I tense in almost unbearable anticipation as I watch him studying me. The desire and focus on his beautiful face, the *ache* on it, the glazed look in his eyes that reminds me he's spiralling out of himself just as much as I am. This man is going to get it in a minute.

'There's nothing wrong with your responsiveness, Ms Chapman.' His eyes flick up to my face, and what he sees there must be good, because he smiles his *Noah* smile at me. 'Now, let's get you that release you're searching for.'

The thrill of what's coming is almost unbearable. I moan. 'Hurry up. *Doctor*. I need you inside me. Right now.'

He shakes his head at me and drops his face right between my legs, and his tongue gets to work on me. It's tense and firm and flat right where I need it, and its movements are decisive, as if he knows now is not the time to mess about with light, teasing strokes.

I'm a writhing, moaning mess on the bed as the pressure ratchets up and up, spreading from the nerves Noah's touching to deep, deep inside me, and I come, so hard that the world is swirling colours behind my closed eyelids and what was my body is a melted puddle of pure sensation.

I've probably made a great deal of noise, but I'm not really aware of it, just of Noah removing his mouth as my shudders subside and getting to his feet and practically diving on me, his arms coming around me to plaster me to his front and his erection like steel against my sensitised flesh.

'Fuck,' he gasps into my neck, and I'd agree with him if I hadn't lost the power of speech. His hands move in my hair, combing it away from my face so he can put his mouth to mine and show me how I taste. 'You're the most—*Honor*. I need to fuck you. Now.'

That we agree on. My blinding orgasm is coursing away from me, leaving emptiness, and my heart is overflowing on behalf of this man who's taken me apart so completely and needs to blow his load just as desperately now as I did a couple of minutes ago. I haul myself up and scrabble at his belt buckle. It's reward time for Dr Noah Thierry.

25

NOAH

I loosen my tie and tug it off while trying simultaneously to unbutton my shirt. I'm way too far gone to hold this role-play together. I buck on the bed as Honor gets my fly down and pulls my trousers and boxers over my hard-on. I kick them off. She crouches over me, naked and flushed and so fucking beautiful.

I had a plan: to stay fully in control—almost fully dressed, even—and in character, to spread her out on the bed and take her. But my balls are on the verge of exploding, and we've both gone way past that point. All I can conceive of right now is skin on skin, of being as deep inside her as I physically can. Consuming her, and letting myself come undone, too.

Honor bends and licks my leaking tip, and my cock jolts so hard it practically slaps her in the face.

'Baby,' I tell her. 'I'm too close. I can't—let me get a condom on.'

I scrabble desperately in the bedside drawer and draw out the fruits of my emergency Boots trip on the way home from the airport yesterday. Tear open a box.

'Allow me.' Honor holds out her hand, a lascivious smile on her beautiful face, and rips the foil. She runs a hand up and down the length of me and deftly rolls the condom on as I watch this unimaginably wonderful spectacle. I inhale hard as she ministers to my poor, tormented cock.

And then she's straddling me, her spectacular body looming over me, and she lowers herself down, feeding me into her inch by inch, until I bottom out and sensation grows and grows, flowing outwards from where we join across the rest of my body. I rear up and kiss her, hungrily, desperately, before bending my head to her perfect, perfect breasts and sucking hard.

She moans and rolls her hips to take me even more deeply inside, and moves. Slowly. Up, until I'm almost entirely out of her. And back down, sinking as deep as she can onto me. It's so fucking heavenly that I have minutes left in me, if not seconds, and as the arousal builds, so the emotion undulates through my chest in a wave.

I reach up and around her and pull her down to me, flip us over so I can get closer to her, hook a hand under one of her knees and angle myself deeper and she joins me in a kiss: deep, sensual rolls of our tongues that ramp up the intensity of what I'm feeling in my cock to another level.

Her kisses grow more fierce and she whimpers into my mouth as she angles her hips up and moves more forcefully with me. Her most intimate muscles are beginning to shudder around me as she sucks on my tongue.

'Oh, God. *Noah*.'

She clenches my arse in an attempt to draw us even closer, and I happily oblige by hiking her knee up higher, pulling her as tightly against me as I can. A sheen of sweat has broken out all over my skin with the effort of holding myself back from the edge, but it's worth every drop of exertion if I can take her with me.

'Tell me what you need, baby. Come for me, if you can.'

Her skin is slick against mine and I focus on maximising the friction for her as her muscles grip me and her fingernails dig into my back and my arse. She's making a sound I haven't heard her make before, a low groan in the back of her throat, and it grows louder and more agonised with every thrust.

I'm so close. Whew. I slide out and drive back inside her with a determination and self-control I didn't know I had, and she breaks, crying out, her arms around me in a vice and her muscles shuddering, convulsing around my cock in a performance so glorious that it sends me over the edge too.

'Fuck.' I take another thrust and bottom out, emptying myself in a deluge of white-hot pleasure while she quivers around me. I kiss her, gasping, and bury my face in her hair.

'Honor. God. *Jesus*, Honor. Baby. Holy *fuck*.'

I wrap my arms and upper leg around her as tightly as I can, melding us together, our hearts hammering against each other's chests, our breath harsh and ragged as we come down. Entangled. Reborn.

I get rid of the condom and clean myself up as quickly as humanly possible, then rejoin my goddess back in the bedroom. She's lying on top of my duvet, one arm flung over her eyes, her rib cage still rising and falling exaggeratedly. What a sight. I scoot back on the bed and pull her to me so we're flush against each other. Maximum skin on skin. I smooth her hair. I still haven't found the words to acknowledge what just happened between us.

Honor gazes at me. Nose to nose. Her beautiful, huge tiger eyes still look a little glazed.

'You know, I've never, ever had a vaginal orgasm before.' She strokes my upper arm.

I grin. 'Feeling you have one around my cock was fucking amazing. How did you like it?'

'It was incredible. Like this amazing ache that just kept building and building. I didn't know it was going to happen until right before it did.' She stretches luxuriously in my arms. 'The pressure's on from now on.'

'Challenge gratefully accepted,' I whisper. A fresh wave of emotion hits me.

I had a plan today: to take full advantage of the fantasy Honor offered me when she showed up as her TV persona. To stay in charge. To give her the fantasy she'd professed to want and to remind her I wasn't a mere lovesick fan, that I was capable of consuming her and giving her everything she desired in bed. And I know I delivered on my initial promise to her. I flipped some switch inside her that transported her away from all the bullshit in her real life to a place so thrilling that it felt more real than anything she left behind when she walked through my front door.

But somewhere along the line, my plan fell apart in an intoxicating tangle of seeing her response to me and to our game, inhaling her skin, tasting her and feeling her come apart around me. Our little role-play allowed us to shed any remaining inhibitions, and in doing so took us to a place so intimate that to consider this experience just sex would be a joke.

Some kind of chemical reaction has happened here, something that feels as significant as the Big Bang, and now an addiction to Honor Chapman courses through my veins. An addiction to the curve of her back as she arches in ecstasy, and the way her adorable eyelashes flutter when I kiss her, and the noises she makes when she's coming that are so fucking intoxicating that, like a crack addict, I'd do anything to get my next fix. The hollows above her collarbones. The perfect plumpness of her bottom lip between my teeth.

This isn't what I planned. It isn't what I promised her. Sure, I promised her devotion and adoration (as well as a steady supply of orgasms) but I meant it lightly. I was supposed to be her enthusiastic partner in bed, and that was it.

In this moment, as I stroke her satiny skin in long, decadent laps and my entire body hums from the touch of her skin against mine, I'm reminded that the extraordinary connection we've just shared will shortly ebb away as she slips back to a schedule that is full and demanding and glamorous and does not require my services.

She's married. She's famous. She runs a huge brand. These stolen, sunlit slivers of time on my bed are the full extent of what I can hope for from her. They're a miracle in themselves, but I'm growing dangerously high on them.

She interrupts my reverie. 'You may have spoilt me for life with that doctor stunt you pulled.'

Her words, and the size of her smile, are breadcrumbs to my starving heart, and I take them gladly.

She continues, her leg gently rubbing mine. 'I'm not sure I've ever been so turned on. Is it totally sick that I love your dirty doctor act?'

I laugh. 'No sicker than me loving taking advantage of my beautiful patient. Believe me, I was as into it as you were.'

'You were *very* convincing. Quite intimidating, even, which really did it for me. Impressive acting skills.'

'I think you must be my muse.' I kiss her nose. 'I haven't acted out a part like that before. Well, not since *Macbeth* at school, which had far less of a happy ending all round, let me tell you. But no harm in two consenting adults having some fun in a safe space. And anyway, I lost the plot once you came. I couldn't hold it together enough to have my wicked doctor way with you like I wanted. You are too. Fucking. Sexy.'

'Next time. Let's do it again. Tomorrow.'

'I think I can pencil you in for a follow-up appointment.' Relief courses through my veins. I just need to last until tomorrow. I can do that. I'll take each moment with her as it comes, and I'll get to see her at Good Vibes, too. I'll just have to be content with that. 'How long do I have you to myself right now?'

She looks at her watch. 'Probably another half an hour. I need to get ready for a call at twelve.'

'You can do it from here if you like. Naked.' I drop a kiss on her glossy shoulder and she giggles.

'It's a Zoom call with Burberry. And my husband. So that wouldn't work so well.'

Ugh. Her fucking husband. The mention of him is like a bucket of cold water.

'Ah.'

'Ah, indeed. It's an important call, and I need to look like I haven't just had two earth-shattering orgasms.'

'You can shower here.' My hand slides down to appreciate the luscious curve of her arse. 'My washing skills are almost as fine as my acting skills. What are you speaking to Burberry about?'

She hesitates. 'Between us?'

'Of course, baby.' I aim for a joke. 'Doctor-patient confidentiality.'

'We're in the early stages of discussing a new pair of scents they're looking to launch—for men and women. They've approached Jackson and me to face the campaign.'

'Holy fuck.' I reel internally. Honor and Jackson's faces. Together. Splashed across every bus and billboard in London and beyond. 'That sounds big. And lucrative.'

She nods. 'It is. And... long. It's a five-year contract, initially. With a high likelihood of it rolling over at the end of the term, because they want this scent to have longevity. Hence they're interested in us, because we're...'

'Married. Dependable.' It hits me in the gut. Burberry's banking on Honor and Jackson still being together down the line. And they'll reward that longevity handsomely.

'I was going to say old. But yeah. They're not thrilled about Jackson's recent press. That was one of the reasons our publicist thought it would be good to get snapped at Heathrow yesterday. The front pages today should reassure them.' She sighs.

I stare at her. Try to see what's inside that head. Minutes ago, when we came together, we were closer than I would have thought it possible to be with another person, and now I'm buggered if I can tell what motivates her. 'Do you want this contract?'

Another telltale hesitation. 'I do. It's amazingly prestigious; it's an endorsement of the brand we've built. And the knock-on effect for the Honor Chapman brand globally would be vast. It's also a legacy, a way of capturing a moment in time for me and Jackson.' She shrugs, avoids my eyes. 'I suppose I'm just antsy at the pressure it puts us under, you know? Another five years of not fucking our marriage up; it's a long time.'

In this moment, it feels like a life sentence. It's the reminder I needed that I'm on the periphery, that this incredible, fragile *thing* I have with her can never fully bloom because it will be stunted by Honor's requirement to play the game of a high-profile wife in public. Right here, right now, is as good as it's going to get.

26

HONOR

I ask Ally to stop by the house on her way to Good Vibes. It's been a week since we got back from France, and I could use some serious advice—advice that's way too sensitive to be overheard in a coffee shop.

Ally and I have tag-teamed at the hospice on alternate days and we haven't actually overlapped. I'd rather be there the whole time, for reasons that have nothing to do with poor old Mum, but unfortunately I have an empire to run, children to parent, and relentless press-related shit to manage. I also have a lover to see, and he's doing an admirable job of taking priority at every single moment I can manage.

I give Carmen the morning off and ask the cleaning staff to stay upstairs. I'll grind away with work at home until Ally shows up. Di's taken the kids to multi-sports camp and will be back at some point, but that's fine. Di knows everything there is to know. She's completely assumed the role of enabler of this affair. Di is Team Noah all the way.

Di's case is helped by the constant tabloid coverage of Jackson and Leila's two-week-long press junket for *Vet* in

Europe. He left a couple of days after we got back from France, thank God, and the tabloids are loving them. They're currently in Italy, and footage of them in Rome last night has had the *Daily Mail* in overdrive this morning.

Ally arrives with a copy of said paper under her arm.

'Nice. Your husband's a classy guy.' She chucks it on the table. The front page boasts a grainy long-lens shot of Jackson and Leila grinning at each other across the table at an intimate little pizza place. All that's missing is a strand of spaghetti between them.

I glance at it disinterestedly. 'Mara's thrilled, but Erika's shitting bricks over this tour.' Erika is our manager and orchestrator of the fragrance talks with Burberry.

'And you? Are you okay?'

'I'm totally fine, because... I have news. And I've been dying to tell you. Shit, Al, I need some serious advice. Or maybe not advice, just a bit of reassurance that I'm not a complete bitch.'

Ally stares at me. 'What the hell is going on with you? Look at that smile! Spill.'

'Okay. Let me get some coffees sorted.' I take a deep breath and approach our huge industrial coffee machine. I locate a bag of coffee beans in the fridge and pull out the appropriate drawer in the machine.

'I'm amazed you know how to operate anything in this kitchen.'

'Fuck off. I'm good at coffees. Everything else is outside my zone of genius.'

'Quit stalling, Duck Face. Spill it.'

'Right.' The heat is rising to my face. This shouldn't be hard. This is my sister; I can count on non-judgement from Ally. I put a mug in place and press a button on the machine. As the whirring and grinding kicks in, I turn to Ally, and it comes out in a rush.

'I don't really care what Jackson's up to in Rome, because I'm sleeping with Noah. Whew.'

I exhale. I would give anything to pick up my phone and capture Ally's face at this moment. Not much fazes my sister, but right now she's frozen and wordless. It's wonderful.

'Noah. *Dr* Noah? You're shagging Mum's doctor?'

'He's not Mum's doctor! That's Elena—he's not that unprofessional. But yeah.'

'How—when? Oh my *God. How*? I mean, I know he fancies the pants off you, but'—she gasps. 'Oh, Jesus. It was in France, wasn't it? You lucky, lucky bitch.'

'That's what Di said.' I allow herself a moment of smugness. Ally's been incredibly supportive over the years, but I don't think she's ever actually envied me the weird, twisted successes in my life. But this is different.

'Sit.' Ally points to the bar stools at the kitchen island. 'I'll finish this. I want you to sit right there and tell me everything. Oh, Lord. You are having sex with that god! Has he let you strip his Homer Simpson t-shirt off? How good must his abs look under that t-shirt? And why do I find it so sexy? Does he have a big dick?' She whips the full mug off the machine and plonks it next to me. 'Oh, God! This is so much to process!'

I sit calmly and wait for my sister's little fit to pass.

'Yes, it happened in France, and I've seen him almost every day since. I've cancelled so many internal meetings this week, I can't tell you.'

'Okay, okay. So what happened? Was it you or him? I can't get my head around my goody-two-shoes, Little Miss Perfect sister embroiling herself in a torrid affair! You've rolled over every time your fucking husband fucks about, and *now* you decide to dabble yourself? It's too much!'

I raise an eyebrow. 'Do you want the details or not?'

'Yes, yes. Sorry. *Please*, for the love of God, details.'

'Right. He started it. In France. It was the day that server from Chateau Marmont came out and said Jackson and Leila had been sharing a bed. I didn't realise it at the time, but Noah saw it on the news, and he was seriously pissed off. He was in a foul mood at dinner, and later, I went down to the pool and there he was. We ended up lying on one of the beds together and he asked me about how my and Jackson's marriage worked.

'He told me it wasn't fair Jackson got to have all the fun, and that I should have an affair. With him. That he'd make it worth my while. So I told him to show me. And he did—he stripped me, basically. And that was that. Until Jackson showed up the next day as a surprise-stroke-press opportunity. But I've been seeing Noah since we got back. I can't stay away from him.'

Ally looks as though she may have a heart attack.

'Oh my God oh my God. He *stripped* you? I can't even…'

'Yeah. And he may have gone down on me, too. By the pool.' I take a sip of my coffee. 'Al, it was one of the hottest moments of my life. He was so *intense*. And pissed off. And sexy. He just totally took charge. I was so turned on it was ridiculous. And then we had sex properly the next morning—we snuck off to his room after having breakfast with everyone.'

Ally carries her mug to the island and plops down on a bar stool. Puts her head in her hands.

'I never thought I could be this jealous of someone and this happy for them at the same time.'

I pat her on the top of the head. 'Aw, thank you, sweetie.'

'God. So this guy who's all smiley and doctor-ish and compassionate and life-savey is also, like, a hot, wanton sex god who smoulders after dark and goes around stripping you and being a cunning linguist?' She looks up. 'Is he? A cunning linguist?'

'He's very cunning.' I smile like a cat and stretch at the vivid mental image of Noah between my legs yesterday. The things he did to me with that tongue. The dark, silky hair falling over his eyes. And the relentless string of presumably filthy compliments he paid me. In French. 'You should see what he can do with a stethoscope.'

'Noooo!' Ally beats her fists on the marble island top. 'It's too much! I can't bear it! I'm not going to be able to look at him next time I go in. Have you had sex at the hospice?'

'Ugh. No. That's revolting.'

'I agree. Good. Right then. So what's the plan? Have you guys, like, discussed it? I don't know... have you put any boundaries in place? Because, knowing you, you probably need them. Right?'

My sister knows me too well, but the problem is that I don't know myself right now. The woman I am currently, who's blithely gone down the same route as my husband, is not the person I've been for the past thirty-nine years. And the Noah-junkie I am today, who spends far too much time staring at my calendar and trying to work out what I can blow off to see him, is not the woman who spontaneously agreed to test the waters with this guy a week ago in France.

And worse, I'm pretty sure this thing we've created together is not the casual fling he proposed by that pool. He said he wanted to make my life better. But he's consuming me.

I nod slowly. 'Boundaries would be good. Boundaries would be great, actually. But I'm not sure we have any. We're kind of making it up as we go along. We haven't really talked about it openly—about plans, I mean, or how we're feeling. The main problem is that the more we see each other, the more desperate we both seem to be for the next time. I didn't really think it through in France, but we saw each other every day last week, except over the weekend.'

'And by *saw each other*, you mean you had sex?'

'Yeah. He has a place in Westbourne Grove.'

'And the sex is amazing, I take it, from what you've said?'

'It's—incredible. I mean, he's so attentive and generous, but he's also very sexy and bossy, you know? He makes me feel amazing, but he doesn't fawn. He's just... perfect.'

Ally lets out a slow exhale. 'Wow. He's playing it well. Clever guy. This sounds pretty full-on, Duck Face. What are you going to do?'

'I don't know.' I pinch the bridge of my nose. 'Keep... going? I suppose? See what happens? It'll either run its course, or...'

'Or bye-bye, Jackson.'

'No! God, no. We're looking at signing a five-year contract with Burberry as the faces of its new, timeless fragrance. That's a big, fat incentive to behave myself.'

Ally makes a face. 'How romantic. You know it sounds more like a business partnership than a marriage, right?'

'Tell me about it.' My voice sounds flat, even to me.

'Okay, okay. Sorry. Not a helpful comment.' Ally takes my hand. 'What about Jackson? How are you juggling your relationships with him and Noah? Because that would be enough to put me off ever cheating on Ted.'

'You'll never cheat on Ted. Come on. But no, it's tough. It's icky. Jackson's definitely sleeping with Leila. He admitted it. And he left right after we got back from France, so I've managed to avoid having sex with him so far, but he's back next week and I'm not sure what I'm going to do. How on earth do guys do it—sleep with two people at once?'

'Well, I suspect your lovely husband just adores sex, and he'll happily take it from you, or Leila, or whoever else is offering. I think he can probably compartmentalise quite easily. But it's less easy for us. A lot less easy. Are you saying you don't want to sleep with Jackson anymore?'

I think. 'It's not that I don't want to. Obviously he's gorgeous. It's just that it would make me feel guilty. Towards him, and towards Noah. I'd feel like I was betraying both of them. Is that weird?'

Ally snorts. 'You realise how ridiculous this is? You're married to literally one of the sexiest men on the planet—by popular opinion—and you also have this gorgeous, adoring doctor at your beck and call.' She leans forward. 'Some people would call that a high-quality problem.'

'I know, I know.' I groan. 'But I'm not like Jackson. More is not more when it comes to sex for me. I don't want to be having it with more than one person. I know our marriage is far from perfect. I just don't know how I'm supposed to deal with two relationships with two different people. It's exhausting!

'I don't have time for an affair—my calendar already gives me panic attacks—but I also don't have the emotional headspace for it. I mean, where am I supposed to put Noah? And what I feel for him is so... all-consuming. I can't stop thinking about him. I can't stop thinking about being with him. Not just the sex part, but *him*. And he's crowding out everything and everyone else. I think I'm falling for him.'

27

NOAH

Honor's fallen asleep next to me in a pool of sunlight, her eyelashes casting long shadows over her cheekbones, and it feels like a miracle.

This past month has taken its toll on her; I know that. Our relationship is costing her far more than it's costing me, and though she acts as though she's handling it, she must be finding it a strain to constantly shuffle her calendar, and eke out stolen hours with me, and lie to those closest to her.

Serena and Rollo are back at school now, and Honor's made it clear to me that this can't eat into her after-school time with her kids. She blew off a work dinner last week to spend a quiet evening at my flat where I cooked for her and made love to her and bathed her before letting her go. But usually, her evenings are for her kids, and I wouldn't expect anything less.

So, it's the mornings that prove the most flexible. She's at Good Vibes almost every day; her team at work knows to keep her mornings clear of big external meetings. She's certainly putting in the hours with her mum—she sits by that bed for as long as she can every day—but I'm reaping the benefits, too.

Even on the days we can't slip away to my flat, I get to see her. And when she's done being with her mum, she comes downstairs and we sit and work at Good Vibes' kitchen table together, laptops in front of us, a mug of tea by our sides, and it's heaven. The Good Vibes family is tight-knit, our guests' visitors become regular, much-welcomed parts of that family, and if anyone finds it odd that I'm devoting so much of my time to a certain guest's famous daughter, no one says a word.

What's clear is that this thing between us has bloomed beyond just sex (if it was ever just sex, which I doubt) into an intimacy that colours my days golden. However frenetic our lives are, being together seems to bring Honor the same enormous amount of pleasure it brings me. And that's the thing I keep coming back to. That's what alleviates my conscience when I torture myself with the sacrifices she's having to make for me. For us.

She cried on me last week. Jackson was back for a few days between press junkets, and she told me she refused to sleep with her husband. She picked a fight and told Jackson it was because of the escalating news flow around him and that co-star of his. It wasn't. It was because she said she couldn't face sleeping with two men at the same time, couldn't get her head around it; it made her feel violated to even think about it.

My relief that she's not having sex with that philandering dick is matched by guilt that I've put her in that position, that she's having to endure this conflict in her marriage. Because Jackson's headlines aren't the only thing escalating. From what she says, they've agreed a number with Burberry and the contracts for that fragrance campaign, or whatever it's called, are being drawn up.

All I can do is make this worth her while. It's what I promised her that first night—that I'd make her life better. And for now, all I can offer her is as much of me as she'll take. My love. Because I do. I love her.

HONOR

I wake in the most delicious way, floating to the surface, to light and warmth. My limbs are liquid; my mind is air. I have an exquisite impression of peace before my conscious mind can quite identify where I am.

And when I open my eyes, it gets better.

Noah.

There he is, smiling at me from inches away, all warm, bronzed skin and molten eyes, looking as happy and relaxed and well-fucked as I feel. The sensation of warmth I have is his arm around my back, his hairy legs entwined with mine.

'Hi.' His smile widens.

'Hi. Wow, I nodded off there.'

'You were only out for about twenty minutes. Looks like you needed it.'

'I did.' I yawn. 'Those super-strength orgasms of yours knocked me out.' My fingers trail through the soft, dark down on his chest. It's one of the most gorgeous things about him. Beautiful man.

'Good. I loved watching you sleep. You looked like an angel.' He pauses. 'You always look like an angel. There is absolutely nowhere else I'd rather be right now, you know?'

'How are you still single?' I stretch indulgently in his arms. 'Seriously. How in God's name have you not been snapped up and marched down the aisle by some insatiable bride?'

He smiles bashfully. 'Well. I wouldn't classify myself as single just now, exactly.'

'No?'

'Nope.'

'Good.' I reach across and brush my lips to his—a reward for his reassurance. 'Have you been single for a while? I wish now I'd paid more attention whenever Elaine mentioned you.'

'I'm sure she had nothing interesting to say. Poor Mum. I've been single for far too long, in her mind.'

'How long?'

'Years and years.'

'What do you do for sex?' My knuckles brush that trail of hair on his abdomen. Up and down.

'I find beautiful, unsuspecting married women and seduce them by moonlit swimming pools, with the help of soulful French music and lashings of rosé.'

'You do, do you?'

'Yup.' He looks inordinately pleased with himself.

'Well, good for you. It worked a treat on me. But seriously. You'd be great in a relationship. And you seem to like sex *quite* a lot. So where do you get it?'

'Between us?' He looks at me from under long, dark eyelashes. 'I had a thing with Elena for years. Nothing serious. It was just a hangover from our med school days. When she was single and we both had an itch we need to scratch, we'd... hook up.'

'Elena?' I sit up on one elbow. Shit. I've idly noticed how attractive Elena is, in that abstract way I do with most women, where I mentally give them an Honor Chapman

Cosmetics makeover. But Elena doesn't need much help. She's gorgeous, all dewy, olive skin and lush curves and glossy ponytail. She looks great with no makeup at all.

And she's been sleeping with Noah. For years. She knows how this trail of hair on his stomach feels. She knows what his tongue is capable of. She knows how intense it is to have him move inside her.

Jesus. The stab of jealousy is so visceral, it hits me like nausea.

'You okay? Come here.' He pulls me back down and I nestle into him gratefully.

'I'm jealous.' I laugh without mirth. 'So jealous. I know that's unfair, because you've got to deal with the fact that I'm married, but—'

'Hey. You have no need to be jealous, okay? Nothing's happened in over a year.'

I exhale. 'But didn't you want it to go further? I mean, she's beautiful.'

'She is. And a fantastic person, and she's a great doctor. And if I'm honest, she wanted it to go further. She's made that clear, more than once. And I've made it equally clear I don't feel that way about her. So there we are.'

Poor Elena, to be besotted by Noah and not to have him reciprocate. It must be agony. And here I am, with this amazing man, unable to give him one hundred percent of myself, no matter how much he deserves it.

'Don't you want a family?' I whisper.

'Of course I do.'

'Tell me what you want.'

'Okay. Don't laugh. I want'—he sighs—'family Sundays. I've always had this very clear vision: I want walks in Richmond Park on crisp autumn days, then I want to come home and cook a Sunday roast with my gorgeous wife, and stick on Classic FM or Radio 4, and get stuck into a little red while we're cooking. Then a family movie with the kids after lunch, and later, once they're tucked up, I'll sweep my beautiful wife off to bed and make love to her.'

His eyes are shining, and as he speaks, a ball of emotion builds and builds and threatens to crush my chest. The jealousy I felt over Elena dissolves, and in its place is an overwhelming sense of loss and want and pain and jealousy over *this*. Noah will get to do this with someone, and it won't be me, and I can't bear it. But that's not his fault, so I push the emotion down.

'I can't think of anything nicer. You deserve that. So much.'

'But you have that already, surely? You and Jackson and the kids? Sometimes, at least?'

'I suppose so.' It hits me with clarity that there's nothing extraordinary about what Noah's proposing, exactly. And sure, my family and I do have Sundays like that, when Jackson's around and we're not lunching with movie producers and all that other crap. No, the tantalising thing about the picture Noah has painted is that it's him in that vision. *Him*. And I want to live that Sunday over and over again with him. Not Jackson, nor anyone else. Just Noah.

I swallow and look away. 'I wish that could be you and me.'

'I wish it, too.' His voice goes very quiet. 'Look at me. When I think of that image now, the woman in it—my wife—has a face. She's you. I close my eyes and imagine my future, and all I see is you. I love you so much, my darling. I know it's not fair to say—I realise I'm putting you in a difficult position just by telling you—but I need you to know how I feel. How extraordinary you are.'

At his words, that ball of emotion in my chest balloons

and threatens to suffocate me, manifesting as unstoppable tears. They come on without warning and spill over my nose, down onto my pillow. Shit. I press my fist against my mouth as I shudder in Noah's arms, the beauty and pain and shock of his words rendering me incapable of uttering any of my own.

'Oh, God.' He presses himself against me and holds me more tightly, winding the blessed heat of his top leg around me. 'Darling. I'm sorry—I'm so sorry. I didn't mean to upset you. Shit. Forget I said anything.'

'No,' I mumble, sniffing hard. I pull back slightly to look into those glorious brown eyes. 'Listen to me—those words are *amazing*. *You* are *amazing*. To have you tell me you love me—I feel like the luckiest woman on the planet. And, God, Noah, you have no idea how close I am to saying it back. I want to, so badly. I'm so crazy about you, I can barely hold the words in.

'But I can't say them, sweetie. If I say them back, I'm the one who's not being fair, because I'm not free. And you deserve everything you just told me about; you deserve a gorgeous family, and a beautiful wife, and so much happiness, and I can't give you that. And I wish, so fucking badly, things were different.'

'I know. I know you can't. It's okay. We'll be okay.' He presses his lips to the top of my hair, and I lie there and allow myself to be cocooned in him, comforted by him, even though I'm the one who will inevitably, at some point, have to hurt him.

Two nights later, I spend the evening at Good Vibes. I've had a full-on day at work; I've come straight here from the office and haven't seen the kids since I packed them off to school with Di this morning. But Elena texted me earlier to say Mum was having a rough day emotionally, so I swing by for a couple of hours. Things will get tougher when the King's academic year starts up again later this month and Ally can't put in as much time here during the day.

With Mum asleep, I stand stiffly and stretch. It's nine-thirty. Time to get home, shower, and polish off some emails over a glass of wine. Jackson's away, thank God.

I've hardly seen Noah today aside from a quick *hi* when I arrived. I have no idea if he's still here. But the door to his office is ajar, and there he is at his desk.

I slink in and shut the door behind me. He shoots up and wraps me in his arms and kisses me, and I collapse into him.

'I'm so tired,' I mutter into his neck.

'Poor baby.' He rubs my back. 'You've got so much on your plate at the moment. You signed Burberry yet?'

'Next week, hopefully.' I'm touched he's mentioned it, because I feel guilty even bringing it up. It's like waving a huge, eight-figure reminder that I'm choosing to commit to my marriage-slash-fucked-up-business-partnership with Jackson over Noah. We've carried on much as usual since his declaration the other day. Neither of us knows what else to do.

'Well, let's get you home. Is Di outside?'

'Yes.'

'Good. You know it's pissing it down out there?'

'Is it?' I've been oblivious.

'Don't worry. I've got you. I'll see you out.' He grabs a golf umbrella from a stand by his door, and I tug my trench coat loosely over my shoulders.

In the deserted hallway, Noah kisses me slowly, tenderly on the lips. 'Good night, my darling. See you tomorrow, maybe?'

I trace a finger over his cupid's bow. 'Try keeping me away.'

He tears his gaze from me, and hauls open the heavy front door.

'Shit. It's revolting. Wait a sec.' He edges out onto the top step and opens the umbrella with a flourish, then gestures to me to come out. 'Careful. It's slippy.'

I step out to join him.

I tuck my hand through the crook of his arm and beam up at him.

One last fix for the night.

He smiles down at me. Intimately. Lovingly. I drink him in.

And just like that, the surrounding darkness explodes in a blinding burst of camera flashes.

28

HONOR

'Fuck. You look like fucking Meghan and Harry.' Mara's on the other end of a FaceTime call with me. It's nearly 6am and I've barely slept. I doubt Mara's had any sleep at all.

'Huh?' I lean my elbows on the kitchen island and press the pads of my thumbs against my eyelids until I see stars.

'Remember that photo? The one that went viral. Meghan and Harry standing under an umbrella, beaming at each other in the rain. It was like a fucking Disney movie.'

Vaguely. 'What about it?'

'You and this doctor look like them. You've got the look of love, all right.'

'Shut up and send it over.'

'It's already up on the *Post*'s homepage.'

I sigh and click through. Holy shit. The photo the *Post* has run with on their homepage makes my heart leap into my mouth. There Noah and I are under the umbrella, beautifully backlit against the gentle light from the Good Vibes hallway, with the raindrops in the foreground illuminated into a million sparkles courtesy of the camera flash. Our faces are turned to each other; my arm is linked with his.

Mara's right. It is indeed the look of love. Noah and me, our hearts laid bare for the world's news outlets. Fuck fuck fuck.

Noah's texted me so many times overnight. When the flashes went off, we both froze, before I hissed at him to get back inside and shut the door, quick. I then proceeded as quickly as I could to the car, my heels slipping on the wet pavement, so a pale-faced and apologetic Di could whisk her away.

I've only messaged Noah back once.

Leave it with me. Please don't worry. I'll make it go away. I'm so sorry x

There's only one way to make it go away, of course. Flat, outraged denial.

'The worst thing,' Mara says, 'is that it just looks like you're coming out of a house. It doesn't look like a hospice. Cheeky fucking gits.'

She's right. Good Vibes doesn't look like a hospice. Noah doesn't look like a doctor. We're just a happy couple, emerging from an evening at a "private residence", which is indeed the tack the *Post* has taken.

OO-ER HONOR! the headline screams. *While Jackson James continues to get cosy on the road with* Vet *co-star Leila Sherazi, his wife Honor Chapman was spotted exiting a private residence in Notting Hill late last night with a dishy stranger. Has she been doing some cosying up of her own?*

I scroll down. 'Oh, God. Oh, God.'

They have more photos. Fuck. They're of Elaine's house, that night I first met Noah. There's a shot of me walking from my car to the house, and another of me entering the main front door on the upper ground floor. Below, they've also got photos of Noah going in the basement door. Presumably the pap that evening was just clicking randomly, but someone at the *Post* has put two and two together.

The caption reads: *It doesn't look like this is the first time Honor's hung out with her mystery man. Here they are last month, entering another private residence via two different doorways.*

I have to hand it to them. Their ability to find incriminating evidence, even where there isn't any, is uncanny.

God. Poor Noah. Poor Elaine. It's mortifying.

'The only approach here is righteous indignation,' Mara tells me. 'We lay the fuck into them. It'll mean exposing the fact that your mum is ill, okay? But we make a statement to say that the photos were taken when you were leaving a private hospice, that your mother is receiving end-of-life care there, and that the gentleman you were with is her doctor and was comforting you during a difficult time for your family. It'll totally turn public sympathy our way, and they'll have no choice to retract.'

I hate it, but Mara's right. It's a case of throwing my family's privacy under the bus, or throwing Noah—and my marriage—under. Besides, it'll feel great to slap the *Post* with some moral righteousness and force them to backtrack.

'What about the other photos? They were taken at my friend Elaine's house. Noah—the doctor—is her son.'

'Even better. Is Elaine a public figure?'

'Yeah, she's an entrepreneur and a non-exec—she's a high-profile businesswoman. We were all out in France staying at Elaine's place last month. Jackson was there, and Noah.'

'Fabulous. Ask Jackson if he'll post a photo of him and

Noah. Back to these pictures. Were there other people there that night?'

'Plenty. Evelyn Macleod was there, and Astrid Carmichael.'

'Fucking brilliant. We'll make sure they're happy to be name-checked and we'll make a statement that you were at a social event at Noah's family home. We can also buy the images of anyone else they papped that night entering the same address—if they got you, they got Evelyn. Any news outlets who pick this up will have to do a one-eighty so fast they'll leave skid marks.'

I sigh. 'Thanks Mara.'

'Don't mention it. Honor?'

'Yes?'

'I'm only going to ask this once. Is there anything else I need to know about this situation?'

'God, no.' Years of dealing with Jackson's crap have taught me how to hold a poker face.

'Got it.' Mara nods. 'You'd better let Jackson know. I'll prepare a statement. Give it a few hours, then later this morning we should arrange for you to be papped heading to work for a normal day.'

'Do you think I'll be able to make it to the hospice later? To see Mum?'

It's not to see Mum. It's to see Noah, who must be out of his mind, but Mara doesn't need to know that.

'Even better. If you turn up there, it'll give every news outlet a chance to verify that the exterior of the building matches the shots from last night, and it'll remind the public that you're still focused on your mum's wellbeing despite all this bullshit. And obviously, it sends a loud message that you've got nothing to hide. Laters.'

Thank God for Mara. She's mopped up plenty of Jackson's messes in the past, but this is the biggest scandal she's had to deal with on my behalf. She's a great person to have onside.

I slide a clean mug under the coffee machine and pick up my pen. I'm so tired I won't remember anything unless I write it down.

Call Jackson

Call Evelyn

Call Astrid

Call Erika.

Between us, Jackson and I will have taken a few years off our manager's life by the time this Burberry deal is signed.

I have no choice but to wake Jackson up. He answers on the third ring.

'Babe? You okay? Wait a sec.' There's a shuffle and a muffled voice and a pause. God. He's with her. He can lie there and spoon his mistress all he wants, and I've never even had a night with Noah. And now I have to lie to everyone because my relationship needs to stay in the shadows. It's not fucking fair. My eyes sting with tears.

I brief Jackson quickly. 'There's a problem. The *Post* got a shot of Noah helping me down the steps of the hospice last night—it was raining and I was in heels—and they've made it look incriminating. It's on their homepage and it's being picked up everywhere. Mara's going to crucify them, but I wanted to let you know.'

'Jesus Christ. What a load of bollocks. Don't they know or care that you were coming out of a fucking *hospice*?'

Amusement and irritation flash briefly. It would genuinely never occur to Jackson that I may have strayed from him.

'Believe me, they're going to know by the time Mara's finished with them. But I wanted you on the same page.'

'What a bunch of dickheads. Why the fuck didn't Mara stop it?'

'She tried. She's been up all night, but there was nothing she could offer them that was any sweeter than this story. They wouldn't drop it. Don't worry, it's going to bite them in the arse.'

'Will Noah be a problem, do you think, if the press sniffs around more generally? Do we need to get Alex to draw up an NDA for the hospice?'

'Jackson!'

If my husband was here, I'd likely throw something at him. Something heavy. Jesus Christ. The guy has lived this toxic lifestyle for so long that he thinks bribing and threatening people is the normal way to go. As if Noah would ever betray me. As if I'd ever let Alex, Jackson's odious little fixer, anywhere near him.

'Okay, okay. Don't get your knickers in a twist. Just checking.'

'They're family friends. Elaine has been so hospitable to us all. Of course Noah would never betray our confidence. Besides, they're all bound by patient confidentiality.'

'I'm so sorry, babe. About all this.' Jackson sighs. 'D'you want me to come home early?'

'No, don't worry. Thanks though. I'll be fine.' It's far easier having Jackson out of the way.

'Well, we'll do Fashion Week next week, all right? Lots of good photo opps there. And then we can get this Burberry thing closed once and for all and we'll go celebrate. You and me.'

29

NOAH

I barely manage a couple of hours' sleep on the emergency staff bed at Good Vibes, and the sleep I do get is restless. Troubled. I didn't dare go home last night, and since Honor's text first thing this morning to let me know the photos have hit the web and that she's working on a retraction, the whole of Avondale Park has been crawling with press.

That flash of white light last night, intruding on a relaxed, private moment between Honor and me, was the truest form of violation I've ever experienced. I understand now what it's like for her every day. I thought the scene at Heathrow was bad, but at least that was set up. Last night shook me to the core: this unacceptable idea that a private moment between two people can instantly become global news.

And the worst part was that I was powerless. I had to do what she said, had to let her walk out there alone in a blinding haze of flashes and shutter myself in the hospice like she asked. She knew best—and I'd do anything to diffuse the situation—but I felt fucking useless.

She messaged me last night to say she was dealing with the situation, but beyond that I had no colour. I was a caged animal, practically making tracks as I confined myself to pacing around the kitchen table so as not to wake the guests upstairs.

I'm not sure what I'm supposed to do. I can't tell anyone, ask anyone for advice. There's no one I can think of to call, except perhaps Mum, but I'm not sure what my official line should be. Presumably, Honor's going to go for an outright denial that there's anything personal going on between us. Until I have a chance to speak to her properly, I'm staying silent.

When I finally collapsed on the narrow bed upstairs, the smallest bud of a thought crept into my mind, tentative and fragile. What if this was the push we needed? Would Honor ever consider using this betrayal of her privacy as a signal to reevaluate what she wants from life? I've never asked her to, beyond my declaration of love the other day. Any move would have to come from her. I'd be asking her to give up too much.

My rational mind batted the tiny bloom of hope right back down. She couldn't even tell me she loved me the other day. She told me she wasn't in a position to make any commitment to me. This doesn't change that. If anything, it'll send her running for the hills.

I gave up trying to sleep around five and showered and shaved. Pointless gestures that gave me the smallest pretence of being in control. By the time Honor's text came through to say the story was live, I was sitting back at the kitchen table, head in my hands and an empty coffee mug in front of me. And shortly after that, press started gathering on the street outside with cameras and even fucking TV crews. I called the police and pleaded with them to get down here and clear the street, emphasising that the disturbance the reporters were making was threatening the health of my seriously ill patients, but there's no sign of them yet.

Since the news broke, my phone has detonated. Current friends, old friends, mates from uni, all WhatsApping me and sending me messages on FaceBook and LinkedIn and God knows what else. I hold off from clicking into any of the messages—there's only one person I want to hear from and that's Honor—but the reading panes of my various apps suggest they're all along the same lines: some variation on *OMG* or *nice one mate* or *you jammy bastard.* I want nothing more than to turn off my phone, but I'm holding out that Honor will make contact.

It's overwhelming, and the growing sense of dread and helplessness is even more overwhelming. Sleep deprivation is not helping. The office phone rings off the hook from six. I answer it the first couple of times before realising that every news outlet in the country seems to be trying to get through, then disconnect it.

Right now, my priority needs to be the wellbeing of my guests and staff. I send out a terse group WhatsApp to the whole Good Vibes team.

There's some unfortunate press interest around Good Vibes this am thanks to a photo the Post has published of me and Stephanie Chapman's daughter. We are working on refuting their accusations but meanwhile please arrive via the rear entrance if you're on duty today, and categorically do not speak to any press members. Thx.

The early part of the morning is spent in triage mode, managing the bewilderment and morbid curiosity of the staff members who turn up and reminding them of their duty of care. I refresh the *Post* homepage relentlessly.

Around seven-thirty, there's a breakthrough. I stare at the headline.

HONOR DENIES AFFAIR, CONFIRMS MOTHER ON DEATHBED.

For fuck's sake. These people have no compassion. But the paper's turnaround is impressive. The article goes on to explain that last night's photos were taken at the Good Vibes Hospice, and that the mystery man pictured with Honor is Dr Noah Thierry, owner of the hospice and friend of the James-Chapman family.

They've lifted exterior shots of the building, and a smiling headshot of me, from the Good Vibes website and, while they fall short of an apology, they've appeared to drop all speculation that Honor and me are an item. They've also resurrected some photos of Stephanie, and they have confirmed her illness as late-stage pancreatic cancer.

I exhale deeply—I must have been holding my breath. Honor's team's ability to twist the arm of national rags is both impressive and terrifying.

My phone rings. It's her. I can't answer it fast enough.

'Hi, darling. Oh my God, are you okay?'

'I'm fine.' She sounds breathless. 'Rollo, put your tie on. Here. Sorry, I'm trying to get the kids processed.'

'No problem. What can I do? I saw the *Post* has changed its story. Well done.'

'Yeah. We had to give them some stuff on Mum, which is the absolute worst, but it worked. Listen, I can't talk right now, but I wanted to say—*Rollo*. Your tie. *Now*. Sorry, I wanted to tell you to keep an eye on the *Mail*—we've fed them some stuff so they can make the *Post* a laughingstock and hopefully discredit the story once and for all. But also, have the press turned up there yet?'

'Yep.' I look grimly out the window. 'TV crews too. It's mayhem out there.'

'Okay. Listen carefully. We're sending over some security to help you. They'll keep the press off your property, stop them ringing your doorbell and making a nuisance of themselves. They should be there by eight. Tell your team to stay away from the windows and not to engage with the press. I'll be there by ten latest.'

'Wait—you're coming here?' I assumed she'd want to stay miles away.

'Yes. We need to underline that I'm a regular visitor there, that I'm prioritising Mum, and that it's business as usual. It'll be powerful to have me photographed in the same doorway as those photos. Hang on, Noah—what, Serena? Yes, Mummy's just dealing with the very silly photos that newspaper published at Granny's hospital. Noah, I need to run. I'll see you later.'

I take the phone away from my ear and stare at the screen. I've been a waste of space all night, pacing and spiralling and pining, and here Honor is in *doing* mode. She's foiled the efforts of a national newspaper to discredit her, she's dealing with my security situation, she's processing Serena and Rollo and all the while diffusing the power of the "very silly" photos to upset her children. And it's not even eight o'clock in the morning. She's amazing. And at this moment, the gulf between us feels infinite.

It's the most unsatisfactory conversation, but I need to look no further than the *Post*'s update for my answer to where Honor and I are headed.

HONOR DENIES AFFAIR.

That's my answer, right there.

30

HONOR

I stalk imperiously through the sea of press and up the steps of Good Vibes in full armour, if armour constitutes a face of impeccably applied makeup, a black, laser-cut Alaia dress and Gianvito Rossi ankle boots. Di, in full pit-bull mode, sticks to my side as reporters scream my name. Their questions and their camera clicks are a wall of noise around me, but it's nothing I haven't handled a million times before. At least they're not asking me today if Jackson is shagging anyone.

We nod at the two burly security guards, one of whom pounds on the door behind him three times as pre-agreed. It swings open and we step inside. Noah's behind the door. His eyes are reddened and his hair is mussed up. He takes a step towards me and stops. Looks at Di.

'Hi, Di.' He turns back to me. 'Hi. You okay?'

'I'm fine. I desperately need a cup of tea.' *And to collapse into your arms and not move for hours.*

'I bet you do. You've basically conducted a military operation this morning.' Noah gestures at the mayhem beyond the door.

I smile tiredly. 'Let's say our crisis response protocol is a well-oiled machine by now. Isn't it, Di?'

'Runs like a Swiss watch these days,' Di says cheerfully.

'Let me get you tea. See you in my office? Di, you're welcome to hang out in the kitchen.'

I make it to his tiny office and fall into the spare chair, pressing my fingers to my temples. I'm broken, and the worst part is still to come: talking to Noah and breaking the news to Mum that her illness is front-page news. God help me.

And then Noah's back, two mugs of tea in hand. He kicks the door shut with his foot and puts them down and pulls me up into his arms. And that's that. His strong arms wind around me and hold me up, and he sighs into my neck, and all the bullshit and uncertainty and overwhelm from the past twelve hours melt away. It may be just for a moment, but I'll take it.

'Jesus Christ,' he mutters. 'Where do we start?'

'Just hold me very, very tight.' I tighten my grip on his neck and rub my nose into his shirt, right below his collar. Inhale him.

He obliges. 'Any reason you look even more like a supermodel than usual this morning?' His tone is light, jokey. It sounds forced, but I appreciate the levity.

'Armour. Revenge. Show them their crap doesn't phase me. Standard response.'

'Effective.' He strokes my back. 'What the hell happened last night—did you find out?'

'No. Probably an opportunistic pap striking lucky. The *Post* said he approached them with the photos.' I pull out of his grip and put my hands on his shoulders. 'Did you see the *Mail*?'

I'm proud of what we've pulled off this morning. The *Mail*, never happier than when on the moral high ground, has gone to town on a scathing indictment of the *Post*'s morals and journalistic integrity. They've reprinted my and Jackson's joint statement in full and have included stock photos of Evelyn, Astrid and Stacey turning up at Elaine's that evening Noah and I were supposedly having a private rendezvous. The *Post* has ended up with egg on its face, though I'm wiser than to suppose it'll stop them from pulling similar stunts again.

'I did. Very impressive. Seriously. Remind me never to piss you off.' His hands play with the dip of my waist, and he kisses me gently on the mouth, and, as his lips coax mine open, my resolve to talk weakens. It can wait a few minutes. I stand in his chaotic little office and allow myself to experience this kiss as it takes on momentum.

Noah's telling me something with this kiss, and I want to tell him the same thing. This is sacred. This is for us. It's as sweet, as sublime, as transcendent as it would have been yesterday, before this shit-show erupted. Those vultures outside can't touch us, can't burst our bubble in this moment.

He slides a hand up my neck, gathering my hair in his fist, and angles my head. Kisses me more deeply. Our kiss is worshipful, heavy with meaning, and I'm hyper-present to every dance of his tongue, every slide of his lips. I can't tell if he's in denial about the conversation that has to happen next, or all too painfully aware. But as his tears pool where my face meets his, I have my answer. He's committing me to memory.

A few minutes later, I pull gently away. 'Noah.'

He rests his forehead against mine, rubs a lock of my hair between his fingers. 'I know.' It's a whisper. He lets me go and sits down heavily. Swipes the back of his hand across his wet cheeks. 'Have a seat. Get that tea down you.'

I scoot my chair forward so our knees are touching. 'I don't see a way forward for us, darling. I've been going over it all night.'

'I know.' This time it's a sigh, and the weight of resignation in that sigh tugs my heart down with it.

I push on, take his hand. Squeeze those beautiful, supple fingers. 'They've taken all our oxygen, you know? We've got nothing left to play with. Short of spending all our time together in this room for as long as Mum's here, we have no options. We've done well to keep it under the radar till now. But the *Post* won't take this lying down. They'll have people trailing me—us—from now on, hoping to catch us.'

'It's so unfair. Your husband is fucking that woman in plain sight and doesn't seem to have had to deal with any consequences, from what I can see. I feel so powerless. It's the nastiest feeling, having the rug pulled out from under us like this. I can't—I can't make head nor tail of it.'

'Nothing about this is fair, darling.' I bow my head. That powerlessness, that sense of being a puppet with no clue who's pulling my strings, is all too familiar to me, but must be crippling for him.

'Can I ask you a question? Have you ever thought about telling Jackson about me? I've been wanting to ask—it sounds like he's pretty open with you about what he gets up to, from what you've said.'

'It's a fair question. And the answer is no. I thought about it for a second this morning. He didn't even question my integrity when I called to brief him, which is kind of sweet and also really fucking irritating. He's so sure I'm the good little wife I've always been, waiting for him at home. He was in bed with her when I called; can you believe that?'

'You have got to be fucking kidding me.' He clenches his fists.

'Sadly not. But I'm not like him, and this whole thing has got unsustainable. I can't keep going like this. Jackson is very good at compartmentalising his family and his other women. I don't think he loses a moment of sleep over it. But I've been feeling torn in two. You and I—we've got in so much deeper than we were ever supposed to, and you know you consume me.

'So if you're asking if I've considered coming clean to Jackson and getting his blessing about seeing you, then no, because you deserve far, far more than being on the periphery, and I can't handle the emotional load of juggling a marriage and a very intense, meaningful relationship. So maybe this disaster is a blessing in disguise—maybe it's done us a favour by taking the decision away.'

'So your marriage wins.' His tone isn't spiteful, just resigned. Flat.

'Noah—'

'It's okay. Seriously. You've always been honest with me. This was supposed to be a bit of fun for both of us. I wasn't supposed to fall in love with you. You haven't done anything wrong.'

I stroke his dear, handsome face. He's heart-stoppingly gorgeous, those huge brown eyes swimming with unspilt tears that almost send me over the edge too. But I have no right to cry. Not in front of Noah, anyway. This is all my doing, and he's beautiful, blameless collateral damage in the car crash that is my life. 'I need you to know. This is not about me feeling less for you than you feel for me. Okay? I'm in as deep as you are.

'But I've spent fourteen years building a marriage, and a family, and a huge web of business interests with Jackson.

And maybe those things shouldn't be tangled up, but they are, and I can't just walk away. I have a duty, to Jackson, and to my kids, and to everyone we employ. What I want doesn't count as much as you might think it should.'

'Don't cry.' He pulls out a tissue and dabs my face with it, gently, lovingly. 'And please don't worry about me. I'm a big boy. I knew what I was getting into. The last thing you need right now is to expend any energy on me. Use it on your mum. Your family. And on yourself. You have a tough few weeks ahead, my darling. Your mother is an absolute trooper, but I can't imagine she's got more than two or three weeks left here.'

'You're right.' I sniffle. 'I need to go and see her and confess that I've dropped her in it with the press.'

'She'll understand. I know how protective she is of you.'

There's a pause, and I look up at him, and his face tells me he's thinking the same thing as me. That in a moment, I'll walk out of this room, and a veil will drop between us, invisible but devastating, and I'll cease to have any rights where Noah is concerned, any access beyond being a client of his hospice.

'It's unfair to ask you this.' I get to my feet slowly. 'But... will you be my friend? I don't think I can get through this without you.'

He rises and gives me his best Noah smile. Puts his arms tightly around me. 'You're the most important woman in my life, darling. Of course I'll be your friend. I'm here whenever you need advice. Given my conflict, I need to stay away from any medical decisions between now and the end of your mother's life—that has to be purely Elena's domain—but I'm here to answer any questions you have and to walk you through whatever you need. I know it's scary and intimidating.'

'Thank you. God, that makes me feel better.' I sigh into his neck.

'But when your mother has passed, I'll need to put some distance between us. Not that we'll have a reason to see each other, unless it's through my parents. I just—my heart can't handle seeing you, if I can't be with you.'

'I understand,' I whisper. 'I don't want to make your life harder than I already have. I'm just sorry I dragged you into this toxic clusterfuck that is my life.'

He kisses me softly. One last time. Then smiles against my lips. 'I'm not sorry for any of it.'

31

HONOR

There's an overwhelming sense of peace when I walk into Mum's room. The serenity hits me: the quiet whirring of a fan, but no intrusive beeps. A heavenly scented candle burns, making the room smell more like a spa than a medical facility. It's all deliberate, of course. Noah and his team have engineered this cocoon with every detail arranged just so.

And when I shut the door quietly behind me and lean against it for a moment, I have the impression of having left all the craziness behind for a moment. No one and nothing can get to me in this refuge.

Perhaps it's also the emotional kick of seeing the two women I love most in the world in one room. Mum's awake, propped up on pillows, and Ally sits by the bed, a book in one hand, Mum's fragile, blue-veined hand in the other. Ally told me this morning that she'd be here for me today, and I'm beyond grateful.

Ally raises her eyebrows questioningly, and I shake my head and roll my eyes, pressing my lips together to hold back the tears. *Are you okay? Not really.* A sisterly communication. Words unnecessary.

'Hi.' I kiss Mum on the forehead before pulling up a chair to the near side of the bed and sinking into it. I've had a firm policy of censorship where Mum is concerned these past few weeks. No news flow or personal stuff that might upset her is allowed through her bedroom door. But we're way past that now.

'How are you doing?' Ally asks quietly, and it's my undoing. I drop my head in my hands and shake, all that suppressed emotion swelling through my system now, shuddering its way out through tensed shoulders and wet eyes and burning my throat and my jaw with its desperate need to escape in loud wracking cries I'm trying my best to repress.

'Oh, God.' I moan into my hands. The tears are coming faster now. 'I'm sorry—I'm so sorry, Mum'

'Darling?' The quiver of concern in Mum's already weak voice is another dagger to my heart. 'What on earth is the matter?'

'Oh, sweetie.' Ally jumps up and rounds the bed and kneels by my side, bowing over my lap and gripping my waist with her arms. 'Let it out. You poor baby.'

'Honor. You're *scaring* me. Speak.' Mum reaches out for me, and the gesture is comforting enough to allow me pause to breathe. It's time to spill, even though it will hurt and worry Mum, because putting up more walls of secrecy between us is not an option this far down the line for Mum.

'Whew. Okay. I've messed up. Badly. I've been seeing Noah, Mum. Having a fling with him, since France, and it got way more serious for both of us than we ever expected. And last night we got papped outside here, and I've managed to bury the story, kind of, but I've had to deny everything, and—there's no way forward for us.' I shrug, desolation hitting in a fresh wave. 'We're out of options.'

Mum stares at me with the oddest expression. 'You and Noah,' she says wonderingly. 'I knew it.'

'What—you guessed?'

'No, no. But I told you you should have married someone like him, didn't I? I knew you two would be good together. Really, really good. It was so clear to me.' She sinks into her pillow as if defeated by the effort of speaking.

I pull a handful of tissues from the box by the bed and wad them against my eyes. Makeup be damned. 'Well, you were totally right. But it doesn't change the fact that I'm married, and our luck has run out.'

'Have you spoken to Noah?' Ally releases me from her embrace and squats back on her heels.

'Yeah. Just now. He was amazing—obviously. He understands. He's not stupid.'

'And what does your perfectly faithful husband say about all this?' There's a flinty tone in Mum's voice. She may be dying, but this woman can rise to a challenge better than anyone, and Jackson lost her full respect a long time ago.

'He was outraged on my behalf. Obviously, he didn't, for a second, suspect there was anything in the reports.'

Mum's quiet for a moment, her eyes closed. She says without opening them, 'Do you love him?'

'Noah?' *Noah.* The only person in the world who can make me feel as though everything is wonderful. In his arms, I'm safe. I'm *me*, and I'm loved for being precisely that. 'Yes. I love him. He's so different from Jackson—I'm so different when I'm with him. I know we're still in the honeymoon phase, but it's effortless. *Was* effortless.'

'And do you think he loves you?'

'He does. He told me he does, but I didn't say it back. I

told him I wasn't in a position to say it, even though I wanted to.'

Ally has her hand pressed to her heart as if it's breaking. She and Mum exchange a look. I know that look. It's their *Honor is being ridiculous* look.

'Are you sure this is the way you want to go, Duck Face?' Ally asks. 'Doubling up on your commitment to Jackson. It's a bit of a fork in the road, this moment, isn't it?'

I stare at her. A fork in the road. Exactly how life felt when Noah lay down next to me on that daybed only a few weeks ago. I made the decision to let him into my life right in that moment, with no real thought of the consequences. And it seems I've made a split-second decision once again. I called Mara and told her to deny, deny, deny, because I was on the back foot and the idea of doing anything else was terrifying.

I've always been the sensible one, the one who keeps my head down and works hard and reaps the rewards. Everything in my life has been fastidiously planned and ruthlessly executed—until Noah came along.

Jackson and I have always had a huge, ambitious strategy for the heights our family could reach, and for that reason, I've kept my precious, fledgling relationship with Noah safely away from all that. Or tried to, in any case.

And I haven't allowed myself for a second to wonder whether Noah presents a viable alternative future to the James-Chapman juggernaut. Nothing good comes from entertaining thoughts like that, because however hard I've fallen for Noah, everything else I value in my life has come from my union with Jackson.

I poke my finger through a laser-cut hole in my dress. 'If last night was a fork in the road, then I definitely wasn't ready for it.'

'Did you even think about not denying it?' It's Ally again.

'No. *No*. That wasn't the plan. Noah and I were supposed to be a bit of fun. Jackson and I have worked so bloody hard for this, and we're so close to signing Burberry. God! Look at how much I've sacrificed for that man and for our family and our business! I've done everything I was supposed to! I'm not throwing it all away now.'

'Just remember, darling.' There's a touch of her old imperiousness in Mum's voice. 'You are not the Queen. You've always had such a strong sense of duty, and I know how hard you work, but your duty has limits. No one's asking you to sacrifice your own happiness for the greater good.'

It's meant kindly, but it's a blow, because walking away from Noah is the biggest sacrifice I've ever made, and no one seems to appreciate it. Not Mum. Not Ally. Not Jackson. Jackson has no idea. He thinks the sum of my sacrifices is looking the other way whenever he strays. But I've just given up the person I want most in the world, without wavering for even a second, and I'm supposed to throw myself back into my marriage with no thanks and no pats on the back.

And instead of bollocking me for having an affair, or praising me for being strong to end it, Mum and Ally seem to think I'm misguided, too. It's bloody infuriating. But I won't be shirty with Mum, as I would have countless times in the past, because she has days or weeks to live, and nothing is worth ruining the time we have left together. Not Jackson. Not Noah.

So I paste a humble look on my face and pat Mum's leg through the bedclothes. 'Understood, Mum. I fancy a change of subject, do you? Do you want to do some funeral planning? I'm quite keen to hide out here for a while longer.'

Far from being morbid, the planning of Mum's funeral has been a cause of great excitement, for Mum at least. The enthusiasm she's been showing freaked me out to the extent that I brought it up with Noah.

'It's a good thing,' he told me. 'It means your mum's not in denial about what's coming. And this gives her a sense of empowerment—she gets to participate in what should be a celebration of her life.'

'Yes, let's. Water, please,' Mum croaks.

I cradle her head the way the nurses here have shown me, and lift her high enough to take a few sips of water through a straw. She weighs so little now that it requires almost no effort on my part.

We've previously agreed that she will be cremated quietly with just the family present. So the funeral we're planning is really a memorial service. Mum has latched onto the prospect of a glamorous party in her honour with great glee.

'I want the Montague,' she whispers now. 'Honor, will you speak to Miles? I want it in one of those charming rooms he has overlooking Knightsbridge.'

'Consider it done.' I reach into my bag and pull out a notebook. The Montague is Mum's favourite London hotel, an old Grande Dame near Hyde Park. It's now run by the Montague family's eldest son, Miles. He's a good friend of mine and he'll do us proud.

We talk a while about dress code (Mum wants full-on cocktail wear which most guests attending a memorial will probably baulk at, but whatever), which of Mum's favourite drinks to serve on arrival (champagne, as Mum's preference of vodka martinis will have everyone hammered before they can say *RIP*), and what poems should be read (Mum would be happy if we read out every Mary Oliver poem ever written).

And then the conversation turns to memories, and as Ally and I flank Mum's bedside and recount our favourite and most hilarious and weirdest memories from our childhood, and as I watch the occasional tear float down Mum's temple, I'm grateful for this moment in time where Mum is alive and the circus beyond the walls of this building can wait a little longer.

32

HONOR

I can't decide if the timing of London Fashion Week this year is diabolical or heaven-sent. It nearly breaks me physically, but it saves my sanity. The entire week is so heady and crazy and stressful and frothy and frivolous and *vapid*. And it consumes me, and that's precisely what I need despite the protestations from every side—Jackson, Ally, Di, my team, even Mum—that it's too much for me at this stressful time.

It is too much, and having Honor Chapman Cosmetics working on some of the biggest shows provides the exact oblivion that my fevered, knackered, lovesick brain needs just now. I'm reeling from the loss of Noah, who so quickly became my north star. I'm on the worst tenterhooks as Mum slips gently and inexorably towards her death. And so it actually feels good to stress that the model opening the Erdem show is late for her call time, or agonise endlessly with Astrid over whether the look we've settled on for the Astrid Carmichael show is too matte for a spring collection.

It also helps that London Fashion Week is firmly my and Jackson's territory. The guy adores Fashion Week. He was in

New York last week for Tom Ford's show, and in London he and I take our places front row at all the biggest shows. The shows themselves, as well as the endless logistical exertions of being dressed in advance by the designers and getting ourselves from show to show (never straightforward in London) are the best kind of mindless distraction. Surface froth that masks how flat life is right now, without Noah.

And so I allow myself to be dressed up like a doll, and I sit on front row after front row with my ridiculously handsome husband, who's at his absolute best at this kind of thing, and bask in the attention, and in Jackson's relentless, infectious energy, and in knowing that every front-page photo of Jackson James and Honor Chapman sitting side by side, looking every inch the glossily perfect power couple, shoves the images of Noah and me further away from the collective consciousness.

And if it's not real in the public's eye, it's not real in my eyes. This is real. If Jackson and I are sitting shoulder to shoulder for all the world to see, it must be real. This is the life I've deliberately chosen, because that day was a fork in the road, whether I liked it or not, and I made my decision. Chose my direction. If this is my life, I'd better damn well enjoy it.

Having Jackson back is strangely comforting. It helps that Fashion Week is such a well-trodden path for us as a celebrity couple and for Honor Chapman Cosmetics. Jackson's always been my biggest cheerleader professionally, and he attends every show my brand is involved with. He's there for me, in all his magnificent physical glory, and by showing up for me he's unknowingly bolstering our marriage.

There's one night, in the middle of Fashion Week, when I'm broken. I attended a couple of shows this morning, had

Di race me across town in full Roksanda regalia to spend an hour with Mum (forcing myself not to knock on Noah's office door), and came back to the Fashion Week show space on The Strand for more shows. The joints of my feet feel disfigured from a day of four-inch heels, and I'm on the verge of tears with exhaustion.

So when I get home to find Jackson has cooked me my favourite Thai curry and run me a huge bubble bath, I'm overwhelmed with gratitude and love for my husband and, that night, I let him make love to me. And it's nice. It's more than nice; it's comforting and lovely, and he's gorgeous, obviously, and loving, and I focus hard on not allowing my brain to flit to what it was like with Noah, even for a second.

I go through the motions of Fashion Week and navigate my version of what's normal on a daily basis, in this odd twilight of grieving for Noah and grieving for Mum's imminent death. But there's an unwelcome sense of consciousness that wasn't there before. Of analysis.

It's as though I'm seeing everything I do through Noah's eyes and finding it lacking. Not that Noah would ever judge me: he's always told me how amazing, and inspiring, and even intimidating, my professional success is.

But by distancing myself from the action, and putting myself in the shoes of someone as altruistic and far removed from the world of celebrity he is, I see clearly how nonsensical much of it is. Nonsensical and invasive, and plain *gratuitous*.

This perspective hits me when I have to barge past the paps to get Rollo to his school gates. When a photographer nicks the tail light of another parent's Porsche Cayenne and I have to apologise and fork out for the damage. When I find Serena crying in bed one night because another girl has said Serena's daddy has a girlfriend who is not her mum. When

Mara suggests it would be great to capture the whole family, Jackson included, arriving at Good Vibes to spend what could be our final time together with Mum.

No! No, no, no. All these years, I've endured this type of bullshit, and for what reason? I've always told myself it's to grow our family brand, keep it current, keep it front and centre in the public's mind, benefiting our array of business interests.

But it's not.

Not really.

It's all for Jackson.

He's a world-famous movie star, operating at the highest levels of the entertainment industry. He's done incredibly well, and he chose me and brought me along for the ride, and so much of it's been an amazing adventure. We have more money than God, and I've had access to the smartest, most successful people and parties and inner circles. His chosen career requires a level of public exposure that's frankly terrifying, and is jarring so hard for me right now, but my career doesn't. Not really. Our profile as a couple undoubtedly launched my cosmetics brand, but now I have the track record and customer base to prove my product has legs and isn't just another celebrity hobby.

Evelyn and Astrid and Elaine and Stacey are all examples of women at the top of their game, who've achieved enormous professional success without courting the spotlight. Granted, Evelyn had a nightmare when she was married to her ex, Seb, but since they divorced she's focused all her press efforts on herself as an entrepreneur, and it's been extraordinarily effective. Same with Astrid. Same with Elaine and Stacey.

If only I didn't have to constantly worry about my and my children's faces being on the front of the *Post*. If only I could focus on making the cover of *Forbes* instead. But this is what Jackson and I have always done: offered the press access to our family. This has always been at the core of our media strategy.

Mum's words keep popping into my head at the most inconvenient moments. *You are not the Queen.* I've taken this burden on myself. No one is making me get out of bed and live this ridiculous life every morning. No one but me. And perhaps in a few months, when I'm in a more robust state of mind, I can work with my executive coach and with Mara and Erika and Jackson to iron out what I view as a more sustainable model for my career. One where I don't have to sell my soul to the tabloids every day.

33

NOAH

Honor came in earlier with Jackson and Serena and Rollo, and I'm still reeling. She was thoughtful enough to text me and warn me in advance, under the diplomatic auspices of checking that it wouldn't be too disruptive to the other Good Vibes guests if the four of them came in. I briefed the staff, knowing for sure that having Jackson James in the house would send everyone into a tailspin of hysteria.

I've had a few conversations with Honor about how to approach the subject of their grandmother's death with her children. They haven't been in to visit since I admitted Stephanie, and Honor's been feeling guilty on her mum's behalf while understandably wanting to protect her children.

'The death of a loved one can be hard for children to process,' I told her a couple of days ago, when I saw her here briefly. 'They don't just have to come to terms with their Granny dying, but knowing someone they love has passed can be extremely destabilising, because it brings home the fact that anyone close to them could die, and that's an enormous burden for them to assume.

'You shouldn't feel bad if you or they decide that visiting Granny at this point is not in their best interests. Maybe they want to say their farewells by painting a picture for her, or making her a card. Those are perfectly fine alternatives.'

'But Mum keeps asking for them.' Honor twisted her mouth in distress. 'I can't deny her that. I shouldn't have kept them away this long. And even though she should have lived for another twenty years, in their eyes she's ancient. So I can't help but feel now could be a good chance to have them experience death in a way that we can manage together, as a family. Especially because this place isn't scary, not like going to a hospital would be. And I'm worried we'll leave it too late, and she'll miss her chance to see them.'

I agreed. So I suggested Honor take some photos of Stephanie and of her room, and possibly even a little video, if Stephanie was up to it. It would be a good way to prepare the children for how much their grandmother had changed.

And this afternoon they showed up. I've seen her a couple of times over the past week. She's looked unbelievably glamorous and stunning, even by her standards, but that's because it's Fashion Week and I've got used to seeing her and her husband splashed across the front page of the *Evening Standard* most evenings on my walk home.

But I wasn't prepared for the visceral shock of seeing her with her family. Serena and Rollo were in school uniform, Jackson was in a navy suit that melded itself to his body so obnoxiously well that it should be illegal, and Honor—well, Honor was breathtaking.

She was in a long, slinky dress that flowed behind her when she walked in, in a glossy green with gold shimmers that made her huge tiger eyes pop. And when she stepped forward to kiss me on the cheek, I could see the golds and greens of her eye makeup bringing out the same colours in her eyes. Those eyes were full of emotion as she put her cheek to mine, and I let my eyes drift closed for a nanosecond as I inhaled the scent of her, before letting her go and flashing them all my best professional smile.

'Mate!' Jackson stepped forward and shook my hand vigorously, slapping me on the back with his other hand. 'Good to see you.' He lowered his voice. 'I'm so sorry for all that press bullshit. Not what you needed at all, man. Thanks for bearing with us.'

'It's no problem at all.' It was surprisingly hard to keep my voice, and my smile, steady. 'I'm just glad you've got everything resolved with the papers.'

Jackson jerked his head towards Honor, who was watching us nervously. 'My wife, the media mogul. She sorted it all. She's amazing.'

I hoped my face didn't give away my entire emotional state as I agreed. 'She is.' I turned to Honor. 'Elena's upstairs. She'll pop in and brief you.' Elena was in fact sporting a bouncy blow-dry and more makeup than I'd ever seen on her in anticipation of Jackson James' visit.

And then they were off upstairs, as nurses with hearts in their eyes peeked out of every door. I watched them go. The love of my life. Her movie-star husband. Her beautiful children. The four of them operated in a different space from me. It was as though they breathed different air. I was one of those stupid mortals who'd dallied with the gods, and now I was suffering the eternal damnation.

~

The days pass in a blur of relentless activity, driven by desperation. I'm a live wire, working and working out and doing whatever I can to run myself into the ground. I'm exhausted, but it's not enough. It's as though there's an itch under my skin, and my blood is bubbling, and my limbs are restless in wake and sleep. I'm abusing my adrenal system so shamefully that it reminds me of my days as a junior doctor, but I can't find peace.

I'm miserable when I cross paths with Honor at Good Vibes, and I'm just as miserable when she comes in and doesn't seek me out. Meanwhile, Stephanie is on the final stretch of her journey and Elena, I and our team focus on monitoring the signs of her decline and rigorously prioritising her comfort.

Her nervous system and cognitive function are still holding up well, and I'm grateful for that on her daughters' behalf, but her cardiovascular system is faltering, leaving her extremities cold and mottled. She's so skeletal now that the nursing staff are placing pillows between her knees when they position her on her side, and appetite is declining steadily.

But she still has the energy to twinkle at me when I poke my head around the door. Earlier today, I checked in on her, taking a pew by her bed for a quick chat. I couldn't take my eyes off the large, silver-framed photo by her bed—Stephanie and Honor and Ally. It was a professional photo, the three of them back-lit by the sun, their faces crinkled with genuine laughter. It took my breath away.

Stephanie caught me looking. 'She's magnificent, isn't she?'

There was definitely nothing wrong with her cognitive

function yet. I answered with a sheepish grin and a quick nod of my head.

'I'll be off, then. I'll see you later, Stephanie.'

As I rose, she raised a hand with great effort to stop me. 'You're a wonderful man, Noah. I wish you could be the one to look after my eldest daughter when I'm gone.'

I turned away quickly so she wouldn't see the moisture in my eyes.

Ally was here this afternoon, and Honor's been here all evening. I take a deep breath and mount the stairs and do what I've been sitting on my hands to prevent all evening: I go to see her.

It's almost ten. I lean against Stephanie's door frame. She looks to be sound asleep, and Honor's sitting by her bed, her laptop open on her lap. She's the most dressed-down I've ever seen her, in yoga pants and a loose sweater, and she passes a hand tiredly over her face.

'Hey.'

She looks over her shoulder and I'm gratified by the extent to which her face brightens.

'Have you eaten?' I hold up a large Ottolenghi carrier bag, and her mouth opens into an O as round and red as the iconic O on the packaging.

She snaps her laptop shut and comes over to me. 'You little beauty. Seriously?'

'Seriously. I got tonnes. Thought you might be hungry. Will you come and eat with me downstairs?'

34

HONOR

I'm not sure I've ever seen a more heavenly apparition than Noah, framed in the doorway, wearing my favourite Homer t-shirt and bearing Ottolenghi. I follow him downstairs like he's the Pied Piper.

'Ally says Mum's not eating at all,' I say as he unpacks a feast from cardboard boxes. 'Is there nothing you can do? Can you put her on a drip or something? I feel like she's given up the fight, and I'm not ready for that.'

He grabs some cutlery from the sideboard in the kitchen and lays it on the table in a pile.

'Here's the thing. It's understandable to find it upsetting when a loved one who is dying stops eating. But your mum's waning appetite is a sign that she's nearing the end of her struggle. It won't be what kills her now.'

'But can't we—I don't know, delay things slightly?' The panic is rising and threatens to overflow.

Noah hands me a plate. 'Forcing her body to process food won't do her any good at this point, and it could cause her discomfort or distress. Our digestive processes require so much energy. Your mum's body doesn't have the resources to handle extra nutrition anymore, so she's using up her own stores instead. Hence the weight loss. Nature is very efficient that way.'

We sit, and he puts a serving spoon in each container, piling perfectly roasted aubergine with black garlic yoghurt —my absolute favourite—onto my plate.

Having Noah explain what's happening with Mum in such a logical way makes me feel—not better, but more reassured.

'Okay,' I say. 'It's hard to watch, but it makes sense.'

'I know it's hard. Right now, everything we do is to maximise your mum's comfort so she can pass with the same grace and dignity with which she's lived her life. That's our priority, for her, and for you and Ally.

'It might sound strange, but this time can be very sacred. In a weird way, experiencing death can be almost as sacred as experiencing birth—you're standing at the edge of a portal that's totally beyond our human comprehension, and all you can do is watch in awe.'

'I'm scared of seeing her die,' I confess, 'but I'm also scared of missing it. And I'm dreading it, obviously, but I'm also wondering how long this is going to drag out, because I don't want it to be any more prolonged for Mum than it needs to be. Does that sound awful?'

'It sounds extremely normal.' Noah puts a quick hand on mine. 'And one thing we've seen again and again is poor relatives hanging around, and sleeping on sofas, terrified that if they leave, their loved one will die alone. And as soon as they pop to the loo, or treat themselves to a shower, sure enough, their relative or friend passes.'

'Oh, God. That's awful. That's exactly what I'm afraid—I was going to stay here tonight, if that's okay?'

'I can see why it seems awful, but it happens so often

that many of us in the palliative world share a theory: that people who are dying feel compelled to hold on for the sake of their loved ones, even though they're more than ready to pass, and as soon as they're left alone, they can make the crossing. For what it's worth, I think your mum's got another few days left in her. But of course you're welcome to stay here tonight, if it makes you feel better. We can make up the sofa in her room for you.'

I take a bite of perfectly marinated and charred cauliflower. I didn't realise how starving I was until I saw Noah with that bag and my body had an instant Pavlovian response.

'Thanks. That would be great.' I pull myself together. I should enjoy this heavenly, unexpected interlude with Noah. 'This is delicious,' I tell him. 'Let's talk about something less depressing. How is your week going?'

He shoots me a subdued smile. 'I'm surviving. I miss you.' His brown eyes are liquid as he holds my gaze. 'I'm making my schedule as crazy as possible to keep myself occupied.'

It's weird how much easier it makes the pain to bear when I know we're both in it together. 'I miss you too,' I whisper. 'So much. And I'm doing the same.'

'So I've seen. How was Fashion Week?'

'Crazy. Brutal. And fun, in a totally superficial kind of way.'

'Good. You deserve some fun at the moment. Have you signed Burberry yet?'

'No. I told them I wasn't prepared to take any big steps while Mum's so close to death.' It's partially true, but the rest of the truth is that every time I think of locking myself into that contract with Jackson for five more years, a wall of panic rises up inside me. So I'm avoiding and ignoring it for now. I change the subject. 'What are you up to this weekend?'

He grins. 'I'm cooking dinner for a few friends on Sunday—my signature Beef Wellington. Two couples I'm close to—they both met at med school, so we've all been friends for years. And they've each got a toddler, so the flat should get a workout.'

An image of Noah flashes into my mind's eye, sleeves rolled up and an apron on, moving purposefully around his kitchen and joking with his friends while flashing his gorgeous forearms. Being all cute and competent with the babies. And hosting two couples without a date of his own. The physical pain is excruciating and the tears that are never far from the surface at the moment spring to my eyes.

'Hey.' He leans over and squeezes my arm. 'What is it?'

'Nothing. I'm fine—it's so stupid. It just sounds perfect. I wish I could be there.'

'I wish you could too.' There's a pause as he runs his thumb across my sweater sleeve and we both allow ourselves a moment of fantasy before his face creases into a smile. 'I bet you'd be a great help in the kitchen.'

'That's so unfair!'

'Do you actually cook?'

'Well, no, but—'

'I rest my case.' He whistles. 'Sounds like I had a lucky escape. Bloody useless.'

'You're such a dick.'

'I know for a fact'—he helps himself to more aubergine—'that if you were there, I would be completely ignored all night. Completely. It'd be like that scene in *Notting Hill* where she goes to his friends' house for dinner. Everyone would be star-struck.'

'They would not.'

'They would. Fact.'

When we've finished eating, Noah grabs a blanket and two pillows from a cupboard and his hoodie from his office. 'Come on. Let's go get some sleep.'

'What?' I stare blankly as he pulls the hoodie on over his head.

'I'm going to stay with you. You're not doing this alone.'

'What? Noah—don't be ridiculous. Of course you're not. You need to go home and get some sleep.'

'I'm a doctor, darling.' His expression is soft. 'That means I have an advanced degree in sleeping absolutely anywhere. I promise you.'

He takes me up to Mum's room and kicks off his shoes, sitting at one end of the sofa. He puts one pillow on his lap, wedging the other behind his head, and holds out the blanket to me. 'Come on.'

'Seriously, Noah,' I whisper. 'This is going to be so uncomfortable for you.'

'I have nowhere else to be, and nowhere I'd rather be. Lie.'

And so I sigh in defeat and lie down on the sofa, resting my head on Noah's pillowed lap and curling my legs up. I face away from him, towards Mum, whose even breathing is a small source of comfort. But not as much comfort as the feeling of Noah's body under mine.

He brushes some strands of hair lightly off my face. 'I'm getting my night with you at last. Just not quite how I envisaged it. Now, sleep well, darling.'

I sleep fitfully, or at least that's how it feels, vaguely conscious of nurses tiptoeing in during the night to tend to Mum. In the early hours, I sink into an exhausted sleep. And when I wake, Mum is still out for the count and the blanket is down around my waist. Noah's hand has snuck under my sweater and is splayed against my stomach, and my own hand is pressing down on his, holding onto it for dear life. I'm stiff and exhausted, but a warm glow emanates from where our skin touches, and spreads throughout my abdomen, and it's the best feeling I've had all week. It's the best feeling in the world.

I swivel onto my back, clamping onto his hand so it slides around my waist as I turn. I look up at him just in time to see him stir. And I smile at the warmth in his eyes when he surfaces and clocks where we are. His eyes flick over to her mum and back to my face, before landing on our entwined hands.

'Oh, wow,' he whispers. 'Sorry about that.' He moves his hand reluctantly off my waist and uses it to rake my hair gently back. It feels amazing.

'Don't be sorry.' I stretch luxuriously. 'I loved it. Do you grope all your guests' family members when they stay over?'

He smiles down at me, as if this innocent night together has been as much a gift for him as it has been for me. 'Just the prettiest ones.'

35

HONOR

My world has shrunk to one room in one building. Ally's, too. As we sit by Mum's bed, we marvel aloud at the fact that the event we've dreaded all our lives, and in particular since we got the diagnosis, is nearly upon us. And yet, instead of being in a blind panic, we're prepared. Resigned, almost.

It's the strangest twilight zone, this limbo between a loved one's life and death. I've known Mum since before I was conscious, when my only awareness was of her heartbeat and the cradle of her body, and yet, sometime in the next few hours (or days, but Elena and Noah think hours), she will slip away and cease to exist on this plane.

I've read my fair share of Eckhardt Tolle, but it's still a head fuck of epic proportions. And yet, the knowledge of what's hanging over us is allowing us this brief period of incredible peace, as though life is suspended and everything is possible. I feel it, and Ally feels it, and I really believe Mum feels it, because everything about her breathing and her countenance is serene.

I should be holding onto this moment harder; I thought

I would be clawing at it, desperate to get Mum to hold on through sheer force of will. But instead, the calm inevitability that surrounds our little trio like a cloak has bewitched me, and I find myself content to simply live it. Maybe it's because Mum's death is so certain, and so imminent, but I'm hyper-present in a way I usually fail spectacularly to be.

Right here, right now, in this moment, there is a pulse flowing through Mum's veins, though it's so faint that we can no longer feel it at her wrists as we hold her hands, and there is air flowing through her lungs, and for once in my crazy, striving life, that's enough to be grateful for.

We both stayed here last night. No sofa-time this time; we've been in these chairs all night. Keeping a vigil. And, more importantly, keeping Mum company. Whatever Noah may have said about people sometimes finding it easier to die alone, I'm not taking the chance of letting her feel abandoned in her final minutes.

The curtains are open. We kept them open all night—it felt less isolating, being able to see the glow of streetlights out there and know that for most people, life is going on as normal. The remnants of a beautiful late October dawn still streak the sky. I stare out at it and shiver as full-body goose bumps hit me.

'You okay?' Ally asks. She looks like I feel; her face is white and exhausted and drawn.

'Yeah.' I wiggle my shoulders to shake off the sensation that just hit me. They're stiff as hell from a night in a chair preceded by a night on a sofa. 'I just had déjà vu—or something. That sky reminds me of when Serena was born. We waited all night for me to dilate enough, and by the time I was ready to push, the sky was exactly like that, and the air felt so similar to how it feels now. Like it was full of... I don't know, electricity and expectation.

'It was the most magical feeling then, waiting for this new soul to come into the world. I don't know why I feel the exact same way now. Probably sleep deprivation.'

'Oh, babe. I suppose birth and death are not dissimilar; they're both a total fucking mystery.' Ally looks down at Mum and her forehead pinches. 'Do you think she's still here?'

An instant swell of panic replaces my equilibrium. 'I don't know.' I look at Mum. It's so hard to tell—I can't see her chest rising, but her breaths have been so faint all night. I stand, and crouch over her, and hover the side of my face to just above her mouth, but I can't pick up any breath. I feel like a helpless kid, and a glance at Ally tells me she feels the same.

I need a grown up—someone who knows what the hell they're doing. I hit the call button, and a moment later, Karen, one of the lovely nurses, appears.

'I think she might be gone.' I'm whispering, because if Mum's still alive, I don't want to freak her out. I stroke Mum's hand as if she's the child and I'm the responsible adult and I'm trying to reassure her that everything's okay.

Karen's face goes solemn, and she comes over and puts a couple of fingers to Mum's neck.

'I can't feel a pulse.' She puts her hand gently on my shoulder. 'I'll just page Noah.'

Ally and I stare at each other across the bed until Noah shows up, a stethoscope already in his ears, and I have a fleeting and completely inappropriate flashback to our role-plays before the part of my brain responsible for basic human decency pulls me to the present moment. He feels her neck with his fingers and uses the stethoscope to listen to her heart, before pulling out the earpieces and bowing his head.

'I'm afraid your mother's gone. Honor, Ally, I'm so very sorry for your loss.' He checks his watch and turns to Karen and tells her in the same low, reverent voice, 'Time of death, oh-eight-fourteen.'

And just like that, the mysterious veil between life and death drops, and my dam bursts, and all the equilibrium and quiet resignation I've been feeling this past night is submerged in a tidal wave of grief. Mum is gone prematurely—both our parents are gone prematurely—and the world will never be quite the same again.

I cry as Ally rounds the bed to hug me and weep onto my shoulder before slipping out to call Ted, and I cry as Noah takes me in his arms and holds me, and I wonder if he'll let me cry on him for as long as I need. Because I know Ted will be on his way as soon as he gets the kids off to school, and my desire to have Jackson wade in here and comfort me is non-existent.

~

Mum and I had a chat yesterday, during a brief period of wakefulness for her before Ally turned up to join me on the night shift, and that it was the last proper conversation we ever had imbues it with even more solemnity in my mind, when I replay the scene now.

'I saw you and Noah last night.' All she's capable of is a croaky, laboured whisper, but I can hear her well enough.

'Did you?' I stroke her hair away from her face.

'I woke when they changed my catheter. I saw you asleep with him. What are you doing, darling?'

My instant reaction is defence. 'We were just sleeping—he was keeping me company. It wasn't anything more.'

She tuts. 'I don't mean that.' She's quiet for a moment, catching her breath. 'Don't tell me you two don't belong together. When are you going to take a deep look inside and go after what you really want, rather than what you think you should want?'

Her unexpected insight and the generosity of her advice hit me right in the chest, and the mere suggestion that I should allow myself to entertain the idea of being with Noah brings tears to my eyes. Because the only way I know how to survive is to pick a prize and keep my eye on it and not allow myself any distractions. And I've chosen my prize; I did that a long time ago. And I can't veer off course now. I'm not allowed.

'I don't think I know what I want anymore. Or—I'm worried that if I let myself change my mind, it will say things about me.'

'Say what about you?'

'That I'm fickle. Or I don't put the work in. Or that I'm a bad parent. I can't just go after what I might want—I have to think about the family.'

'Darling. I may not agree with the lifestyle you and Jackson lead, but Rollo and Serena are two of the most well-adjusted, delightful children I've ever met, so kudos to you. And you're allowed to change your mind about what you want. You don't need to ask anyone else's permission. It's *your* life. If you were lying here in thirty years' time, dying, who would you want holding your hand? Jackson or Noah?'

Oh my God. *Oh my God.* Fucking hell. It's Noah. When Mum puts it like that, there's no question. Jackson isn't even in the picture. I can't answer, but I'm pretty sure my face tells Mum my choice.

'Well, then.' She nods. 'Whew. Give me a moment. I'm so tired. But I need to say this, darling.'

We sit together in silence for a few moments, and I'm on tenterhooks as I wait for her to impart this nugget of advice, pleading for her to find the strength.

'You always pushed yourself. And we encouraged it, supported it, cheered you on. You've always been so single-minded. I don't know where you get the energy. And you've done so well, but you've paid such a high price.

'And you are allowed to walk away. You're allowed to grow as a person, and find new things that bring delight and meaning and purpose to your life, and you're allowed to choose happiness over success. Remember the sunk cost fallacy, darling. Digging your heels in just because you've already invested so much in this path is plain stupid. And you, my darling, are anything but stupid.'

She sinks back into her pillows, but she squeezes my hand with more force than I thought she was capable of, and I squeeze back. She's right, of course. I've used the sunk cost fallacy a million times in business. We use it to evaluate when to shut down underperforming products and when to double down and put more investment behind them. But I never thought about using it in my *life*.

'It makes total sense when you say it like that. But I can't help but thinking I'm being selfish. Or flaky. Or weak, by walking out on my husband and our brand just because I'm in love.'

Mum sighs, and I'm sure it's exasperating for her to have to dig deep for energy in her final hours on earth because her daughter is being obtuse.

'It's not weak to acknowledge that you want something

different and to go after it. It's strong. You'd be weak if you knew it and were too afraid to act on it. And this isn't just about men, darling. It's about what they represent. Jackson represents power and money and success, and you already have that on your own. And he'll always be the kids' father.

'Noah represents deep love and fidelity. He's an extremely compassionate person. Look at what he's devoted his life to. God knows where I'd be right now if you hadn't met him—probably dying under strip-lighting in some ghastly hospital. It seems to me that what Noah represents is exactly what you need at this very juncture of your life. You might even say it's fate.'

Noah as a way of life. The mere idea of it makes me feel warm and fuzzy and loved. Mum's right. Again. Everything about Noah is good and true. He's a person who cares deeply about his fellow humans, and has done amazing work to make other people's dying moments profound and beautiful. It's not just about the attraction of him. It's about what I'd be like if I were with someone like that. What my life would be like.

'I'll make a deal with you.' Mum's voice is fading; she'll drop into sleep in moments. 'When I cross, if I see that you're with Noah, I'll send you a sign to tell you I approve.'

'Mum!' How ridiculous. I roll my eyes.

'Humour me. I'm dying. You have to.'

'Are you scared?'

'God, no. I'm going to be with your father again. How on earth could I be scared of that? It's about bloody time.'

That sends me over the edge. The idea that Mum and Dad could soon be together again on some parallel and unseeable plane of consciousness. I bow my head and shake with emotion. 'Tell him I love him, will you? Tell him I miss him *so* much.'

'My darling girl. He knows that. But I will. Now.' She squeezes my hand. 'Pick a sign.'

'I don't know... a unicorn?'

'Too easy. They're everywhere.'

'All right, then. A... turquoise unicorn with... purple stripes. And an orange horn.'

'Good grief.' Mum's practically dead, but aesthetic sense is still easily offended. 'Sounds ghastly. But if you do it, I'll send it. And you'll know how happy I am for you.'

36

HONOR

'How are you feeling about tomorrow?' Jackson asks as he tops up my glass of flawless Puligny Montrachet. He's also cooked me my favourite supper: hake on a bed of chorizo and lentils. He's a good boy, when he wants to be.

But it's not enough.

And I'm not sure why I ever thought it was.

I'm not trying to reinvent history here, to tell myself I'm a wronged wife. I'm not. I have a lifestyle that only a tiny, tiny fraction of a percent of the world's population enjoys, and I've made the necessary choices at each step of the way.

I suppose, with hindsight, those choices were forks in the road, but I never treated them like that. With my tunnel vision firmly in place, I've treated the direction of my life like one of those long, dead-straight, dusty roads you see in American movies. I've blithely ignored any turnoff that might deviate me from my desired destination.

That destination has changed, and one hell of a fork lies ahead of me. And I'll take that fork without a backwards glance.

I glance down at my speech notes for tomorrow and answer my husband's well-meaning question.

'I'm ready. I've practiced this speech a million times, and I trust Miles to have everything ready at The Montague's end.'

'That's great, babe. But how do you *feel*?'

Jackson's been a bit freaked out by my apparent ability to keep my shit together in the past ten days since Mum died. I've gone into my preferred coping mode: over-functioning. So the private cremation a couple of days ago went off without a hitch, and I've planned tomorrow's memorial to the last detail.

I've also worked my arse off this past week, partly because so much stuff piled up while Mum was in her last days, and partly to keep myself from thinking too much. I've avoided Noah—Good Vibes was kind enough to courier Mum's stuff over so I didn't need to face him—and while Jackson's been around, I'm aware I've held off on leaning on him too much emotionally. I'm preparing to cut my emotional ties with him, and while he's been sweet this week, I've had years to practice living my daily life without having him around.

'I feel good about it. The cremation was the bit I was dreading; now that's over, we can have some fun celebrating Mum's life. I think she'd love it.'

I know she would. Miles has everything in hand, and we even have her favourite florist doing the blooms for the function room. It will be beautiful.

'Good for you, babe. I look forward to toasting her.'

I can't avoid the conversation anymore. In my head, it needs to happen tonight because I know Noah will be there tomorrow, and I can't bear to see him and not tell him how I feel, what I want. I'm suspended in this terrifying chasm between the present I have and the future I've chosen, but I can't have the latter without severing ties with the former.

I take a sip of wine and swivel on my bar stool to face Jackson.

'I need to talk to you.'

A sour, sick feeling hits my stomach as I say it. This is it. It's so hard to do this without resorting to cliches. *It's not you, it's me. I can't do this anymore.* But cliches are overused precisely because they're universal truths.

'Honey.' I take his hand. There's no point in beating around the bush. 'I've been doing a lot of soul-searching these past few months, and I don't want this life anymore. This—ridiculous fame thing. I don't want it for myself, and I don't want it for the kids. It's far too high a price to pay for whatever we're trying to achieve.'

'Okay.' I can see his cogs turning, trying to find a way through the problem. 'Right. Well, I can—we can speak to Mara, maybe? And—'

'No, no.' I interrupt him. 'Sorry, I'm not being clear. I know that's your life. I'm not asking you to walk away from your career. I'm saying I want out.'

'Out?'

Shit. That was probably a little too abrupt. Those blue eyes I've loved for so long are wide with shock, and now that freedom is on the horizon, I have a pang of preemptive grief for everything I'll be giving up. Him, and that aura of magic that still captivates me, despite myself. These things are never clear-cut. Of course I'll miss my husband. Our marriage. Our life. But I know, in a profound way, that if Noah lets me choose him, I'll be doing the kindest thing for myself that I've possibly ever done.

'I want a divorce, Jackson. I'm sorry to land it on you like this, but there it is.'

'A *divorce*? But—but what about Burberry?'

I laugh out loud then: I hurl a scoff right out of my body, because his reaction is so un-bloody-believable and yet so fucking predictable. Getting the ink dry on our next piece of high-paying publicity. Seriously.

'Burberry is not happening, because every time I think about locking myself into this for five more years, my anxiety goes through the roof. Come on, Jackson. I'm telling you I don't want our life or our marriage anymore. Burberry should be the least of our worries right now.'

'I'm sorry.' He holds up his hands. 'You're right. I'm just—in shock. I thought this was what you wanted; you've always been as ambitious as me. You know what—I suspect the past few months have taken their toll on you. It's been a lot to juggle, and now you're grieving. You've just buried your mum, for fuck's sake. I think anyone would advise you not to make big decisions when you're in such an emotional state.'

It's a little patronising and a lot sensible. It's exactly what I've told myself, and my therapist has told me.

'Look. I agree with you. But I've had weeks to think this over, and honestly, I owe Mum a debt of gratitude, because knowing I was going to lose her has given me a real kick up the arse.'

'But why not take it slowly, babe? Why not let things settle down and see how you feel in a month or two? This is your whole life you're talking about.'

Exactly. It's my whole life. That's why I can't live this life for a moment longer than I have to.

'Because,' I say slowly, 'there's something I haven't told you. I had a—relationship with someone over the summer, and it's not going on anymore, but I'm in love with him.'

The guy reels, and despite everything he's done over the course of our marriage, in this moment I pity him.

'What the actual *fuck*?'

I can see he's about to go into full wounded-male-ego mode. 'Be *very* careful about how you judge me on this, Jackson.'

He takes a deep breath and visibly collects himself, running his hand over the top of his shaved head. 'But you didn't tell me.'

'No, I didn't tell you, and that was wrong of me. But you and Leila were all over the tabloids at the time, so I figured I deserved a bit of fun.'

'Is that what it was? A bit of fun? Who is this dickhead?'

'That's all I thought it would be, but I got in too deep. And he's not a dickhead. It's Noah.'

'*Noah?* Fuck.' He pushes himself away from the bar and gets off his stool, pacing around the island, before stopping and dropping forward, putting his head in his hands. 'Was it going on in France?'

I swallow. 'Yeah. That's where it started—it was the night that server from Marmont hit the news. I was seriously pissed off, and so was he, on my behalf, and it all just... went from there, really. I'm sorry I didn't tell you.'

'God, so those photos of you guys...'

'They were real.'

'I'm such an idiot! I just never thought you would—'

'What? Sink to your level? Or get disillusioned with what we have and look for some human connection elsewhere?'

He groans. 'Both, I guess. Not just because I expect you to be more principled than me, but I didn't realise you were unhappy. And now I feel like a total jackass. And—'

'What?'

He laughs without humour. 'It feels really, really shitty being on this end of it, and I know I have no right to be, but I'm seriously fucked off. I want to punch his lights out.'

'Jackson!'

'I'm just saying.' He holds up his hands. 'I won't, okay? But you said it's over? But you think you're'—he grimaces—'in love with him.'

I slip down from my bar stool and move around the island to join my husband. I put a hand on his back and rub it.

'I know it's a lot to take in. It had to finish when the paps got us. I had to deny everything. But I realised later that it was a knee-jerk decision and I hadn't really thought through what I wanted. And yeah, I love him, but he doesn't know that. He thinks I chose you.'

This is a really, really shit conversation. I'm hurting my husband, who I love despite everything, and I'm standing at the edge of a precipice, and somewhere, a few miles away, is a wonderful, caring man who's hopefully still in love with me, which means he's also hurting. But not for much longer.

'What do you want, Hon? Like, what do you really want?'

His tone is defeated and curious rather than hostile, so I take the question at face value.

'I want to be with him. Properly. I want a life with him. And I want to be known for my success as a businesswoman and not as one half of a celebrity couple.'

He juts his lower lip thoughtfully and turns to face me. Our faces are centimetres apart.

'That's a lot of change. I mean, I get that you have feelings for him, but he's been a big part of the whole process of your mum dying. Are you sure you're not projecting? It would be totally normal to do that. Maybe you're fixating on him because he's been an authority figure at a really difficult time in your life. It's pretty fucking unethical of him, come to think of it.'

'Stop that. It's not unethical. He's done everything he can to maintain an arm's length relationship with us. We had a totally different doctor—you met her. It's not about any of that. It's him. He's a wonderful person who's devoted his life to helping families who are in great pain. That's why I'm in love with him.'

'Fuck's sake.' Jackson rubs at a non-existent spot on the marble. 'Of course the guy's got to be a fucking saint.'

'I know it's hard. And I'm aware it'll be a lot to ask of the kids, too. I'm hoping that, when the dust settles, having two amazing and very different guys in their lives will be a positive for them. If Noah agrees to take a chance on me and our crazy baggage.'

'Of course he will. Who wouldn't want you? I just wish I'd known. I wish this was all happening differently.'

'I know, and I'm sorry. But he's going to be there tomorrow, and I need to talk to him. I need to see if he's willing to give us a chance. But I need you not to do anything to scare him off tomorrow, okay? Please, honey.'

Jackson sighs, and growls, and digs the heels of his hands into his eye sockets. 'Okay. But only because it's a funeral.'

'Thank you.'

We stand there for a moment in silence, contemplating the seismic changes we're both facing in life.

'I can't believe you were unhappy and I didn't know,' Jackson says. 'We're good together, babe. You and I are similar creatures—that's why we work so well together, even if our marriage isn't the most conventional.'

'We are similar, but I do wonder if that's a good thing.' I look down at my glass. 'It's done amazing things for our careers, but I'm not sure it's healthy. And I can't stop thinking that maybe you figured that out long before me, and that's why you fell for that teacher. And I've been feeling so bad about it, because the way I handled that—well, I'm not proud of it. And what if I cost you your chance at happiness? What if she was a better fit for you?'

Jackson is quiet for a moment. 'Jenna was definitely special—I could really have fallen for her. I did fall for her. But I wouldn't have left you. And I can't exactly walk away from the fame stuff unless I retire. It's part of the gig for me, and I have to accept that, and any woman who's in my life has to accept that too.'

I ask the question I've been wanting to ask. 'And Leila? Tell me honestly, how do you feel about her?'

Another pause, and a smile. 'She's... she's a good one. There's something there, probably more than I've admitted to you, babe, or to myself, to be honest. And she gets it, the fame thing. Or, at least, she'll have to get it, because *Vet*'s going to send her stratospheric. She's amazing in it. So, yeah. If my wife's dumping my sorry arse, Leila might be up for comforting me.'

'Hmm. I suspect if you and Leila were to get it on properly, it may be a silver lining for Mara, too?' I wiggle my eyebrows at him. 'A new golden couple for her to go crazy with?'

'Two new golden couples.' He nudges her shoulder. 'You and the pretty doctor.'

'I'll have you know, the press is never getting a photo of me and Noah again.'

37

NOAH

This is one of the most sophisticated cocktail parties I've ever been to, let alone funerals. We're in a stunning room at The Montague with ornate plasterwork and pale blue silk-covered walls. There are candles on every surface, and huge silver bowls of white flowers everywhere.

But it's not just the decor that's impressive. Well-heeled doesn't begin to describe the people here. There are plenty of immaculately groomed, silver-haired men and women who I assume are long-time friends of Stephanie. Honor told me a few weeks ago that the memorial would be invitation-only and that she'd be giving Jackson's celebrity crew a miss, but looking around, I'm reminded that Honor has her fair share of impressive friends.

I've left Elena on duty at Good Vibes and brought two of the nurses who cared for Stephanie, but Mum and Dad are here too, along with Angus and Evelyn, Stacey, and plenty of Honor's other glossy friends. I've even spotted an actual Oscar-winning actor, Ellery Hart, chatting to Astrid Carmichael. Holy shit.

But even Ellery, in all her youthful, blonde-haired glory, can't hold a torch to Honor. I clock her as soon as we arrive. She's hard to miss, in a stunning golden dress that's all full-skirted and sparkly (the invitation said *Dress Code: Strictly Cocktail Wear, at Stephanie's insistence!*), and I'm conscious of her location in the room every painful second I'm there.

The past week-and-a-half since Stephanie passed has been brutal. Bleak. It was like the sun went out when Honor left, and every time I walk in the front door of Good Vibes, I'm reminded that there's no chance of her showing up and brightening my day.

The guillotine has dropped on any semblance of a relationship with her, and the cold turkey is killing me. Even though I've upped my running routine. Even though I'm working all hours, holding funding meetings and organising an international conference on the future of palliative care and doing as much clinical work as I can. I'm still burning up with how much I miss her, and seeing her today is heavenly torture.

Eventually, she makes her way around to our little gaggle. She's the consummate hostess, serene and smiling, seemingly floating through the crowd of well-wishers with ease and grace, although it must be emotionally draining to be on the receiving end of countless other people's grief and memories and condolences.

She doesn't let her game-face slip until she reaches us. She hugs the nurses and thanks them for coming, and then she's there, in front of me, and we grin at each other despite ourselves. I go to kiss her, but she pulls me in for a hug. 'I'm so pleased to see you,' she whispers in my ear. 'Thank you for coming.'

I give myself a second to lean into the deliciousness of the hug—her warmth and her scent and the satiny skin of her upper back under my hand—before I release her and straighten my suit jacket up. Jackson's around here somewhere—I saw him from a distance earlier—and I don't want to be guilty of any impropriety here, at her mother's memorial.

'I have to go make my speech now,' she says under her breath, 'but I wanted you to know how happy I am that you're here. Not just for Mum, but for me. And I really, really want to chat to you later, so don't think about pulling a stunt like slipping away when I'm looking the other way. Okay?'

She waggles her finger at me. She's got my number; I'm planning on doing precisely that after an acceptable chunk of time has passed. I've been counting down the days till I'd see her again, but now I'm here, it hurts too much. The wound is raw again.

But this isn't about me. Tonight is Honor's night, so whatever she needs from me, I'll give gladly.

HONOR

Ally reads Mary Oliver's Wild Geese so beautifully that I see tissues being fished surreptitiously out of pockets and handbags around the room from where I stand behind her. And then it's my turn on the little stage The Montague's team has erected. Before I begin, I take a moment to look around this beautiful space.

Miles has surpassed himself. Millions of reflected candle flames dance in the mirrored panels around the room, and enormous bunches of white gardenias and anemones and roses and ranunculus and tulips spill from silver julep cups and punch bowls. It's stunning, it's elegant, and it's Mum. She'd adore this, just as she'd adore the lavish compliments everyone I've spoken to has paid her.

Jackson is standing inconspicuously in an alcove near the front of the room. He's been amazing, despite the bombshell I dropped on him last night. But it's not him I seek out as my eyes scan the room. It's Noah, and he's standing right where I left him. When my eyes meet his and he smiles and nods encouragingly, I know I'm in good hands.

'Thank you for coming,' I begin. 'Mum production-managed every part of this evening, except for the drinks, where Ally and I vetoed her because we felt having a roomful of mourners on straight martinis would be indecorous. She did, however, insist that my eulogy be revoltingly fawning, so what this speech lacks in accuracy, it makes up in flattery.'

I get my first laugh, and I'm away. I cover Mum's professional successes, parenting abilities and personality quirks with many more laughs along the way. Years of living in the full glare of the media spotlight have made me an old hand at public speaking, but this speech is different. It's the final moment where I will really get a chance to pay homage to Mum's full and wonderful life, and I want to make it count.

I make sure to give Noah and his team a heartfelt thank you for making the process of Mum's death as meaningful and stress-free as possible.

'We made a choice to entrust the Good Vibes team with one of the most important and potentially traumatic events of our lives,' I tell the room, 'and they rewarded us for that choice a hundredfold. They told us that death could be a profoundly beautiful experience, and they were right. Ally and I will never forget how peaceful Mum was in her final hours, and for that, we can never thank them enough.

'The other reason that Mum was able to cross in such a peaceful manner was because she left this world with no regrets, except perhaps for the premature nature of her passing. She married the love of her life, she loved her career and her children, and, God knows, she lived life vibrantly. She was still demanding martinis and manicures even after she'd walked through the door of the Good Vibes Hospice for the last time.'

A laugh.

'She reminded me of something very important right before she died.' I choke up here, pressure welling up in my jaw and above my cheekbones, and I pause for a second to collect myself before I continue. I find Noah in the crowd. I don't let go of that sight; I don't need my notes for this.

'She told me none of us is the Queen. Thank God. None of us has such a huge burden of duty that we must sacrifice our happiness for the greater good. And it follows that we don't need anyone else's permission to be happy. Really, the only person who can give us permission to be happy is us. Whether that happiness looks like a career change, or a lifestyle change, or choosing the life companion you want holding your hand as you die, the only person who can bestow that act of kindness on you is you yourself.'

I'm looking straight at Noah. Jackson and the rest of the crowd may as well not exist.

'And I'll be forever grateful for that advice. Thank you.'

38

HONOR

Girlfriends are everything. They understand instinctively when you need a hug, or a distraction, or silence, or words. They rally around without needing to be asked. And that's what my friends do for me after my eulogy. They show up in a stylish swarm and spirit me away to an empty table in a quiet corner of the room, while Ted comforts Ally and Jackson does the duty circuit, charming the pants off everyone. I just hope he stays the hell away from Noah.

Stacey has swiped two bottles of champagne from the bar, and Evelyn sets to work filling everyone up. Astrid has brought Ellery over, too: she's the dearest girl, and Astrid and I have been acting as honorary aunts to her for the past five years, since her breakout success in the movie industry.

'Jeez, Honor, that was so freaking beautiful,' Stacey says. 'You have such a way with words, girl.'

'Amen to that.' Astrid lifts her glass.

'Would you ever consider going back to TV?' Ellery asks. 'Honestly, you're so impressive. Sunrise must rue the day they let you walk.'

I shake my head. '*Definitely* not. In fact, I have some big changes I want to make in my life, and I thank Mum for that. Starting with the fame thing. I want to reduce my level of exposure to the press. Evelyn, you've done an amazing job of that. Your profile as a businesswoman is higher than ever, but you seem to live below the radar in your private life, and I want to know your secret.'

Evelyn grins. 'You may want to consider swapping your famous husband out for a handsome but totally unknown farmer, in that case. It's worked very well for me.'

I smile my secret smile. She has no idea how close she is to the truth, but now's not the time to share that confidence. Not quite yet.

'Ellery, she won't be asking you for any advice on avoiding the tabloids.' Astrid elbows her good-naturedly. 'You are all over the bloody papers at the moment, my dear.'

Ellery groans and dips her head dramatically. 'Tell me about it. And for *all* the wrong reasons.'

'Seriously?' I ask. 'What's up?'

'Have you been living under a rock?' Astrid asks.

'Astrid! She's been burying her freaking mother! Give her a break!' Stacey mock-glares at Astrid, who turns bright red.

'I'm so sorry. Of course you have. I'll let you off.'

'Give me the gossip, Elle,' I urge Ellery. 'Please.'

'It's bad.' Ellery shakes her head. She's absolutely gorgeous, with skin no amount of retinol will ever procure for me at this age. Blonde and petite and a huge blunt fringe —she's a knockout.

'Please.' I hold my glass out to Stacey for a refill. 'You have to. My mum just died. I need to be distracted, or at least to enjoy someone else's misfortune.'

Ellery sighs. 'Champagne and schadenfreude are your bag right now. I get it.'

'Champagne and schadenfreude!' Stacey cries. 'Please! I have to have that on a t-shirt!'

We all scream with laughter, and my peripheral vision catches a few quizzical looks from Mum's generation.

'Whoops. Maybe we're being a little raucous for a funeral,' Evelyn stage-whispers.

'It's like the funeral scene in *Ted Lasso*, when Rebecca and Keeley and Sassy all get bollocked by the vicar for screeching too loudly.'

'Bags be Sassy!' Stacey puts her hand up, and we all look at her.

'Yep, no one's going to argue with that,' Astrid mumbles, and I snigger.

'Yesss. That means I get Ted.' She punches the air.

'They can all sod off,' I say. 'This is a hotel, not a church. Anyway, Ellery, you were going to distract me with your torrid tabloid gossip?'

'Ugh. It's so bad.' She sighs. 'Okay. Remember Josh Lander?'

'Yikes.' I draw in my breath. Josh and Ellery's history is the stuff of celebrity *nightmare*. Literally, it's any actor's worst dream. I've never stopped being angry at him for what he did to our sweet, beautiful Ellery. I feel sick for her for a moment. 'How could they possibly have anything to say about you two after all these years?'

Ellery had a brief and very intense whirlwind romance with Josh Lander, douchebag from hell, about five years ago. He swept her off her feet at the Cannes Film Festival when she was an ingenue and he was one of the hottest movie stars on the planet. They dated for a few months, with some very public displays of affection and commitment along the way, and she ended up at his family home for the 4th July weekend with several of their (his) friends.

I'll never forget the photos. They were all over every news outlet on the planet. A few guys (his douchebag frat-boy buddies) and Elle all wearing *I [heart] JL* t-shirts. Twitter went mental, and a few days after she got back to the UK he dumped her. Via his agent. And she never heard from him again.

She was a mess. I remember Astrid and I seeing her at an industry event a few months later and she was still distraught. He broke her. Until she won a fucking Oscar the following February, pulled her amazing, Cambridge-educated self back together and got back out there. Meanwhile, her star has soared higher and higher, and last I heard, his first post-rehab movie bombed. Now *that's* what I call karma.

'Well,' she says now. 'You may well ask that, and the answer is, we've both been cast to do *Grosvenor*. Together.'

'You are *kidding* me.' *Grosvenor* is a massive new production from the streaming platform Azure, set to jump on the *Bridgerton* bandwagon and take a slice of Netflix's share. My mind reels. Oh, dear Lord. 'As... I can't even say it. As love interests?'

'You've got it.' Her gorgeous little face says it all.

'Sweetheart.' All my own problems are forgotten in the face of this horror. 'How the hell did this happen? What the fuck was your agent thinking?'

'It was a bit of a bait and switch, I suspect. We didn't know they were thinking of him, but they said they'd written the role of Georgiana especially for me. And when I read the script of the pilot, I loved it. Like, loved it. I knew I had to play her. And it wasn't until I was properly besotted with the role that they announced they'd lined He Who Shall Not Be Named up to play the Duke.'

'Ugh! The Duke? And you really want to go ahead with this? Did they not even ask for a chemistry read?'

'No one who saw those two together five years ago would need a chemistry read.' Astrid nods sagely. 'Just saying.'

She's right, of course. The sparks between the two of them were electric. The world fell in love with them, and the world got its heart broken with Elle.

Ellery grimaces, like it's excruciating for her to think about it.

'The thing is, I know this series is the right next step for me. I mean, Jackson's doing the same thing, right? Making the jump from movies into TV? And this role is my dream role, I'm telling you. Except for, maybe, the many parts where I need to get pretend-naked and pretend-intimate with the person I hate most in the world. Oh, God!'

I bristle. 'Jesus, Elle. I hope they're offering you a good intimacy coordinator—'

'Relax, Hon. Believe me, everything's being negotiated to the nth degree, and everything will be fully choreographed.'

'Glad to hear it. Also, remember this, my friend. When you met, he had all the power. Now the world is your oyster! And he's been festering in rehab hell and is making dire movies. He needs this a lot more than you. Which means you. Have. All. The. Power.' I jab her with my finger to make my point.

She shifts uncomfortably. She's always been self-deprecating. 'You're right, I suppose. But I'm still dreading it!'

'Because you hate him and you're worried you'll gouge his eyes out when they allow you close to him?' I ask hopefully.

'No.' Her voice drops to a whisper. 'Because this is my

chance to show him what a huge mistake he made all those years ago, and to make him regret ruining my life in front of the whole world. But what if I fall for him again?'

'You won't.' I'm horrified. 'You couldn't—your sense of self-preservation won't let you.'

'I hope not. I just remember how... magnetic he is. He's very, very hard to resist.' She twists her beautiful mouth. 'You're right. I won't. This is about closure, pure and simple. He'll regret the day he ever dumped me.'

What I wouldn't give for her youth and beauty, though I don't envy Ellery her situation. Maybe I can sneak on set and warn that miserable prick to stay the hell away from her heart. And her knickers.

Ellery's plight has certainly done wonders for distracting me, but a moment later I'm back in the thick of my own life in the most pleasurable way possible, because Noah puts his hand on my shoulder, and smiles, in his usual, hopelessly gorgeous, panty-melting way at the girls, and asks if he can borrow me.

It's time to follow Mum's advice. To choose my happiness. To get my man.

39

NOAH

Honor barely has time to stand before I'm engulfed in a stream of effusive, fragrant hugs from Astrid, Evelyn and Stacey. Stacey gives me a huge smacker on the cheek while Honor laughs at me over her shoulder. Even when they introduce me to Ellery Hart, who I'm pretty star-struck by, I can hardly take my eyes off Honor.

I've been biding my time, chatting to Mum and Dad and soaking up the nurses' excitement—this is a far more glamorous event than their regular evenings off. But I need to slink back to my flat, lick my wounds, and focus on moving forward. Very probably over a few glasses of red. So here I am, checking in with Honor before I go, just like she asked.

It looks like they've been hitting the champagne hard.

'You're all awfully giggly for a funeral,' I tell them. 'I bet Stephanie is having serious FOMO right now.'

'I'm sure she is,' Honor says. 'She's either loving it, or she'll spring a leak in the ceiling and put an end to the party if she sees us all having too much fun.'

'Did you want to have a quick chat?' I ask her, trying to

sound as neutral as possible in front of her sharp-eared friends.

'Definitely. Excuse me, ladies,' she tells the other women, who are all still grinning at him, and she leads me off. 'Over here. Miles gave me a little private annex I can use—he said I might need some quiet time if it all gets too much.'

She locks the door behind us, and we're alone. It's hard to register anything else but her. It would be so easy to pull her to me and bury my nose in her hair, but I don't. I stand awkwardly, stick my free hand in my pocket and sip my champagne.

'That was a beautiful speech.'

I couldn't take my eyes off her at the end; it felt like she was trying to tell me something. But I suspect everyone in the audience felt the same way—that's the power Honor Chapman wields over everyone she touches.

'Thank you.' She clamps her lips together, then parts them. 'Noah. I need to tell you something.' It comes out in a rush. 'I told Jackson last night I want a divorce.'

I stare at her like an idiot.

'I told him I didn't want to be married to him anymore, and that I wanted a less fucked-up life for me and the kids.'

She's looking at me expectantly. 'That's—that's good. Good for you. Sounds sensible.' I glug some champagne.

'I told him I was in love with you.'

I nearly choke on my champagne.

'You told *Jackson* you were in love with *me*?' Holy fuck, is he going to beat me up? I won't stand a chance. He'll beat me to a bloody pulp.

Hang on. *She's in love with me?*

'Yes. Because I am. But I know this is a lot—I don't want to presume anything. I know I'm a pretty fucked-up proposition. But I couldn't be with him anymore. I couldn't pretend, and I miss you. I miss you so much. Every day. And Mum asked me, right before she died, who I wanted holding my hand when I died, and I realised it's you; I only want you, and—'

I snap to my senses and grasp that the woman of my dreams is declaring eternal love to me, and that she's telling me she's getting out of her marriage for me, and I do the only thing that makes any sense. I put down my champagne flute and I close the space between us in a second and take her in my arms. And I kiss her.

The feeling when my lips meet hers is indescribable, because I never thought I would get to do this again. I never thought I'd get to slide my lips against the softness of hers, to rub my thumb along her jaw and thread my fingers through her beautiful, silky hair. To inhale her. To taste her as my tongue finds hers. To understand myself and my place in the world this profoundly through the touch of another person.

I can't get close enough to her. I angle her head with my hand and my tongue dances deeper in her mouth, entangling hers. She moans softly and her fingers burrow under my shirt collar to stroke my neck. I tighten my grip on her. It's unthinkable, now I'm kissing her, that I could ever have lived without this. Without her. And while my body responds to hers, my soul is soaring with the revelation that this isn't it. She's offering me everything.

I break reluctantly away. I have to tell her. I can't have her thinking for a second this isn't what I want. 'I only want you, too. My darling. I'll take everything you're offering, all of it.'

Her face radiates the most beautiful smile, and I trace it with my finger before dropping my head to her collarbone.

Her dress has some kind of corseted bodice with straps tied in big, gauzy bows. I slip one off and graze my lips along the distance from her neck to her shoulder.

'You look like a glass of champagne in this dress,' I murmur. 'I wish I could take it off you and pour my champagne all over you, and lick it off.'

'Hardly standard funeral behaviour,' she says, but her voice is husky. I like to think it's the effect of my kisses and my words. I run my hands over her smooth skin, knocking the second strap out of place. She's so beautiful I can't believe it, her huge, gold-green tiger eyes full of emotion and her mouth red and swollen from my kisses.

'This isn't exactly your average funeral.' I skim my hands over her waist. 'How did Jackson take the news?' I brace myself for the answer.

'He wasn't thrilled. Understatement. But he recognised he didn't have a leg to stand on, and it sounds like he and Leila are more serious than I thought, so really, he's been having his cake and eating it. Anyway, you'll be glad to hear he's promised not to have a go at you. Not tonight, in any case.'

'Thank fuck.' This is truly excellent news. Maybe I can slink out a back door and give him the slip before the evening is over.

'The only thing is, he's worried I'm rushing into the whole divorce-and-new-lifestyle thing. He thinks I'm acting out of grief, and I shouldn't be making big decisions right now.'

'I can see his point.' I reach back up and cup her face in my hands. Studying her. Drinking her in. 'I'd usually agree and advise anyone who's recently bereaved against making big life changes. Except I'm horribly biased in this situation, so I'm liable to be very unethical and advise you to throw it all away for me immediately.'

I nuzzle her neck, and she groans and wraps her arms more tightly around me.

'Seriously, though.' I bury my face in her neck. 'Your husband is right. We should take this slowly, for your sake as well as your kids. And even him, I suppose. Dirty shagger that he is.'

'Says the guy who seduced a married woman. Does taking it slowly mean not having sex anytime soon?'

I come up for air so quickly I practically head butt her. 'Christ, no. We should find a hotel room immediately. Like, upstairs. Now. I meant the big stuff, like divorce, going public, that kind of thing.'

As soon as I say it, I grimace. I can't even imagine the media shit-show this will be for everyone involved.

'You're right.' She nods. 'We need a plan for all that, and especially when telling the kids. But this evening, I just wanted to get my claws into you and make sure you were still kind of into me.'

'I'm still very kind of into you. You are not an easy woman to move on from, Honor Chapman. Ever.' I kiss her gently on her soft, sweet lips and she smiles against my mouth.

'Excellent news. You can break the news to your mum, then.'

EPILOGUE

NOAH

'But I don't wanna go to Richmond Park.' Rollo's face is mutinous. 'It's boring. It doesn't even have a playground.'

I stifle a laugh. It's been a month since Stephanie's funeral, and a month since Honor told me she was leaving Jackson. And while it's been bloody amazing, we've had to tread carefully while she and Jackson have rolled out their "conscious uncoupling" strategy with a small army of advisors.

We've been careful not to be spotted anywhere publicly together, so there have been a lot of hotel rooms over the past four weeks. Not that I'm complaining about that at all. We could be Tripadvisor experts by now. The Montague had the softest bed, The Lanesborough, the best power shower, and The Connaught won the prize for best room service (truffled pizza).

Basically, we've been shagging all over London, and I'm permanently in a sex-and-love-fuelled haze, because there is no feeling like being with Honor and knowing that she's mine alone, that I get a future with her, when the time is right and her kids are sufficiently okay to deal with the idea that their mum has a new man in her life.

Today's a big day: it's the first day we're going out together, in public, and the first time we'll be seen with Honor's kids. But one of the moves she and her publicist have made this month is to withdraw consent for the press to photograph Rollo and Serena, so any published photos of them will be pixellated. It's a small step, but an important one in Honor's journey to claw back some semblance of privacy.

She asked me to come to the house today to spend the day with them, but I have no idea what her plans are. She seemed self-conscious about my seeing her home for the first time, and now I'm here, I understand why.

Holy fuck.

Hector, who's Honor's weekend security detail, picks me up and drives me through the gates of an enormous white stucco villa in the exclusive oval-shaped enclave that is The Boltons. It's only the last weekend in November, but the whole house is already fully decorated for Christmas, and I suspect it wasn't Honor up a ladder, stringing the millions of fairy lights over all the trees in the front garden.

We park in the subterranean garage, thereby giving slip to any paps who may be hanging out of nearby vehicles, and Hector takes me up to the ground floor in a lift. Yes. A lift. And when I step out, Honor's waiting for me in a hallway full of glittering surfaces, and she puts her arms around me so tightly I forget about everything else.

'We're having Family Sunday,' she tells me, her face muffled by my coat.

'What?' I disentangle her gently and gaze at her dear, beautiful face.

'You told once me you wished for Family Sundays. Well,

I know they're not your kids, and I can't call it Family Sunday in front of them because I don't want to freak them out—or you. But I want to give you some version of the day you've been dreaming of.'

I'm blown away. She remembers what I told her, and she remembers that I confessed to seeing her face in my Family Sunday fantasy. I wonder if she remembers that I said I imagined her as my wife.

'You're too much.' I dip my head and kiss her, trapping her in my arms and gently opening her mouth with mine. She melts against me and moans a little.

'Tell me what I said I wanted to do on Family Sunday,' I murmur against her lips.

'Richmond Park.' A kiss. 'Roast lunch, which you'll be cooking, obviously.'

'Mmm hmm. And what will you be doing, exactly?'

'Keeping your glass topped up. Ogling you. Distracting you.'

'Sounds acceptable. And what else?'

'I believe you promised me a family movie which, I should warn you, will probably be *Encanto*. Again.'

'I haven't seen *Encanto*.'

'That makes one of us. And then you promised to drag me off to bed and make love to me once we'd got rid of the kids.'

'I promised my *wife* that. But, seeing as you want me to hold your hand on your deathbed, I'm pretty confident I can lock you down sometime soon. Until then, let's practice.' I kiss her again. She's too kissable. Too loving. Too thoughtful. She's perfect.

She's given me a tour of her home, which is so stunning it's fucking terrifying. Jackson moved into his Knightsbridge pied-à-terre a few weeks back, and apparently he's happy for Honor to keep the house. And now we're negotiating with the kids. Rollo didn't get the Family Sunday memo and I can see Honor's torn between being desperate to uphold my dream schedule to the letter and not wanting to scream at her children in front of me.

'You'll quickly see, Family Sundays aren't all they're cracked up to be,' she says to me through gritted teeth.

I laugh. I'm so thrilled to be here with them, and I'm so relieved neither of the kids has spat in my face or kicked me in the shin for breaking up their mum and dad that I'll take any version of today. It's not worth upsetting the kids over.

'I'm easy,' I tell Rollo. 'If you want to go to a different park, that's cool. But Richmond Park is great for making camps. There are lots of fallen tree trunks. And we can bring a ball and have a kick around. What do you think?'

He looks unconvinced.

'There are lots of deer there, too,' I continue. 'Did you ever see that video of the guy whose dog went nuts chasing the deer in Richmond Park? It went viral.'

His eyebrows shoot up. 'Viral? Can I see it?'

'Sure.' I fish my phone out of my pocket and google up *Fenton Richmond Park*. It's a decade-old video of a guy screaming at his dog, but it still gets me every time, and by the time I've shown the kids, the four of us are shaking with laughter.

'Let's go to Richmond Park!' Rollo shouts. 'I want to see the deer!'

'You're a genius,' Honor mouths at me. First battle survived.

HONOR

Noah enchants us all.

He plays with my kids in Richmond Park—rather, he runs them ragged between football and deer-spotting and using fallen tree trunks as hurdles. It's been a late Autumn, and the ground is still a bed of vividly coloured leaves. I know the kids are taking today at face-value: just because they've had a good time running around with Noah, doesn't mean they're going to instantly accept him as a new father-figure in their lives, but it's a great first step. I'll take it.

I have no idea if anyone, professional or opportunistic passer-by, got footage of us in the park today. But we'll deal with that tomorrow. For once, I'm relaxed. Noah and I need to go public at some point, especially given how cosy Jackson and Leila looked at the *Vet* UK premiere a couple of weeks ago.

We're quickly educating Noah on the gaping chasm between theoretical and real Family Sundays. Serena vetoes Classic FM in favour of a Spotify UK Hits playlist, and Rollo hasn't yet practised his spellings for school tomorrow, so I help him with them while Noah peels potatoes (I wasn't kidding about him doing the cooking).

As a dyslexic, Rollo finds spellings excruciatingly painful, and I'm right there with him, ricocheting between frustration and heartbreak and wondering why the hell the kid needs to learn to spell anyway, when everything his generation writes will be voice-led or auto-corrected. But there's no point in trying to present some phoney, picture-perfect version of family life for Noah. He needs to know what he's getting himself into.

Noah surpasses himself with the most delicious roast sirloin, which even the kids devour, and after they've scarpered, he and I linger at the table over our bottle of red. It's so bloody fantastic having him here. His presence warms the entire house up. I beam at him and brush his leg with mine under the table.

'I love having you in my home. You make everything better.'

'I'm not sure anything or anyone could make this place better.' He looks up at the light installation, which is hundreds of wisps of smoked glass. 'It's a palace. It's stunning, and elegant, and stylish. Just like its owner.'

I twist around in my seat to face him. 'Could you see yourself living here someday? When the dust has settled and the kids are fully on board? I mean, your flat is gorgeous, so I don't want to assume anything.' I finger the stem of my wineglass nervously. 'I'm not saying this all has to be on my terms, obviously. And I know it's further from Good Vibes than your flat.'

'Darling.' He's grinning at me. 'Stop overthinking. We'll work it all out. And even if this wasn't the most incredible home I've ever been in, hands down, I'd still want us to base ourselves wherever you and your kids are most comfortable. So chill.'

'Okay.' I let out a deep sigh.

'Actually, there's one caveat.' He runs a couple of fingers up my thigh, over my jeans. 'I may need to road-test your bed before I agree to anything long term with this place.'

Noah in my bed. Oh my God. I've wanted it so badly, and it's going to happen. I practically jump out of my seat.

'Let's go.'

I abandon the idea of a family movie and leave the kids to it. They're far happier watching YouTube on the giant screen in the basement, anyway. I give them bowls of popcorn and, having ascertained that they're sufficiently disinterested in us, I lead Noah upstairs. I hope he doesn't mind omitting a key part of his Family Sunday schedule.

When we walk into the master suite, which takes up most of the first floor, he lets out a low whistle.

'Jesus Christ, darling. This puts every hotel we stayed in to shame.' He circles and points at the rococo nude. '*That* is sensational.'

'Glad you like it,' I purr.

'But she has nothing on you.' He glances at the giant bed. 'I'm going to focus very hard on ignoring the fact that this is your marital bed.'

'*Was*. Big *was*. And we can get a new one, if it bothers you. But I'll do my best to help you focus.'

'Excellent. I intend to leave my mark in here.'

'Please don't lift your leg and piss down the curtains.'

'I'll try to control myself. I have other bodily fluids I can use.'

The reality of having Noah in my bedroom is so fucking amazing. He's looked so gorgeous all day, in a beige cashmere sweater over a soft-looking shirt, and all I've wanted to do since he got here is take them both off. And his cords. And his boxers.

He strolls towards me, grinning lazily, those smile lines I adore bracketing his mouth. I love him so much. I'm in my home, with the three people I love the most in the world, and one of them is about to get me naked. Nothing else matters. Absolutely nothing.

Noah strokes his hands up my arms, leaving a trail of goosebumps in their wake, before gripping the hem of the sleeveless cowl-neck sweater I'm wearing and tugging it over my head. I have yet another set of new lingerie on, and the hunger in his eyes when he looks down at my breasts encased in ivory lace is enough to make my mouth water.

He rubs his hand over his face. 'I'm dreaming. I'm fucking dreaming right now. I can't believe this is my life.'

'Believe it.' I give his sweater the same treatment he gave mine and make a start on unbuttoning his shirt. I'll never get used to this, to seeing his gorgeous, lightly haired chest emerge from under his clothes.

'I need to get you naked.' He moves in and bites my lower lip. 'Now.'

A second later, we're both unbuttoning our own trousers, fast as we can go, and hopping around to get out of them. Noah strips down his black boxers and I stop to stare at this incredible, amazing, fan-fucking-tastic sight: the good doctor, naked and gorgeous and very, very hard for me. His Mediterranean skin still glows with health, even though summer is long gone.

He reaches behind me and unhooks my bra. Chucks it on the floor. Captures my mouth with his and hooks his thumbs through the sides of my thong, lowering it enough that it loosens its grip on my legs and I can step out of it while his hands skim up to my chest and he fills each of them with one of my breasts, cupping them firmly, his thumbs working my nipples so hard that the ache makes me arch and moan. It's so perfect, this feeling. The ache streams through my entire nervous system, lighting up the nerves between my legs and everywhere else like a Christmas tree.

This first time with him here won't be a slow dance of discovery. There's no teasing; we're both too close. It turns out that Family Sunday is a heady form of foreplay, as is having this man I love in my most inner sanctuary, my bedroom. We both need this badly.

I widen my legs and reach between us to grab the heavenly erection that's already leaking promises onto my belly. I run my fingers over the moisture and right down his shaft, enjoying the delicious weight of his balls in my hands before I move back up. Noah communicates his approval with a low groan that sounds like an animal in pain, angling his head so he can kiss me more deeply while one hand continues its fine work on my nipple and the other slides between my legs.

I gasp. The ache is now white hot, and I wriggle my legs to allow his skilful doctor's fingers as much access to the centre of my pleasure as they need.

'Noah.' I'm panting. 'Darling, I'm so close.'

'On the bed,' he manages, and I practically throw myself on the bed, my body screaming *come and get me,* my legs and arms thrown as wide as I can get them. I'm as open as I can be for him. Noah climbs over me, and we pause for a second to connect in a smile that's loving and desperate and triumphant and incredulous all in one.

Then he's down. Mouth on one nipple, then the other, sucking hard and ignoring the desperate, pulsing ache between my legs. He pulls away, looking tortured, before fisting his erection and guiding it to my entrance. I'm so relieved I could weep. I need him now. Filling me up. The thrill as he bottoms out and the pressure as he moves. Now that I'm separated, we've abandoned the condoms, and I gasp as he strokes his wetness against mine.

'You ready for this, darling?' His voice rumbles with intent.

'Please. Now.'

I arch my bum off the bed and he closes the gap between us on his knees and grabs my hips, driving into me. It's so good, it's so *good,* and I luxuriate in the incredible rush of sensation as he moves. He's moaning and grunting and digging his fingers into my hips and my arse as he fills me up, and I watch this beautiful man moving between my legs, becoming one with me here, on this bed.

And then, Nirvana. Noah takes his thumb and rubs it just north of where he's entering me, watching me all the while with those dark, dark eyes which are now so full of emotion it almost blinds me to look at them.

His thrusts are steady, and rolling, and perfectly deep, and his thumb is relentless, and his face is entrancing as he licks and bites his lower lip. And it's too much. My body undulates on the bed, and that blessed heat builds and builds and flows and streams through me and I ignite. I crest the wave and it submerges me in endless shock-waves of pleasure so deep that I'm only partially aware of Noah coming right on my tail before collapsing, spent and shuddering, to kiss me and tell me how much he loves me.

~

We make it under the duvet to recover. I can't let myself fall asleep here—it would be an absolute disaster if the kids found us like this—but my orgasm-addled body has other ideas. And yet, there's none of the despair at our inevitable parting that used to take hold of me in Noah's flat. Because I know that soon, we'll be together permanently, under the same roof.

My phone pings from the table beside me and I turn my head with effort to grab it as Noah runs an adoring hand up and down my abdomen. It's a text. From Serena.

Mum look what Ottilie said she'd buy me for my birthday isn't it soooo ugly-cute

A few dots, and then a picture appears.

It's a hideous furry unicorn.

With turquoise and purple stripes.

And an orange horn.

I stare at the image in disbelief and clap a hand over my mouth.

'You have got to be shitting me,' I mumble.

'What?' Noah cranes his neck to see, and I angle the screen towards him. Oh my God. Oh my God. There's no way this is a coincidence.

'Um.' I'm struggling to process this gigantic head fuck. 'Right before Mum died, she urged me to find the courage to be with you. I told you that.'

'Yeah.' He still looks bewildered.

'Well... she told me she'd send me a sign to show me she approved if she saw me with you. Anything I wanted. And I chose a unicorn. With turquoise and purple stripes and an orange horn.'

'Oh, Jesus.' A huge smile appears on his face and he sinks back onto the pillows.

'You're not shocked? This'—I shake the phone at him—'is *shocking*.'

'Baby, I've seen so many of these signs in my line of work.' He points at the screen. 'That's Stephanie doing her best celestial string-pulling.'

'Oh my God. Do you think that means she saw us having sex?'

Noah laughs and pulls me back into his arms. He raises one arm and gives a thumbs-up in the direction of the ceiling.

'Nice one, Stephanie.'

THE END

I have a Bonus Epilogue for you:
Enjoy Honor and Noah's mini-break at Sorrel Farm here!
https://dl.bookfunnel.com/crhdlgx4rx

You can binge the entire Love in London boxset here on Kindle Unlimited, kicking off with Jackson's naughty exploits.
http://mybook.to/loveinlondon

Or jump straight into Ellery and Josh's steamy story, *Falling Stars,* out now on Amazon and KU!
http://mybook.to/fallingstars
Read on for Chapter 1.

FALLING STARS - CHAPTER 1

ELLE

I've been careful, until now, not to get sucked into the crazy machine that is the film industry. Admittedly, my acting career to date is a grand total of one bit part and one lead role. But still. It's important to keep some perspective.

And I've always been a good girl. Head down. Work hard. Be ladylike. Unless there's a dance floor present (I may or may not have been known as the Dance Floor Whore at university).

So, when I find myself at the Cannes Film Festival, going straight from the premiere of the film *Gracie*, in which I play the lead, to the Vanity Fair party, and there's a dance floor beside the pool of whatever outrageous villa we're at, I know I'm getting sucked in.

Big time.

I'm screwed.

But this is my night, and I'm damned if I won't allow myself to succumb to whatever magic is in the air. My imposter syndrome is sky high. Any moment, one of those burly, ear-piece-wearing guys doing the rounds will chuck me over the bougainvillea-clad walls and out into the street.

And yet, A-listers *I've watched on screen since I was a child* are seeking me out. Shaking my hand. Air kissing me. And telling me I'm their bet for the Best Actress award at the Closing Ceremony next Saturday. Kirsten Dunst even hugged me in the loos and told me *Gracie* made her cry so hard, she had to have her makeup completely redone for the party.

It's too much.

I'm at the poolside bar with my publicist, Mara, *Gracie*'s director, Tina, and a few other cast members. Mara's as cool as a cucumber, even though she's only been doing this a couple of years, but Tina's almost as flustered as I am. She's a cerebral art-house film maker from Chiswick, and she's far more at home intellectualising in West London than she is hanging out in this kind of scene.

We started playing the *how many people can we recognise* game—well, Tina and I did while Mara surveyed the scene with a slightly bored air—but we gave up after thirty-three. It's far more of a challenge to find people we *don't* recognise, servers and security aside.

Although there are stars everywhere I turn, my number one eye-treat this evening so far has been the dreamy A-list trio at the bar earlier: Brad Burton. Davide de Luca. And Josh Lander. Yes. The Holy Trinity of all that is gorgeous and golden and Hollywood. My inner schoolgirl fanned herself, my ovaries did the Can-Can, and I had to use every ounce of strength I had not to pull out my phone and try for a surreptitious shot. Because that would be the least cool thing I could ever, ever do.

Despite my best intentions, I'm getting sucked into the surrounding carnival faster than an earring up a vacuum-cleaner. The whole spectacle is so chic I'm dying. We're perched high on a hill above the Bay of Cannes, super-yachts twinkling on an inky Med. Around me, clusters of household names laugh and flirt and do deals and catch up. There are fire eaters and go-go dancers and saxophonists on roller blades. No one is eating the canapes.

It's completely over the top and absolutely wonderful. Our little group is very much on the periphery as we people-watch. But then the DJ plays *Cheap Thrills*, and I know it's time to stop being a wallflower. I graced the big screen at the Grand Lumière tonight, and whatever my inner judge is telling me, I deserve to be here as much as anyone.

More importantly, *Gracie* may bomb commercially, and I may never get another part. I owe it to myself to make the most of this crazy ride while it lasts.

'Come on.' I deposit my fancy cocktail—name, ingredients and potency level unknown—on the glass bar and give Mara and Tina a little shimmy. 'Let's show these guys how the Brits rock.'

Tina sniggers nervously, admiring my chutzpah even while recognising that I'm talking utter rubbish, and Mara rolls her eyes, tosses her cigarette and stubs it out with her Rock Stud stilettos.

'Sure. Let's do it.'

'You really should be French,' I tell her as we walk in the direction of the chequerboard marble dance floor. 'You're so cool. And so nonchalant. Please show me how to be like you.'

She brushes my shoulder in a move that's almost affectionate. 'Elle. You'll never be cool. Or nonchalant. Just be you.'

'Right,' I mutter, feeling like a schoolgirl in her achingly cool wake. 'Excellent. Really helpful, thank you.'

Maybe it's the pulse of the music, or the scent of French cigarettes and flowers in the air, or the heady vibe of power and success all around me.

Maybe it's the fabulous Paco Rabanne mini-dress I changed into for the party, which is little more than some huge silver paillettes (think giant sequins) on mesh, held up by fine chain-mail straps. Whatever it is, as we join the throng of lithe, glossy, immaculately dressed bodies on the dance floor, I find the music and I lose my inhibitions.

I lose *myself*.

Mara has a dancing rhythm of her own—a sultry sway that does little to accommodate the actual beat of the music but is very sexy.

Tina's bopping like someone's let her out of Book Club for the night.

And I absolutely go for it.

I gyrate my hips, throw my head back, brush my thick fringe off my forehead, and let my arms float in the air. I grind, I thrust, I squat. Again and again. My skin slicks with a fine mist of sweat. I feel limber and weightless and energised. I could dance like this all night.

And as I revel in that unmatchable feeling of being one with the rhythm of the music, I gradually clock that Mara and Tina are moving away from me.

And looking at me oddly.

And that Marion Cotillard has just shot me an approving smile and a thumbs-up from the left.

And that there's heat building right behind my body.

Human heat.

I glance behind me and do what must be a comedic

double take, because, inches from me, is Josh Lander, and the guy is moving. In. On. Me.

Oh, holy cow. Oh, my goodness. Josh Lander is mirroring my moves, and he's now actually touching me. I can feel his knees right behind my knees. That means that right behind my bum is his... Jesus. Don't dare think about Josh Lander's penis.

My quick peek at him has confirmed that not only is he hotter than any actual human has a right to be, but that he's in a white shirt, a few buttons undone at the neck. Sleeves rolled up. I have no idea what he's wearing on his bottom half because craning my neck to look down at Josh Lander's crotch seems ill-advised, even through my mystery-cocktail haze.

But instead of freaking out, like I would have put serious money on my doing, I embrace this madness. Having such a huge, hot Hollywood star gyrating inches from me gives me the most enormous surge of adrenalin and, to be honest, power.

I double down.

Hell, I may never again get to dance with someone this gorgeous and this famous. (To be more explicitly frank, I may never again get to dance with someone whose face graced my teenage self's bedroom wall.)

I may as well just go for it.

The track changes to Rihanna's *Work*, but she may as well be singing *twerk* because that's basically what I do. I grind. I twerk. I thrust. And I squat and rise. And squat. And rise. I throw my head back and toss my hair (which is very Bardot-esque tonight) in Josh Lander's face and throw my arms around. My dress acts like a disco ball, its silver pail-lettes reflecting all the lights of the dance floor back in every direction. And *right* behind me, because I can feel him, Josh Lander matches me beat for beat. The music pulses through our veins in tandem.

Then the light but delicious pressure of a hand on my waist. He's guiding me. Pulling me in closer to him.

Oh my gosh, I'm gyrating against Josh Lander's crotch.

Around us, people are clapping and whistling and clearing a larger space for us. Oh, dear Lord. I'm hazily conscious of a lot of phones aiming in our direction.

I want to turn around so badly, to slide down Josh Lander's rock-hard body and possibly graze his arm or his stomach through his shirt with my fingers. But I won't. I'm not brave enough, and I don't know him. I mean, I know him, obviously, but I don't actually *know* him.

Everyone's eyes are on us, and I'm struck by a possibly childish desire to be the one to end this little dance floor flirtation (if simulating sex, while fully clothed and upright, with an A-list celebrity, in the presence of many other A-list celebrities does indeed pass as a flirtation). And so, as the song comes to its conclusion, I brave another backwards glance.

I look him in the eye, and dearest Lord, if his heavenly face isn't radiating amusement and intensity and a teeny bit of lust. The jut of that famous, stubbled jaw is tense. He licks his bottom lip, and my gaze is *there* for it. He's catching his breath (gratifyingly, he looks more out of breath than I feel) and his chest, so close to my shoulder, is heaving.

I give him a coquettish grin. Casual, just a twist of my mouth. Like we're partners in crime and I'm not some total random.

'See you,' I say.

And off I sashay without a backwards glance.

Leaving Josh Lander on the dance floor.

Working that mini-dress.

And resisting the urge to punch the damn air.

Ready for more Josh and Elle fun?

Read for FREE on Kindle Unlimited!

http://mybook.to/fallingstars

AUTHOR'S NOTE

Dear Reader,

Thank you for reading *A Fair Affair*! I've been proofing it as I sit in my kitchen on Day 6 of having a broken boiler, so I'm very grateful to have had the chance to the south of France with Honor and Noah (again and again and again).

I'm not sure if you came to this book cold, or via *Parents and Teachers*. I felt like Honor got a bad rap in PAT, and I wanted to give her her own story and delve beneath the surface of that glossy exterior. All I can say is, I'm glad she's fictional, because I'm so darn jealous of her for landing Noah that I couldn't look her in the eye if she was real (this happens with all my female main characters as I write them, to be honest).

I got interested in palliative care when I listened to Gwyneth Paltrow interviewing the amazing BJ Miller, MD, on the Goop podcast a couple of years ago. I read his book, A Beginner's Guide to the End, and found it profoundly helpful for research purposes. Dr Miller is a pioneer in his field. Oh, and he's a triple amputee. Beyond impressive. Poor Stephanie was my first death as an author, but I was interested in using her death as a catalyst for Honor to experience profound human connection and to reconsider what's truly important in life.

If you'd like to geek out more about all things romance, please join me in my closed Facebook group, Sara Madderson's Book Nerds. It's still small, but I'd love to grow it as a place for fun and warm-heartedness!

Thanks again for your support, and hope to chat to you soon

Sara xx

ALSO BY SARA MADDERSON

All my books can be read as standalone.

LOVE IN LONDON

Parents and Teachers

A Fair Affair

A Very London Christmas

Falling Stars

Wilder at Heart

SORREL FARM

Food for Thought

Heaven on Earth

Make Me Sweat (related material)

A Manny for Christmas

STANDALONE

The Winter's Fail

The Rest is History

Ready to raise the spice level to 5 chillis? Meet my naughtier pen name, Elodie Hart:

ALCHEMY

Spicy age gap romance set in an elite Mayfair sex club

Unfurl

Undulate

Unveil

Untether

Unstitch

Unbind

Always Alchemy

ABOUT ME

I like to change things up! I spent my 20s as a banker and my 30s bringing up small children and running my own fashion brand. I started writing aged 41, and I wonder why I didn't do it sooner.

I've always loved writing. My daughter Tilly has an old notebook of mine filled with half-finished stories and accompanying drawings. I've read for as long as I can remember, guzzling up books so quickly that my mum always protested that I couldn't be reading them properly.

Reading and writing romance saved my sanity during lockdown and has been my refuge ever since. I've published my books independently, and I love the freedom it provides. The world of independent publishing is fascinating and so empowering--I'm delighted to share more of my experiences of self-publishing if you're interested.

I'd love to hear from you with feedback, suggestions and requests! My email is sara@saramadderson.com.

Facebook

Instagram

TikTok

Printed in Great Britain
by Amazon

57491444R00182